ALSO BY MARIE HARTE

The McCauley Brothers

The Troublemaker Next Door

How to Handle a Heartbreaker

Ruining Mr. Perfect

What to Do with a Bad Boy

Body Shop Bad Boys

Test Drive

Roadside Assistance

Zero to Sixty

Collision Course

The Donnigans

A Sure Thing

Just the Thing

The Only Thing

Veteran Movers

The Whole Package

Smooth Moves

Handle with Care

All I Want for Halloween

the Kissing Game

Marie Harte

Published by Sourcebooks Casablanca, an imprint of Sourcebooks
P.O. Box 4410, Naperville, Illinois 60567-4410
(630) 961-3900
sourcebooks.com

Library of Congress Cataloging-in-Publication data is on file with the publisher.

Printed and bound in the United States of America.
VP 10 9 8 7 6 5 4 3 2 1

To all the readers who've been asking about Rena and Heller for years, this book is for you. And as always, to DT and RC.

CHAPTER ONE

On the first cold Friday of the new year, Axel Heller stood in Heller's Paint and Auto Body and glared from his newest employee to the unfinished Escalade sitting all by itself in Bay 2.

The Seattle weather made the concrete in the floors radiate cold. Icy winds and sleet beat against the reinforced walls offering them protection from a harsh winter, but Axel wouldn't call it warm inside. It didn't bother him any though. Braced against the cold in a thick cable-knit sweater, jeans, and his comfortable leather boots, he felt nothing but toasty as his rage grew.

I so *do not need this right now.*

Mateo and the always-reliable Smitty waited with the new guy, no doubt ready to intervene should Axel's infamous temper flare out of control.

Lately, it didn't take much to set him off. His mother's death still hurt, a fresh wound even after six months. And his family…

He took a deep breath and let it out slowly, saying nothing, just studying the idiot unable to *follow. Simple. Instructions.*

It didn't help that Axel had just ended a call from his father. As usual, it had been filled with nothing but arguments and swearing in guttural

German. He could only be happy his father still lived in Germany and rarely made the occasional trip stateside to visit. Otherwise Axel would probably be in jail for patricide.

At the thought, he smiled.

Mateo took a step back and shoved the new guy—Rylan—forward. "Take him. I'm too pretty to die young."

"Asshole," Rylan muttered before confronting Axel. "What the hell, man? You wanted us to buff out the Corolla and set the quarter panel for the Kia, so we did. What's the problem?"

Behind him, Smitty shook his head and stood with his arms crossed over his chest. Axel didn't have many friends, but he considered Smitty one of them. And he knew Smitty had problems with the new guy, but they'd been hoping to work them out.

Axel took a step closer and looked down at Rylan, who finally had the sense to shut up. *Count to five. No, ten. Breathe. Remember, Rylan needs his face in one piece. Probably.* "The problem is I told you hours ago we had a change of plans."

"But I thought the Corolla and Kia would be faster. I mean, we did get them both done today."

Axel curled his fingers so he wouldn't be tempted to wrap them around Rylan's neck. He'd spent the afternoon away, working on taxes with an overpriced accountant, content at least that the shop work would get done. "I trusted you to pass the message to finish the Escalade first because the client paid extra to have it done early. But seeing as Smitty and Mateo helped you with the lower-priority work, I'm guessing you didn't tell them."

"Hell no, he didn't," Mateo muttered.

"Now we're going to be behind next week unless your sorry ass is in here tomorrow, on a Saturday, fixing your mistake."

Rylan flushed. “Oh, ah, well, I can do that.”

But I don’t trust you to do anything on your own. Axel mumbled under his breath about shoving a rock-hard head through a cement wall, idly wondering if his father had secretly sent Rylan to screw with him.

“When he talks in German, the shit’s ready to blow,” Mateo helpfully pointed out.

“Shut up, Mateo,” Rylan snapped. “Look, Heller, I’m fine to work tomorrow. You don’t even have to pay me overtime.” He swallowed at the look Axel shot him. “Or at all. I’ll make up for my mistake.”

But Axel had already made up his mind. “Get out. Everyone go home. I’ll see you Monday.” He knew Rylan had been trying to help, but the guy kept messing up and putting them behind. If Rylan wasn’t so skilled at sanding and refining, as well as having an incredible eye for detail, Axel would have fired him by now. But with Kelly out for another month dealing with some family issues, he had to admit they needed all the help they could get.

Instead of relaxing tomorrow, *Axel* would have to come in on his day off and fix the mess. He knew what the Escalade needed, and sadly, it wasn’t as if he had anything better to do with his time.

The crew departed, Rylan still trying to apologize as Mateo tugged him out the door. Smitty paused by the exit, his red Mohawk like a stream of fire. Full of muscle and tattoos, he looked like a bruiser but was one of the calmest, nicest guys Axel knew. “I’ll swing by to help you with the SUV.” Because Smitty knew Axel would fix the issue himself.

Axel grunted.

Smitty grinned and left without another word.

Axel leaned against a workbench and stared at his pride and joy, a paint and auto body shop he’d put together without help from anyone.

He scrubbed his hands over his face, wondering if the whiskers should stay or go. He'd been too busy to care about keeping his cheeks smooth, and with his constant visits to Stuttgart, Germany, helping his aunt and cousins as best he could, he'd been slacking off with the business.

The grief always sitting under the surface welled up, threatening to drown him in it. Taking deep breaths, he forced himself not to think about the past. Instead, he dwelled on the living, and on one particular individual he found fascinating.

The cement floor blended with the whitewashed walls as thoughts of fine-as-hell Rena Jackson intruded. He heard himself sigh and flushed, glad the guys weren't around to see him acting like a lovesick moron.

He'd fallen hard for the stubborn woman from the first. But smart chick that she was, she wanted nothing to do with him. He thought they'd become kind of friends. After all, he considered her *nice* cousin a friend. And her other one, the she-wolf with attitude, well, if not a friend, then a colleague of sorts. They shared the same paint specialist, though the she-wolf did tend to hog him at her repair shop more than she should.

Something he'd once again take up with her as soon as he got a minute to more than breathe.

Hell. He needed a break. One beer couldn't hurt. And it had been a while since he'd been at Ray's. He ignored the secret hope that lingered—that he might see Rena there.

Three fallen dickheads later, Axel had worked off a decent head of steam in the bar's parking lot, much to the entertainment of the crowd who'd gathered to watch. He'd also won fifty bucks and beers on the house. Ray, the owner of Ray's Bar, shook his head as he stared down at a bunch of racist pricks who'd already been kicked out once...for being racist pricks.

"I catch you here again," Ray said to Fletcher and his asshole buddies moaning on the ground, "there won't be enough of you left for anyone to identify. Now fuck off before I let Earl and Big J do what they've been wanting to all night. Axel was just a warm-up." It wasn't as if Ray didn't still have some fight left in him. A retired boxer, he had the fists, and face, of someone who'd fought too many rounds. The fists looked like he'd won most of them, but his face suggested he'd lost more than a time or two.

Behind Axel, the bar's bouncers waited with shit-eating grins. Trouble, those two, but they liked Axel taking care of their business. They had enough to handle with all the—what had Rena lovingly called the clientele?—*riffraff* in the place.

Fletcher stood with help from his seedy friends and shot Axel the finger. "Your ass is mine. I won't forget this, dickhead."

Axel just stared, not saying a word, and waited for the idiots to limp away. Funny that Fletcher couldn't seem to recall *he'd* been the one to start the fight. Axel hadn't even stepped a foot out of his truck before Fletcher had been in his face. The dumbass was apparently trying to make up for getting walloped a few months ago.

Axel turned, praying his favorite person in the world really had stayed home tonight. God forbid she see him do yet another thing involving brutality.

To his chagrin, she stood by the entrance behind the enthusiastic crowd cheering him on and collecting bets.

Rena shook her head at him before turning to go back inside.

Fuck.

He sighed, feeling down, and forced his feet to take him into the bar to apologize. He didn't want to tell her Fletcher and his cronies had had it coming. The crap they'd said about her and J.T., her nice cousin, just because they had darker skin… Rage threatened to consume Axel. He hated bigotry of any kind, and that kind of intolerance aimed at Rena?

He forced himself to calm down, needing for once to make a good impression. He wanted Rena to see him as more than a giant mauler. She claimed he fought too much, and maybe he did. But the things they'd been saying about her had bothered him. A lot.

Everything about her captivated him. Her laugh was real. Contagious. She had full lips, the cutest dimple, and a lovely face he'd more than once fantasized caressing. Her skin was a warm chestnut brown, and the golden-brown curls framing her angel's face made her amber eyes almost glow.

God, he would give anything to hold her close.

When around her, his troubles faded, and joy took their place. He couldn't explain it except to tell himself love at first sight must exist. At least for him.

He'd told his mother about Rena a month before she'd passed, and she'd agreed. He had it bad for the bartender-slash-waitress-slash-hairstylist. His mother had also agreed that he needed to make a move.

But fear kept him back, that he might do the wrong thing and scare Rena away. The idea that Rena would someday be his felt more unattainable every time he screwed up in front of her. And then the drama with his mother and father, his mother's death, it all conspired to keep him distant, apart. Cold. Because numbness made the hurt bearable.

Pushing through the crowd, he tried to fight his fragile hope she might smile his way. He would have felt better about beating the losers outside if she hadn't seen him. Now his therapeutic workout in the parking lot was all for nothing, and the balled-up tension inside him threatened to freeze solid under an icy wall of self-preservation.

But Rena could melt him with a smile. If only she'd give him one.

He found an open spot at the bar and looked around, but she didn't appear. Instead, crowds of his kind of people, hardworking men and women who liked keeping a low profile—especially around law-enforcement types—milled around tables and danced by a new jukebox playing some funky metal-dance mix. Piercings and tattoos decorated visible skin, and denim and work boots seemed the dress of choice.

The booths and tables in Ray's were mostly clean. Axel's feet didn't stick to the floor too badly, and the smell of stale beer didn't offend as much as the few smokers puffing away in Ray's nonsmoking bar. Most of the occupants adhered to Ray's rules: no fights *inside*, no cops, no drugs, and, most importantly, no fucking with the staff.

For all that Axel didn't like Rena working in the place, he knew she had so many friends and family around that no one messed with her without major consequences.

He cracked his knuckles, once again gratified they'd met Fletcher's big mouth and drawn blood.

"Yo, Heller. What can I get ya?" Sue asked, smacking gum as she waited for him. She wore a black T-shirt that said *Bartender* in big white letters. Her many tattoos, piercings, and braids made her an obvious fit for the place.

"A *dunkel*—a dark ale—for me tonight."

She nodded.

"Is Rena here?"

Sue gave him a sad look as she handed him a glass. "Sorry, slugger. She was just leaving when you showed up to pound Fletcher into hamburger. Nice work, by the way."

"*Ja.*" He sighed and drank the beer down in one go.

Sue watched him with wide eyes.

"One more, then I leave." He had no reason to stay, not now that Rena had gone.

"Sure." She poured him another. As he drank this one more slowly, she said, "You know tomorrow night's Rena's last, right? We're having a party. You're coming, aren't you?"

Had the time come already? "When does it start?" Panicked at the thought of Rena leaving, though he'd known she would at some point, he did his best to appear unconcerned. How the hell would he see her now? To get up the nerve to talk to her? At least at the bar he had an excuse to hang around and watch her. With her working at her new salon, he couldn't come in every day for a haircut. Could he?

"Seven. We're gonna do a cake, food, and drinks, of course." Sue smiled. "Lara's baking her famous chocolate chip cookies."

He'd had them before, and he looked forward to having them again. "Yes. *Gut.* I'll be back."

"Sure thing, Arnold." She chuckled. She must have seen his confusion because she explained. "You know, like Arnold Schwarzenegger? 'I'll be back,'" she said, sounding not at all like Axel. At his lack of expression, she shrugged. "Ah. Whatever. See you, Heller."

He left, not satisfied or relaxed in the slightest. Now he just felt tired.

Axel drove home, washed up, and slid into bed. He stared at the picture on his nightstand the way he did every night, now that she was gone. In a plain brown frame sat a photograph of him and his mother when he'd been a boy, both of them smiling at each other. A festival filled the background, the bright-red balloon clutched in his hand a reminder of a precious gift—that there had once been better times, that at least one person in his life had truly loved him.

The picture framed the clear affection between a mother and son.

Axel forced himself to close his eyes and fall asleep before he did the unthinkable and cried. Again.

♥ ♥ ♥

"Happy birthday, dear Jane, happy birthday to you!" Rena blew on the festive red noisemaker until it straightened its curl, glad she'd made it in time after her shift at the bar. Everyone waited for the delighted girl of the hour to blow out her candle, then her mom cut the large sheet cake into squares while her father twirled his little princess around.

Along with the other revelers, Rena cheered, awash in the joy of family. Having been introduced to the boisterous, loving McCauley clan through her cousin Del's marriage, Rena had been to more birthday parties and picnics in the past year and a half than she'd been to in her life. Del had married Mike, and Colin—Mike's son—provided Rena an honorary nephew to spoil.

She looked around but didn't see Mike, her personal hero, so she nudged her cousin, who stood wolfing down a plate of mini corn dogs and chicken wings. "Hey, where's Mike?"

Del smiled, and the overhead light shone on her brow ring. "Colin and Mike are coming as soon as Colin's basketball game is done."

"I thought he was into soccer." Colin was the absolute cutest kid and fanatical about the sport.

"Oh, trust me. He is. But Mike insisted he try something else just to see if he liked it. And he does. Kid is a natural athlete." Del grinned then groaned and rested her hand on the visible bulge of her tummy, where Del Junior—as Mike called their unborn child—rested. "Just like his baby sister. I swear, this kid bounces on my bladder like it's a trampoline, and I'm having to pee every three seconds." Del made a face, handed Rena her plate, and sighed. "Yep. Like clockwork. I'll be right back."

Rena watched her go, so happy for her cousin.

And so envious.

She looked around at the many smiling faces of those she'd come to care for, seeing the love that gathered them all together.

So much love brought tears to her eyes. Most were from happiness, but a few came from the knowledge she'd arrived solo. *Again.* Never with a plus one. For the past year, she'd been too busy getting her new business together to have time for a man. And she wanted one. No question.

Too bad the one she wanted moved at the speed of a glacier.

Axel Heller had no trouble making time for those fists of fury, but God forbid he ask her out or anything. She might have asked him, but the rare moments they had any time together at Ray's lately, Axel turned mute, disappeared behind a menu, or got sucked into conversation with J.T. and friends, the guys who worked at Del's garage.

So not romantic.

She sighed again, wondering how she'd be described as a character in one of her much-loved romance books. Desperate? Pathetic? Cute but lonely? A future CLA—Cat Lady of America? *Hmm. Maybe I should get a cat.*

J.T. saw her and smiled. He left his fiancée to join Rena by the food and glanced down at the plate she was holding. "That's a lot of corn dogs."

She forced herself to stop moping and laughed. "They're Del's. I'm just holding them while she hits the bathroom again." Past the birthday parents, Rena spotted her uncle arriving with his own fiancée in tow. Geez. Was anyone left who hadn't coupled up…besides Rena and the one-year-old?

For a woman who lived with a romance book under her pillow, another on her nightstand, and hundreds more filling several bookcases, to say Rena was a romantic was like saying Picasso had toyed with painting. Rena read romances. She watched them on TV. She saw them play out with friends and family and always offered helpful advice. She ate, drank, and slept with the idea of happily ever after in her blood.

"J.T., why am I still single?"

His expression softened, and he wrapped a huge arm around her shoulders. The big lug stood a good head taller and took after his father in size if not looks. Unlike Uncle Liam, J.T. had the same medium-brown skin Rena did. His sister, Del, on the other hand, had ash-blond hair in funky braids, sleeves of tattoos covering white-girl-with-a-tan arms (J.T.'s description, not hers), and gray eyes. They didn't look much like family, but the Websters were thick as thieves. That Rena was included in their dynamic somewhat soothed the part of her always wishing for a forever love of her own.

"Well, it's not for lack of looks." J.T. smiled. "You look prettier than Aunt Caroline every day. But don't tell her I said that."

Rena's and J.T.'s mothers had been sisters, both always trying to one-up the other. J.T. thought it amusing to continue the tradition of teasing Rena's mom. Rena chuckled. "I won't let you get her started. You know Mom's vain."

"But still beautiful. Looks just like Bridget." His own mother. J.T. looked over at his father. "He's been talking more about her. It's been nice."

"Good." Rena knew her uncle had loved deeply, and when Aunt Bridget had passed away, he'd grieved for her for *years.* Until he'd met a special McCauley. Like daughter, like father. "So he and Sophie are seriously getting married on Valentine's Day?"

Uncle Liam would be getting married on Rena's favorite holiday, enjoying his honeymoon on the most romantic day of the year. Rena would be nursing a hot cup of tea, eating chocolates she'd buy for herself, and binging on Hallmark movies while she wallowed in self-pity.

"Yep. I can't believe it." J.T.'s large grin showed his pleasure at the thought. "You going to bring a date to the wedding?" He paused, still looking at his dad. "Heller's back in town to stay."

"Don't talk to me about that man," she fumed. "Heck. The reason I'm single is probably because he's been keeping everyone away from me." He wouldn't ask her out, but he didn't like anyone else paying attention to her. The big, sexy Viking. *No, the big, unsexy jerk.*

J.T. turned to regard her with concern. "Now, Rena, Heller's not like that."

Blaming her loneliness on Axel felt better than thinking her inability to attract a man might be her own fault. Heck, she couldn't remember the last time anyone had flirted with her. "Oh? He comes into the bar and smiles at me, then glares at everyone else."

J.T. grunted. "Good. I don't want you dating the guys who hang out at Ray's anyway."

"You hang out there."

He nodded. "Exactly."

She shook her head. "You make no sense."

"Oh please. How many times have you talked about quitting the bar? And not just because you're opening your own salon. Ray's is a great place to chill…if you have a rap sheet."

"Stop."

"Or you're hiding from the law."

She bit back a laugh.

"Or your P.O. demanded you get a job and Ray's the only guy who'd take you."

"He took me."

"And Big J and Earl and Wiley—who we all know has issues with theft. The crap in Ray's kitchen can't possibly be store-bought. You said you saw a brand new stove in the back last week. And that jukebox is shiny and sounds terrific. Definitely not the one that was in there last month."

"Well, okay. So maybe Wiley knows a few guys. He's sweet."

"He's a crook," J.T. growled. "Hey, I like him too. I like everyone there, except the few guys Ray kicked out." A few white-power creeps who'd made Rena feel more than uncomfortable. Guys like Fletcher, whom Axel had just pulverized last night. She didn't know how to feel about that. Glad the guys were gone but wishing Axel would stop fighting before he got hurt.

"And you know," J.T. was saying, "Ray has a habit of looking the other way from what goes on in the parking lot, especially if it involves cigarette cartons and brand spankin' new electronics."

"Chump change."

"*Illegal* chump change," J.T. said, sounding just like his father. "Since the guys and I aren't around as much, I feel better that you're quitting sooner than later." *The guys* meaning J.T.'s mechanic buddies who worked for Del at her garage. And Axel. The source of Rena's current confusion.

She didn't want to talk about Axel Heller though, so she fell back on the old "You're not the boss of me."

Del had returned to overhear. "Oh, *this* sounds like a mature argument." She took the plate from Rena and started eating again. "What did you do?" she asked her brother.

J.T. frowned. "Me? I told her she needed to quit Ray's, which she's already doing. It's not a secret she's handed in her notice. Ray announced her last day is tomorrow. We're having a big party."

"No one told me that." Del frowned back at him.

"You're pregnant."

"No shit?" Del gave him a fake look of shock. "How did that happen, I wonder?"

J.T. glared, but before Rena could step aside and let the siblings argue, he latched onto her arm. "To answer your question, Cuz, you're single because you want to be. And you know it."

Great. Now Del looked concerned. "You ready to start dating again? Want me to set you up? I know a bunch of guys who'd be lucky to have you." She looked thoughtful as she stared at her plate. "Well, maybe not him. Or him. And Nick is definitely out. But Jay's not bad for a—"

"Don't say ex-con," J.T. muttered. "God knows the types who hang out with your employees."

"Who happen to be your friends, jack-hole."

"I know." He chuckled.

"Shut it." Del turned back to Rena. "I was going to say Jay's not bad for *a doctor*. He's not snooty or anything. We just fixed his '67 Charger. Foley did a helluva job. Jay's kind of cute." She paused. "You could do worse. Hell, you have done worse. So much worse it's scary."

Rena loved her cousin, but she could see why Del and J.T. argued so much.

"Then again, I thought you and Heller had a… J.T., why are you shaking your head at me?"

Rena growled. "Don't mention Axel Heller again. I have nothing to say to that man."

"Why? Did he do something to piss you off?" Del's eyes narrowed. "Because I don't care how big he is. He can still bleed."

"Oh my God, killer. Calm down." J.T. put his hand against his sister's forehead as if to hold her back while she tried to slap him off. "He's been out of town for a while, so Rena's upset he hasn't asked her out." He dropped his hand, ignoring the dirty look she shot him.

Del relaxed and ate a chicken wing. "Oh. Well, Rena, his mom just died. You should give the guy a break."

"A break?" Rena wanted to smack both her cousins. They'd found love with awesome people. Of course they could be nonchalant while giving terrible advice. "First of all, I've known Axel for close to a year. He's nice, sure. But he's never once asked me out. And I know his mom just died. Six months ago. He's sad. I get it. But if he hasn't asked me out before now, he's not interested. I'm going to find my own Mr. Right. And before you even *think* about asking, no, I do *not* need your help. Now, if you'll excuse me?"

She left them looking after her, no doubt with concern she could do without. So she made her way to the only person with a Y chromosome worth talking to and stopped in front of Mike McCauley, who'd recently arrived. She turned to his son and said, "Hey, Colin. About time you got here." To Mike she said, "Your wife is on my nerves."

Mike sighed.

Eight-year-old Colin grinned, showing off a new missing tooth. The spitting image of Mike, with black hair, blue eyes, and a killer grin, he'd be a real heartbreaker someday. "Hey, Aunt Rena!" He gave her a huge hug, which she'd really needed. "Is there cake?"

"Yes. Let's get some." She hurried him away before his father could caution her about feeding his son too much sugar. As if there could ever be such a thing. "So. Tell me. I need to know. You still hate girls?"

"Yep. Except for Jane." He glanced over at his baby cousin. "And Del Junior. I'll like her. But everyone else is gross."

"I'm with you. Boys are gross." They high-fived and ate cake.

And though Rena tried to put him out of her mind, she couldn't help wondering what the big, silent Axel was up to this new year, and whether he'd even bother showing up tomorrow night to say goodbye.

CHAPTER TWO

Saturday evening, Axel did his best to stop looking at Rena. She stood in front of the bar wearing a *Bartender* tee but wasn't working so much as laughing and talking to everyone.

The bar was packed, the music was loud, and the beer and cookies flowed. An odd combination, but Lara—one of Ray's ex-bartenders—had a reputation for making the best chocolate chip cookies in Seattle. Too bad she'd opted to become a nurse instead of opening up her own bakeshop. She could have made a fortune in cookie dough alone.

He saw her move in to hug Rena, who squealed and hugged her back. Nearby, Lara's boyfriend and the other mechanics from Webster's Garage stood drinking and talking with each other. Axel knew he could have joined them. Lou, who did double duty working for both Del and Axel, had waved to him. But Axel was in no mood to hear how much Rena would be missed, what the hell was he waiting for by not asking her out, and, man, what a bunch of lame-asses his guys were for losing the last darts match two weeks ago.

In his current mood, Axel would end up slugging the big one, Sam, who would hit back. Foley, his friend, would join in, while

Johnny and Lou placed bets. Then Rena would accuse him of ruining her party. He frowned, wondering if she'd ever make her way away from her many admirers.

And he hated that she had so many.

"Why so glum, chum?" J.T. asked as he sipped from a bottle and kept a watchful eye on the gorgeous blond he'd arrived with, who stood chatting with Rena, Lara, and a bunch of the bar's riffraff.

"You're very annoying." *And in love.*

The blond turned to wink at J.T., and he smiled back at her. "So says the guy not getting any. Aw, damn. Hope is so fine. I am the luckiest man alive." He patted Axel on the back. "Can you believe she and I are engaged?"

"No."

"I mean, she's beautiful and built and so smart."

"Yet she is with you?"

That too went right over J.T.'s head. "And she's a Donnigan. I thought for sure I could distance myself from all those clingy McCauleys despite Del being married to one. Then I had to fall for Hope." J.T. sighed, but Axel knew he loved the McCauleys and Donnigans like his own family. "Guess I'm gonna be stuck for life."

"Braggart."

J.T. gave him a smug smile. "Yeah, I know. I'm trying to make a point."

"That I should shove my fist in your face to shut you up?" Axel drank more, his mood simultaneously dark and uplifted, because watching Rena smile made him warm all over.

"That you can have what I have—not with Hope but with your own woman. *If* you'd grow some stones and make a move."

"You have a death wish?"

J.T. shook his head. "Heller, you need to do something. Tonight is her last night here. She's ready to start dating again… And you're not on the list."

Axel tensed. "What?"

"She was telling me last night she's done being single. Del's going to set her up with—" He grabbed Axel by the arm. "Wait a minute. Hold on."

Axel let J.T. hold him back, though his instinct was to go over to Rena and glare her many admirers into submission. As archaic, moronic, and chauvinistic as he knew the action to be, he couldn't help feeling like others crowded his woman. *His.*

"Man, you have to be smart. I think she's got a thing for you, but she's pissed you haven't made a move."

Axel hated that his cheeks heated.

"It's been a year." J.T. wouldn't shut up. "What are you waiting for?"

Axel blurted, "I just don't want to mess it up." Didn't want to mess *her* up, the way his father had hurt his mother. "She's too good for me."

"Yeah, she is," J.T. agreed. "But don't you think she deserves someone who'd fight to protect her? Who'd put Fletcher and guys like him in their place?"

"Yes."

"Who'd always put her first?" J.T. gentled his tone. "That's you, isn't it?"

"*Ja.*"

"But if you don't let her know you want a future with her, she'll end up finding some douchebag who'll treat her wrong. Or worse, she'll find some rich city boy who'll make her into a trophy wife. And Rena would eat that shit up because he'd act all nice, but inside she'd be dying because he'd never see *her*, only who he'd want her to be."

"What the hell is coming out of your mouth?" Del asked before

Axel could. He'd been with J.T. about the douchebag part but lost the rest of the thread.

Delilah McCauley, Axel's business rival, had joined her brother. She was glowing, pregnancy agreeing with her. Behind her stood her behemoth of a husband. Axel had thought that marriage would settle Del down. If anything, the she-wolf bared her teeth more, though her bite felt less sharp.

He snorted in her direction, knowing if he told her how lovely she looked or how much he admired her work at the garage he'd probably give her a heart attack. That or she'd go for his throat.

She snorted back then ignored him in favor of her brother. "Rena deserves to find a man who'll give her that romantic happily-ever-after bullshit—no offense, Mike—that she deserves."

Her husband strangled on a laugh. "Oh, uh, sure, Del. None taken. I'm gonna grab a beer. I'll get you a seltzer water." He took a step away then paused. "And if you need anything at all, you'll let me know?" Mike met J.T.'s eyes for a moment then Axel's, as if to say *watch over my mean-ass wife.*

Axel gave him a subtle nod.

J.T. rolled his eyes. "Yes, yes, Mike. Go on. I'll protect fragile Del from danger while you're away."

Mike growled but left.

"Don't mess with him, J.T.," Del scolded. "He's going to worry until the baby comes. Let him."

Axel had no idea why Mike might think Del so fragile. For one thing, he'd never met a tougher woman. And secondly, women seemed to be strongest when defending their kids. At least, his mother had been when shielding him and his brother from his dickhead father. But protecting herself, now, that was another story.

Perhaps Mike worried for another reason. "Are you sick?" he asked Del.

"Huh? Sick? No. Do I *look* sick?" A lot of challenge in that question. "I'm going to have a baby, not the plague."

"Then why does he think you need so much help? Pregnancy is a natural part of life."

"Exactly." Del gave him a huge smile, one that made him wary. "For once, Heller, you make a lot of sense."

"I always make sense." He frowned.

Del's smile grew. "Whatever you say. But let's not get sidetracked. What my idiot brother—"

J.T. glared. "Hey."

"—is trying to tell you is that my cousin is done waiting on your ass. Either ask Rena out or I'll set her up with a guy. I'm a McCauley now. My new family knows all the nice, respectable people in this city. I can find her a date in seconds." She snapped her fingers.

"Who'll bore her to tears," J.T. added under his breath.

"Hey, boring is better than hurting. Any guy would be lucky to date Rena. She's sweet and funny. And she deserves hearts and flowers and her stupid HEA." To J.T. she said, "That stands for *happily ever after*. Abby told me."

"Who's Abby?" Axel asked absently, watching Rena hold court with all the degenerates like a queen. Hell, Del was right.

"Abby's my sister-in-law, who happens to be a romance writer. Rena thinks she walks on water." Del shook her head. "Rena, the woman you can't stop staring at, is addicted to those love books."

Axel glanced at J.T., who nodded. "Sorry, man. It's true. My cousin wants romance."

Axel cringed. "Romance?"

Del sighed. "Romance. And if you're not quick about it, you're going to miss out on one amazing person. For some reason, she seems to like you. Even if she doesn't like you much right now. So try not to fuck it up. Go ask her out already." She rubbed her belly just as Mike returned.

His eyes widened. "Are you okay? Should we go?" Then he turned a surprisingly mean glare Axel's way. "What did you say to her?"

Axel just stared in surprise. Mike sounded halfway tough. Shocking that the family man had a rough side. Though maybe not so shocking, since the poor bastard had married Del, after all.

Del swore. "Mike, stop. I'm fine. The baby kicked is all." She shot Axel a sly glance. "I think she likes Axel's voice. It's deep and sexy."

Axel watched Del with caution. "Maybe you *are* sick. In the head."

Mike seemed to relax. Del laughed and dragged him with her to Rena and a bunch of other McCauleys who'd just arrived.

J.T. chuckled. "My sister's a pain, but she's right. I know you don't want to mess up your chances with my cousin, but by doing nothing, you're already screwing up. Make a move or leave. But quit hanging in limbo, my man. Now, I've got a hot blond to seduce. You're on your own."

It wasn't as if Axel had *asked* either Del or J.T. for help, though he secretly appreciated the advice.

Great. Rena wanted to find a man. He was the perfect man for her. He just had to get her away from everyone and let her know they should date, marry, and have a bunch of *kinder.*

He took two steps and bumped into a guy he'd never seen at Ray's before.

"What the fuck you lookin' at?" the man asked, unfortunately sounding sober. He had beady eyes and large hands and came to Axel's chest. Behind him stood two men who'd fastened their gazes on Axel as well. His friends, maybe.

"Not you." Axel glanced toward Rena and of course saw her staring at him and trouble. "Later, little guy."

The man's eyes bulged. "*Little guy*? I'm gonna bury my fist in—" the guy started, but Axel hurried past the jerk and his buddies, intent on behaving himself if it killed him.

Rena sighed. It was as if Axel had *trouble* written on his forehead. She watched as three men tried to pick a fight with the giant headed her way. But he ignored them. When one of them reached for Axel's shoulder to stop him, he grabbed the hand on his shoulder and turned, then somehow had his assailant's hand behind his back as he shoved the man's face against a nearby tabletop.

She winced.

Next to her, her friends watched with *oohs* and *aahs*. Axel, to his credit, moved quickly. He said something to the man, waited for him to respond, then stood and, ignoring the small crowd watching him, made a beeline in her direction.

"Oh," Lara sighed. "The handsome Viking is coming to plunder."

Hope, her cousin's fiancée, sighed as well. "He's so hot, in a tough, scary kind of way. I mean, his muscles are almost bigger than J.T.'s."

To that, Rena, Lara, and even Del scoffed. "Seriously?" Del said. "Hope, take off the blinders. My brother is big. Hell, so is Mike. But next to Axel, they look like, well, like Johnny."

Lara snickered. Behind her, Johnny—her boyfriend—glared. "I heard that, Del."

"I know."

"Truth, bro," Rena heard one of his friends tell him. She smiled at the group.

Her eyes teared, and she sniffed. She was going to miss this place and everyone in it. Yes, the many patron of Ray's Bar had rough edges, but heck, so did she. She locked gazes with Axel. He stopped at the edge of the small crowd around her, looked at her over their heads, and gave her a soft smile.

That made her tear up even more because she hated that she was going to miss the big lug who made it a habit of staring and not talking to her. What kind of nutcase missed that?

"Speech!" J.T. yelled.

"Speech, speech," others repeated, until Ray sounded an air horn and shut everyone up.

"Okay, assholes, simmer down." Ray glared everyone into submission. "Not you, honey," he said to her. "Now, I'm gonna say my piece. Rena Jackson is one of my favorite people. She always showed up on time"—he glared at Sue and Wiley in particular—"made everyone smile, and never mixed up an order. Sweet as honey is our Rena. And we're sure as shit gonna miss her."

The crowd cheered and clapped until Ray yelled at them to be quiet again. "But this is a celebration, not a funeral. So we're gonna laugh and drink and make sure we take some of our girl's business cards. Rena's finally opened up that damn salon, and she needs customers."

More cheering.

Ray pretended to scowl at her before smiling. "I hope I get a discount when I come in."

"Ain't like you got a lot to work with, baldy!" yelled a smartass from the back.

"I know that's you, Earl!" Ray barked back then patted Rena on the shoulder. "Well, girl, give us your speech."

Rena wiped her eyes. "I'm going to miss you degenerates." Everyone laughed. "I mean it. You've all been like family, and I'll miss you. But I do plan on coming in to grab a cold one now and then. And this time I'll be nagging Sue from the other side of the counter."

Everyone toasted that.

"So eat and drink up. I doubt Ray will ever open the bar again for free drafts."

"The free drafts are done in ten minutes," he said loudly. "You people are drinking me dry!"

More laughter.

Rena finished by saying, "I'm keeping this brief because Del and J.T. told me I had to." She smiled at those booing her cousins, who shot her dark looks. "I love you all, and thanks for the party. I hope I'll see you at Rena's Salon off Rainier! Make sure you take a card before you leave. Ray's customers get a discount. Now drink up!"

The mood grew festive again. Someone plugged the jukebox back in, and the music started. Big J and Earl broke up a fight in the back, and two other bouncers Ray had brought in for the night seemed to be occupied near the corner with someone else.

A large hand wrapped around her arm, and heat filled her from head to toe. She didn't know how she knew, but she could always tell when Axel was close.

In a deep voice, he asked, "Ah, can I talk to you?"

"Sure."

He nodded to the left. "Away from the noise, *bitte*?"

She shrugged, doubting his goodbye would take more than a minute at most. Sadly, she'd given up on Axel as boyfriend material. He had looks, a body she'd had many, *many* naughty dreams about, and a great smile. But she needed a man who could communicate. And that was not him.

"Sure." To the gang now watching her, she said, "I'll be right back." *This won't take long.*

Lara and Hope winked at her. The guys gave Axel the evil eye, though she saw her cousins nodding at him. Oh boy. They'd better not have said anything to encourage him.

She shot them death glares as she let Axel lead her back behind the bar. But he didn't stop there. He continued with her down the hallway into the back supply closet. He turned on the overhead light and closed the door behind them.

"Axel?" Rena might be nervous with another guy in a dark closet, but not Axel. From the first he'd gone out of his way to protect her and all the girls in the bar.

He let go of her arm but didn't back up. "Sorry. I wanted to talk to you without interruption."

"Go ahead."

She swore his cheeks turned pink, which intrigued her. Axel Heller did look like a big old Viking. And like the warriors of old, he had a tan from time spent under the sun. How, she had no idea. Seattle didn't like to let the sun out until closer to April. Axel wasn't pale but a warm, buttery beige. His dirty-blond hair looked like a cascade of tarnished gold, and the beard and mustache he'd grown in the past months made her weak at the knees. She normally liked her men clean-shaven, but he was *rocking* that facial hair.

Her fingers itched to cut his mane back, to better frame the hard planes of his face.

She swallowed loudly, aware her heart thundered. With any luck, he'd mistake her silence as patience and not mesmerized awe.

Axel gave a nervous cough, which made him absolutely adorable. "I am happy for you but sorry to see you go."

"Thanks, Axel." She smiled.

His eyes narrowed on her face, and she felt his intensity like prickles of electricity all up and down her spine. "You have the prettiest smile," he said, his voice deep, quiet.

"Th-thanks." She backed up a step, fighting the absurd impulse to throw herself into his arms and just kiss him already. "Well, I'd better—"

"Do I make you nervous?" He closed the distance between them.

"Nervous?" She gave a *nervous* laugh and wanted to smack herself. "Nah. I'm just… I'd better get back to the party."

"I hear you are going to start dating again."

Stupid J.T. and Del. "So what?"

"So… Maybe you and I could… We could… Well, ah, go out for coffee sometime."

Coffee? Lame. But hey, he was trying. Too little too late. She imagined a year of saying hello over lattes while he tried to find a way to ask to hold her hand. "Axel, I'm just going to be honest with you. I want a real relationship. And I don't think that's with you."

After a pause, he asked, "Why not?"

"Because it's taken you almost a year to ask me out. For coffee."

"*Ja.* I know." His cheeks definitely looked pink. "But I wanted to be good with you. For you to like me and trust me."

"I do like and trust you. But I want a real relationship *now.* Not in another year or two years when you've decided we're good enough friends to try a kiss." She blushed, embarrassed to have to put it out there like that. Then she felt bad for being so blunt. Rena grabbed his hand, all too aware of how much larger he was than her. "Axel, sweetie, I don't mean to hurt your feelings. I just think you and I have two different speeds."

Axel had royally fucked up. Frozen with indecision on how to handle her, he'd avoided the problem instead of confronting it head-on. Unlike the way he dealt with the rest of life, delving into his issues headfirst, with Rena he'd held back.

Time to flip that idea on its head.

She might call him a thinker, but Axel thrived on the long game, on strategy. Rena, for all her sweetness, couldn't back down from a challenge. His backup plan, had she said no to a date, would have to be put into play.

Hell, everyone at the bar placed wagers on everything from how much Big J could guzzle in one sitting to how poorly Foley threw darts. For ten months, Axel had watched his pretty Rena bet with the best of them. Time to go big or go home.

She didn't look scared of him, but he wanted to make doubly sure before he made a move he couldn't take back. "Are you sure I don't frighten you?"

Her eyes narrowed. Perfect. Now she looked angry. "Why? Because you're huge? So what? I can defend myself, and I have friends."

He couldn't help a small smile. "I would never hurt you."

"You're damn right." She crossed her arms over her chest, too peeved to be worried now. Falling right into his clutches.

"I think we should date."

Rena sighed. "I just told you—"

"I bet you a kiss you can't resist me."

She opened her mouth and closed it. "Excuse me?"

"One kiss." His heart threatened to thunder out of his chest. "When it's done, if you're not impressed, I do not bother you again."

She blinked. "You want to kiss me?"

"I want to prove to you that you can't resist me." Then, to stoke the fire, he added, "I'm too much for most women to handle. I've seen you looking at me. And I know you say you aren't, but really, you're afraid of how you feel."

"I'm *feeling* annoyed. But go ahead and pucker up." Her eyes blazed. "Because I'm resisting you just fine—forever." She stuck her face out and pursed her lips.

And he still found her unforgettably beautiful, even looking like a fish starved for oxygen.

Axel let himself smile and threw his all into the kiss, knowing he had everything on the line.

CHAPTER THREE

Rena wanted to punch the arrogance off his face. In the time she'd known him, Axel had never come across as the typical macho jerk like half the guys in the bar. Too bad she'd been mistaken about him for so long.

She readied for his kiss that likely would be all slobbery lips and forceful tongue. A man with his lack of social skills wouldn't know the meaning of the word *finesse*.

Disappointed and angry with him for ruining the fantasy, she waited.

The kiss, when it came, shocked the hell out of her.

His lips were firm but soft, learning the feel of her as he deepened the contact. He placed his hands on her cheeks, those hot, callused palms cradling her tenderly while he caressed with a skill that turned her into a mindless mess. All from a simple, closed-mouth kiss?

Good God. Axel was *dangerous.* She leaned into him, wanting more. As if he read her mind, he angled his head slightly and slid his tongue between her lips, stroking with a delicacy that made her tremble.

She heard herself moan and clutched his strong forearms for support, feeling weak at the knees.

Before she could fall against him, he pulled back and stared down at her, one brow raised in question. "So, I win, *ja?*"

It took her a moment to realize she was clinging and dizzy. More, that her body was on fire to have him. Yet Axel seemed barely fazed, his breathing a little faster than it had been, but the rest of him might as well have been untouched. She couldn't even tell if he was aroused because he wore jeans and an overlarge shirt that covered his fly.

Embarrassed she'd even looked there, she met his gaze and saw what looked like victory.

"Double or nothing," she offered.

He frowned. "What?"

"If I win…" She paused, mortified to have to work to catch her breath. "You have to admit *you* can't resist *me.* You win, we go on not one but two dates."

He shrugged. "You're pretty, yes, but irresistible?" He smirked at her, his dark-blue eyes fathomless pools of conceit. "We should test this again."

As much irritated as turned on, Rena yanked him closer, hugging the man as much as she could while he bent down to meet her. She planted a doozy on him.

And wondered if she'd have any brain cells left when all her ability to reason suddenly centered between her legs.

Axel had never given a better performance in his life. And that wasn't the kiss but pretending he hadn't been overly affected by the sexy woman in his arms. Good Christ, but she'd fried him. Totally ruined him for any other woman again, ever.

He'd never been as turned on from such a chaste kiss, and knowing she wanted more had made it all worse.

But this, letting her take charge to prove he couldn't resist her? He surely deserved a medal for not throwing her up against the wall and fucking her until she couldn't walk.

She kissed him, nibbling at his lower lip so that he opened his mouth, allowing her tongue to slip inside. The touch as she stroked against his mouth lit him up like a supernova.

He moaned, unable to keep himself apart any longer, unable to pretend. His cock threatened to either break or explode, his body one giant nerve. Holding Rena felt better than anything he'd experienced. Though small, she had generous breasts and a gentle curve to her waist. And the rest of her… He swore to himself, doing his best to keep his hands on her hips and not knead that delectable ass. He shouldn't use his thigh to spread her legs or stroke down her belly and delve under the panties hiding the very heat of her.

She hugged him tightly, her strong arms around his shoulders while she plundered his mouth. And plunder she did, conquering him with little effort.

When she broke the kiss, he wanted to drag her back for more. But a shout, glass breaking, and laughter from outside reminded him they kissed in a closet in Ray's Bar, of all places. Making love to Rena the first time had to be perfect. That was if he hadn't ruined everything by losing the bet—because she sure as shit proved he couldn't resist her.

They parted, and he had to force himself to let her go, straightening to his full height.

Rena fluffed her hair, the golden curls so bright and bouncy, just like her. His heart ached at the sight of her, and he had to school himself to look tough.

And not like a dumbass grinning from ear to ear because he'd finally gotten to kiss the girl.

"Well?" she asked, breathless.

"What do you think?" he answered, sounding as if he'd swallowed a truckload of gravel.

She looked him over from head to toe and grinned. "I think I proved my point."

"*Ja,* that you cannot resist me. So that's two dates."

"*What?*"

"I think you win is what I'm saying."

"Wait. I win…two dates with you?"

"You're irresistible." He couldn't help smiling at her puffed-up pride before she realized what he'd said.

"You admitted it. So I win."

"As I said," he agreed. "But also, you find me irresistible. We're a pair."

She tried to look stern and failed when she laughed. "Okay, we're both amazing. You sure are good at kissing."

"And other things," he had to add, done with trying to play it safe. She flushed, and he did his best not to show his satisfaction. "We go out, yes? When?"

"Um, I don't know."

"Tomorrow." He didn't want to give her time to rethink things.

"Well, I guess."

"Good. I come pick you up, and we go out."

"I—okay." She frowned up at him. "Has anyone ever told you you're kind of pushy?"

"No. But I have been told I'm slow, that my speed isn't what a woman wants, and I am not frightening in the least."

Rena blew out a breath. "I didn't mean that the way it came out." At his look, she amended, "Maybe I did. I don't know. You're confusing. You act one way but… Never mind."

She looked embarrassed, and he chuckled. "Yes, so irresistible when you mumble at the floor."

She flashed angry eyes at him and, seeing his teasing smile, grinned back. "Well, well. There's another side to Axel Heller after all. Okay, big guy. I'll see you tomorrow. Gimme your phone."

He did, and she added herself as a contact.

He felt as if he'd just won the lottery.

"My phone number and address are in there. Tomorrow at two work for you?"

"*Ja.* I'll see you then." He didn't want to ruin anything, so he stole a quick kiss, committing her taste to memory. Then he left the closet and the party before he embarrassed himself, grinning like a lovestruck fool.

Rena spent the rest of the night in a blur. She'd said the right things, fended off good-natured teasing about Axel, and generally enjoyed herself. But lying in bed that night, she could do nothing but replay their shared kisses.

They couldn't possibly have been that good, could they? She sighed, recalling how smooth he'd been, how hot. God, he had a mouth made for sin. For sex.

She shivered, doing her best to relax when images of Axel had the exact opposite result.

He'd bet her she'd find him irresistible. Bet won. But that didn't mean she'd fall into his arms so easily. Lord knew it had been forever since she'd had sex. But Axel worried her. She'd been attracted for so long, then to be done with him, only to have him act like a perfect Prince Charming to sweep her off her feet?

She rolled over and punched her pillow. She hadn't been kidding. She wanted a man, a real man who talked to her, made her laugh, and wanted to be with her…for more than just sex.

With Axel she had chemistry. She liked the guy, well, what she knew of him. But she needed to know more. And he needed to share without being nagged about it. She hated that her date with Axel scared her as much as it excited her.

She didn't want to be rid of him yet, but she had a bad feeling he'd end up ruining things before they'd begun.

♥ ♥ ♥

Sunday afternoon, while she and Axel walked around Green Lake drinking cocoa, she had to wonder if she'd willed the date to be bad. He'd gone with her suggestion to walk through the pretty, light flakes of snow continuing to fall despite the bright, sunny day. An odd contradiction, but the sun continued to peek out when the clouds shifted, and the day felt warm regardless of the white falling all around them.

Axel had been nothing but pleasant. He matched his long-legged stride to hers and talked more than he ever had to her about anything. He mentioned the weather and his fascination with American beers and how bad they all were and asked her about her salon.

He seemed to like listening to her talk, which warmed her. But he hadn't shared anything personal about himself at all, and they'd been walking for over an hour.

She stopped telling him about one of her stylists in an argument with another.

"What's wrong?" He sipped from his cup.

"You."

He froze in his tracks, forcing those behind him to go around. "What did I do?"

She felt like an idiot. He'd been polite and charming and had even bought her hot chocolate. He talked and walked and paid her attention, ignoring the many stares aimed his way. And at his height, with his looks, he always drew notice. But she couldn't help feeling like Axel wasn't sharing anything his buddies at his shop didn't already know.

"Tell me," he insisted in that low voice that wrapped around her and made her shiver deep inside.

"Well..." She toyed with a strand of hair and stopped herself, annoyed with the nervous habit. "Tell me something about *you*, Axel." She tugged him by the arm to continue walking with her.

"I did." He looked puzzled. "I like German beers best. Though Budvar isn't too bad, and it's Czech."

She rolled her eyes. "Not about beer or the weather or how blue the sky is. Like this: Hi, Axel. I'm Rena Jackson. My mom's name is Caroline, and she lives over in South Seattle. So she's close but not too close." Rena smiled. "I have relatives I love in the city. My uncle Liam, my cousins Del and J.T., and now a nephew since Del married Mike. Oh, and I'm about to be an aunt a second time once Del has her baby."

"What about your dad?" He gave her all of his attention as they navigated the many people thrilled with the pretty, nonthreatening snow.

"He's never been in the picture." Rena didn't feel hurt by that anymore. It had taken her a long time to come to terms with the fact her father had never wanted her.

"His loss," Axel said plainly. And he meant it, she could tell.

She smiled at him, aware he watched her with so much focus. Whenever he looked at her, she felt as if he saw nothing but her. She found it flattering but also a little disconcerting. What exactly did he see when he looked at her?

After a few moments of walking in silence, she wondered if she'd need to prod him, when he spoke.

"You know my mother died back in the summer. I loved her very much, and it's been…hard."

"I know, sweetie." She gripped him by the hand.

He squeezed and didn't let go. "My father and I are not close at all," he growled. "I have an older brother I don't know very well. Maksim works with my father in Germany. I came here, with my family, many years ago. After a while, my father and brother went back, but Mom and I stayed. She ended up going back to Stuttgart a few years ago." He paused.

"I know she had a tough time before she passed away. I'm so sorry for your loss."

He turned a wan smile her way. "Yes. I am too. She was an amazing woman."

The guy still cared for and missed his mom. Rena loved that about him, that he could feel so much for someone.

"I have been traveling back and forth these months helping my aunt and cousins with the farming. They needed some extra help, and I needed to be there for them. I told my mother I would."

"That's nice of you. Farming?"

He gave her a genuine smile. "A few cows and pigs. Goats for milk. They are more gentleman farmers than the real thing. But it makes them happy." He sighed. "They all loved my mother."

He didn't say anything more about her, and she didn't want to push him. So she changed the subject to his brother. "So you're not close to...Maksim?"

He frowned. "He spent much of his youth with my father, so no. We don't know each other well. When my parents spent time apart, I was with *Mutter,* Maksim with *Vater.* Maksim and I, we look alike. It's strange to see him."

"So you're saying he's big, strong, and handsome like you," she teased.

"*Ja.* But not so handsome. I am better." He winked at her.

Her heart pounded at his grin.

He watched her watching him, and his smile faded. He drew her to the side of the path, out of the way of the many strollers and couples walking. "Is this date okay?"

"Okay?" She wondered if he'd let her run her fingers through his hair. The dark-blond mane looked so soft.

"You are enjoying yourself?"

"I... Oh heck. Can I touch your hair?"

He paused. "Sure." He bent his head, and she ran her fingers through it, right about its softness.

"Can I cut your hair?"

"I had planned to get an appointment this week. With you."

"Good. But I tell you what. You let me style your hair the way I want to, I'll do it for free. Then you tell everyone who cut your hair. You'll be a walking billboard for my salon."

"Sounds good to me."

She watched him raise his hand to cup her cheek, the movement unbearably slow. "Y-you don't want to know how I'll cut it?" Right now he had a shoulder-length cut, all one length, and looked smokin'. She had a different look in mind, but one no less attractive. Then again, he'd been sexy-scary with a buzzcut. With Axel's features, hair or no hair, it didn't matter.

"I trust you." He ran his thumb over her cheek, and she did her best not to melt on the spot. When he gave her a slow smile, she lost all thought. "Notice I do not ask to touch *your* hair. I am a smart man. I never mess with a woman who makes a living with scissors."

"Ah, good." She cleared her throat. "Because I'd have to kill you."

He laughed and dropped his hand, and she wanted it back.

She reached for him at the same time he reached for her. They shared a warm smile and held hands as they finished their loop around Green Lake.

The car ride home passed too quickly, and as she left his truck, promising to see him the next day at four for a hair appointment, she realized they hadn't talked much on the ride at all. But they'd held hands the entire way home.

Rylan stuck his head in the door first thing Monday morning. "So, Boss, you finished the Escalade?"

Axel continued to frown at the paperwork on his desk, managing the paint and supplies they needed while wondering what the hell had happened to the budget. He had no one to blame but himself, he thought, knowing his time away from the shop was responsible for the imbalance on the books.

"Boss?"

Axel glanced up, still too pleased about his date with Rena to be too angry. Even if Rylan was a major pain in the ass. "*Ja,* I finished your work. Come in and sit down."

Rylan strutted in and sat. Not a small man, Rylan acted big and tough but nonetheless gave Axel the impression that he was not as confident as he portrayed himself to be.

"Rylan, you are creative, and your attention to detail is spot-on. But you're not good at following orders. If Kelly were here, things would be running smoothly. Unfortunately, he's out until April. You want to have a job when he comes back?"

"Yeah."

"Then get your head out of your ass and think. Follow orders. Watch and learn from Mateo and Smitty. Listen when Lou speaks. I've never met a finer artist. Not because he draws on command but because he listens to our clients and does what *they* want. Not what he thinks they should want." A bad habit Rylan had, of doing what he wanted regardless of what he'd been told.

"So you're saying you want sheep to work for you? Guys who obey, do what you say without question, go along with the herd?" It wasn't the sarcasm that made Axel pause but the hint of unhappiness he could sense. Having lived with it for so long, he knew well when a man dealt with impossible burdens.

"What is wrong with you?"

Rylan blinked. "What?"

"You're not being an ass on purpose. It's there, *ja*, but you are having a problem with something. Someone." He gauged Rylan for a response, seeing the flush that came from his candor.

"I'm sorry, okay?" Rylan blurted and stood. He began pacing. "I'm having…problems at home. I really need this job. I like it here. And I'm good at paintwork, which you'd know if you'd let me do some—" He broke off at the sight of Axel's stern expression. "Sorry." Rylan ran a hand through his shaggy hair. "I know I'm new. I know I fucked up a few times. But at my job before this one, they said I didn't take enough initiative."

"You mean they fired you because they found out about your record, and no matter how hard you worked, they wouldn't keep you."

Rylan paled, frozen to the spot. "You know?"

"I know about everyone who works for me." Axel sighed. "You should have told me."

"I want this job. I *need* it. My P.O. kept giving me static for not having anything, but it's so hard to find work when you've been in the system. And the places that will take you pay for shit."

Axel could imagine. "What were you in for?"

Rylan flushed. "You don't know?"

"I'm asking you."

If Rylan turned any more red, his head would go up in flames. "Assault. I was at a party, drinking. It got out of hand. I hurt a guy. He's fine, but he pressed charges."

"Assault is a misdemeanor."

Rylan blinked. "Ah, yeah, but, well, there were extenuating circumstances." Rylan paused and mumbled, "I didn't know he was a cop."

Axel studied him. "Anything else?" Something Smitty had mentioned stood out, but he waited to see if Rylan would say anything about it.

"Nothing."

Axel didn't blame Rylan for wanting to keep some secrets. But he knew how keeping them locked down could hurt.

"Fine. I'm not your parole officer. I'm not your friend, your coworker, or your therapist. I am your boss. I think you have real potential, but you need to stick to what we tell you. I like guys thinking outside the box. But not new guys. Kelly still does what he's told. To the letter. And I barely tolerate him." Axel liked the kid, thought the smartass a funny guy. And it never failed to amuse him that Kelly was still afraid to talk to him, mostly because Mateo talked like Axel was a bear to work with.

"So you're not firing me?" The hope on Rylan's face hurt to see.

Axel looked back down at his paperwork. "Not today. I don't care about a fight that landed you in prison. That's what you did. I care what you do. This is your last warning." He glanced up. "And get a haircut." He tossed a business card at Rylan. "Help out a fellow local and I'll forget I talked to you today."

"Oh, sure. Yeah. No problem." Rylan beamed. "I'm pulling dents and detailing." The crap work. "And I'm fine with that. Great."

"Get out."

"Oh, sure." He paused. "Um, do you want some coffee or something to eat? I'm going out for a food run. Smitty's orders."

Axel had caved not only to a soda machine but also to a high-end coffeemaker for the guys as well. "What's wrong with what we have in the break room?"

"Um, Smitty said he's not human unless he has his morning Doppio, whatever that is. I guess he got up late today."

"Tell him he's a pussy for not drinking it straight up black and cold. Then grab me a vanilla latte and an egg sandwich." When Axel reached for his wallet from his back pocket, Rylan stopped him.

"No, Heller. I got this. Consider it restitution for not working on Saturday with you and Smitty."

Axel shrugged. "Fine. But don't take all damn day."

Rylan gave him a mock salute and left. A few minutes later, Smitty barged in.

"I'm busy," Axel barked.

"Talked to Rylan, eh?"

Axel leaned back. "*Ja.* He's good now. I hope."

"Thanks. He's got some problems, but I'm trying to help him. I think he could be a real asset around here. Besides, we're getting really busy."

"You help everyone." At times too much. Smitty would give a guy the shirt off his back. Sometimes to his detriment. "Don't let him step all over you."

Smitty flushed. "Fuck you."

"Ah, and you're back. I worried with all the fancy coffee drinks and your fancy date on Saturday."

"Again, fuck you." Smitty flipped him off. "The date went nowhere, thanks for asking."

"Sorry."

Smitty shrugged. "His loss. So what about you and Rena?" Smitty looked him over and gave him a sly smile. "You haven't been such a prick today. So she didn't throw your ass to the curb, I take it."

"I went on a date yesterday. Just a walk around the lake. It was good." Remembering it made him feel warm inside.

"That's one dopey smile, son."

This time Axel gave Smitty the finger. "I have a haircut with her later today. But I'm wondering what to do with our next date. Something good. Not pathetic like walking again." He'd felt unsure about Sunday, but Rena had liked talking to him. Except he'd had to share. He shuddered just thinking about it. "She wanted a lot of talking, Smitty. Is that something I'm going to have to do a lot?"

Smitty nodded. "Yep. Your girl is a talker. You know that." He fingered his red locks. "She's talented. My cousin loves sitting in her chair while she makes him look pretty, so he says." He ignored Axel's snort of amusement. "But from what he said, that woman can *talk*. And she has a way of getting things out of a guy." Smitty shook his head. "Good luck."

"Thanks."

Smitty left, and Axel daydreamed about what the afternoon might bring. He hoped she didn't consider this their second date. A haircut? Then again, he didn't know what to do to romance her into a third date.

Who did he know to ask? Not Smitty. Smitty's idea of romance included fine dining and mutual blowjobs. Mateo and Axel weren't on a friendly kind of level. Lou might be a help. Axel's paint specialist had a million female relatives and had snagged a woman he was head over heels for. Had the dickhead shown up for work today, as he'd been scheduled to, Axel could have asked him.

Which gave him an excuse to confront Del McCauley at her garage. They'd get to talking about who had Lou's time this month, set a schedule, then he'd slip in a thinly veiled question about Rena. She'd be none the wiser, and he'd get insider info on his skittish quarry.

His *häschen*—little rabbit—a term of endearment he'd taken to calling Rena whenever he thought of her. Would she like that? Would she understand he meant it because she reminded him of a beautiful, golden-haired rabbit he'd admired when young? Or would she think he considered her his sleek prey? Either way worked for him.

CHAPTER FOUR

"You are *so* not fooling anyone with your not-so-subtle questions." Del shook her head, her arms crossed over her chest, as she stared at Axel from behind the desk in her office. She had her hair pulled back in a ponytail today, the colorful sleeves of tattoos on her arms lovely. Axel knew her brother had done them, and he wondered if he ought to book an appointment with J.T. soon to add to his own.

He pretended ignorance. "I came to let you know I need Lou this week and next. Three days at least. Nothing subtle about that."

He stood and waited, just staring at her. He gave her his cold, threatening stare, the one that scared so many into doing what he wanted without question.

The stubborn woman didn't look the least bit intimidated.

Huh. With most women, he worked to appear smaller, nicer, more easygoing. With Rena, he'd pulled out all the stops to smile and express a more tender mien. And it had worked. With Del, he wore his war face. She didn't blink an eye.

"Fine. You can have Lou. But I want to know what the hell you're up to with my cousin."

"Now who's not being subtle?"

She smiled through her teeth. "Talk, German boy, or I'll shove my cankles up your ass."

"Cankles?" He was unfamiliar with the word.

"Ah, never mind. Talk." She rubbed her belly, patted it, and smiled. "She's kicking again. I'm telling you. It's your voice."

"What Rena and I do is our business."

"Try again. She's my cousin, more like a sister. And I've watched her be brokenhearted too many times. She's been stressed with the new business, and it's her dream to make it a success. I won't have anything interfering with it or her." She gave him a serious stare.

For Rena, he'd put up with Del's interference. And, well, he liked her. "I am dating your cousin. We went out for a walk yesterday. Today she cuts my hair. But that's not a date." He frowned. "I don't know what to do for our next time out. Perhaps you can help."

"Wait. So you're really dating Rena?" Her surprise didn't help his ego. "She agreed to go out with you?"

"*Ja.*"

"Now, now, don't get testy." She tapped her belly. "My cousin is a romantic, I think I told you. Valentine's Day is coming up, and it's her favorite holiday." She studied him. "You want my cousin to fall for you? Romance the hell out of her, then do a big thing on Valentine's Day. She'll eat it up."

"What kind of big thing?"

"No clue. But I do know she loves chocolate and flowers."

He drew out a notepad. "What kinds?"

Del goggled at the behemoth taking actual notes on Rena. She and J.T. had done their best to shelter their softhearted cousin for years.

She'd been in and out of love a lot, but unlike Aunt Caroline, Rena rebounded, not making the same mistakes over and over with losers. Del knew Rena wanted what Del herself had found with Mike. It almost didn't seem fair that her romance-loving cousin remained single while Del had found love with an ex-romance novel cover model.

But now Rena was looking. Apparently Axel was looking right back. And taking notes? Jesus, the guy must be hooked on her cousin to be dopey enough to write shit down.

"I'm waiting." He looked at her with those dark-blue eyes, and she contained a shudder.

She'd never admit it, but sometimes Axel made her want to take a step back. Oh, she didn't think he'd ever hurt her. But he had a bridled rage, a raw force she could sense simmering beneath the surface.

"You ever hurt Rena, I'll gut you. Me, Mike, J.T., and my guys," she warned.

She didn't expect him to smile at her. And wow, did that smile turn him from a threatening hulk to one fine-looking man. She bit back a grin, determined to tell Mike that later on.

"*Gut.* You look out for Rena. She deserves that. Now, chocolates? What kind? And what about the flowers? Maybe her favorite books? She's a big reader, yes?"

Del rattled off a bunch of information she thought sounded right.

"*Danke,* Del. And I forgive you for being so selfish as to hog Lou all the time."

"Selfish, you—"

"*Ja,* selfish," he rumbled.

She sucked in a breath. "Come here." He hurried to her side, and she placed his large hand on her tummy. "Say something."

He just looked at her.

"Do it."

"Ah, well…" He said something in German that made the little girl under his hand squirm something fierce. Del loved feeling that life inside her.

"How cool is that?" she asked Axel, softening when she saw the look of wonder on his face.

Okay, she approved. A dude who could crush Fletcher and his guys yet still have a soft side for babies and her cousin, well, as she'd said, her cousin had certainly done worse.

"Very cool, Del." He stood and looked around. Then he whispered, "You will make a wonderful mother. And you are not a bad mechanic either." Then he glared down at her. "And stop stealing my people to work for your gutter of a shop."

He turned and left before she could stutter a response. But when the gang rushed to her office to know what she'd done to set Axel off, she figured she owed him one. "He had the nerve to demand I give him Lou back. Lou," she barked, "you're only going to Heller's for three days this week. Not a minute longer!"

Lou sighed. "Yes, Boss."

A tough chick, she had her reputation to consider. She yelled through the door as they all went back to work, "Good. And you tell Heller I said he can kiss my ass if he thinks I'm letting you go a second longer."

"Yeah, right." Lou was no fool. "I'll leave that to you."

"Fine. I'll do that." She'd tell Axel over the phone much later, where she could be heard sounding tough, not sniffing or wiping her eyes. *You will make a wonderful mother. And you're not a bad mechanic either,* he'd said. High praise from the normally taciturn Axel.

She blew her nose. Hell, these stupid tears weren't helping her street cred any.

♥ ♥ ♥

Rena had been jumpy all day, waiting for the clock to strike four.

"Yo, *chica*, chill." Stella Cortez Hernando popped her chewing gum and swept up the mess of hair from under her chair. One of four stylists in the shop, not including Rena, Stella did great work and had already brought in her share of customers. Stella preferred to work with nails and facials, but she occasionally did hair as well.

Nicky was out today, but Tommie "Call Me Thomasina and I'll Kill You" had been busy all day with back-to-back appointments. She was currently snipping and gossiping with a client they all secretly referred to as "Man-Eater." Cara Fuentes thought it her shining duty to sleep with (and brag about) as many men as possible. Be they single or attached, Cara didn't care. With her lustrous black hair, curvy figure, and amazing looks, she'd turned more than one man away from his significant other.

Rena caught Stella's gaze and saw the girl roll her eyes in Cara's direction. Cara kept talking about Johnny and how the guy had the hots for her despite acting like he loved Lara.

Tommie let her talk.

Rena, however, had a moment's pause. At five minutes to four, she had little time to mentally prepare for Axel…or Cara's reaction to Axel.

Her non-talky Viking would certainly attract Cara's notice.

Hmm. Might be a good way to see how he reacts when a woman with Cara's looks is around.

Sure, Rena had known Axel for a long time, and she'd seen him interact with women at Ray's. But he hadn't been serious about her then. Though, come to think about it, she'd never seen him flirt with anyone. He always seemed so serious unless giving her a smile.

The door beeped, and there he was, larger than life and needing a haircut. All talk in the salon ceased.

Tommie stood frozen with her scissors poised to cut Cara's brittle ends. Cara gaped at Axel via the mirror. The two women waiting for manicures stopped reading their magazines and gossiping and looked up, and up, at Axel.

He paused. "Four o'clock you said, yes?"

"Holy shit," Stella swore. "Honey, haven't I seen you somewhere before? I know, on the TV show *Vikings*."

He shot Stella a devastating grin. "That would be my little brother." At her look of astonishment, he said, "I'm kidding."

Cara and Tommie just stared.

Rena rolled her eyes. "Come on, Ragnar. Let's get a look at you."

Stella joined her at the hip. "Can I watch?"

"Us too?" one of the women waiting asked.

"No." Rena grabbed him by the arm. The others laughed, and the chatter resumed.

Rena led Axel through the large outer room, comprised of a small waiting area, a main desk, and two salon stations. Off the outer room, Stella typically worked at the dedicated nails and makeup table. They had a bathroom and additional back room occupied by two additional chairs and a wash station.

"I like this place," Axel said, sounding like he meant it. "It looks like you."

She looked around, proud and still stunned that her dream of owning her own place had finally come true. She'd saved for years, worked a bevy of jobs, and networked her tail off to find clients, so that when she'd officially opened a month ago, she'd known she was in good standing to make her business work.

She'd chosen to expose the brick behind the band of mirror that reached from wall to wall in the outer room, keeping the rest of the space white with bursts of fuchsia and funky graphic art done by local artists. The old wooden floors hid dirt while also making it easy enough to clean and provided yet another hint of character. Rena liked to think her place was fun, fresh, and creative.

"Thanks. I like it. Mike and his brothers helped with renovations, and my landlord is pretty pleased with how it turned out too. I give her free haircuts, and she takes money off the place every month."

"Not free. A trade then." Axel sat in the chair she directed him to, and she was glad she'd invested in something sturdy and practical, not just fashionable. A fair share of male clientele came in as well as women of all shapes and sizes. Rena had no intention of discriminating when it came to making people look and feel good about themselves.

Still, it took some effort to lower Axel's chair so she could give him a proper study. She ran her hands over his hair, secretly loving the silky strands, aware she was touching him, standing so close she could smell a hint of cologne. Her body tingled all over, and she clenched her legs together.

She cleared her throat and focused. "So, how about I shave the sides and focus on the top being a little longer?"

He stared at her in the mirror. "Whatever you want."

She found it hard to swallow, the air between them suddenly charged. "Um, okay. And the beard and mustache. We keeping them or do they go?"

"Whatever you want." That came out much huskier than his previous line. Damned if she wasn't imagining what that facial hair would feel like between her legs.

"Great. Need water. Be right back." She raced into the bathroom and rinsed her heated face with cold water. Then she left to grab a cup from the water cooler by the front desk and downed it in one swallow.

"I feel you, girl," Stella murmured and slapped her on the back. "Now go cut your man."

Rena felt foolish for darting away, but she returned to Axel with a professional smile. She put a salon cape on him and took her time, driven to give him the best dang haircut of his life.

She did most of the talking, with his occasional grunt or comment thrown in. She appreciated that he'd given one of his employees her card. "Say, I never thought about it. But would you like to set out some Heller's Paint and Auto Body cards? We have a local business board by the front door."

"Sure." Another one-word answer. She cut and clipped, keeping the top long, the sides short, and couldn't believe how amazing he looked with the transformation.

"You like it?" she asked as he stared at himself in the mirror.

He frowned. "It's different. But, yes, I like it."

She led him to the wash station, had him sit, and washed his hair. His low groans of pleasure didn't help her calm down much. The sight of his long torso and even longer legs stretched out while she ran her fingers over his scalp gave her inappropriate thoughts she'd never before had for a client, and at work no less.

She did her best to behave professionally and finished the shampoo then used a small amount of conditioner. She towel-dried his hair before leading him back to the chair.

"You have magic hands," he told her, his eyes really dark.

She cleared her throat. "Thank you."

"You're most welcome." He cracked his neck, and she winced. "Ah, better."

Rena finished trimming his hair then fetched the barber kit she used quite a bit with clients. After sculpting his beard and trimming his mustache, she put a conditioner on his facial hair. "Just let it dry and it's done."

"Smells good," he said, sounding sleepy. She met his gaze in the mirror. *This is how he looks when he first wakes up. Something I need to take my time finding out.*

"Yes." She pulled the cape away, and he stood, looming over her. "How tall are you, anyway?"

"Six-six." He checked himself out in her mirror. "Wow. You did a great job."

"Don't sound so surprised."

He chuckled.

"Now let me take a picture."

He waited while she snapped one with her phone. Then he pulled out his phone. "For me." Before she could take it, he dragged her next to him. "Stella," he called.

"You know Stella?"

"She's Lou's little sister." Stella stood at the doorway and stared. "Their grandmother loves to feed me." He motioned for the girl to take their picture—his and Rena's.

"Oh, you guys look great together." Stella winked at her then waggled her eyebrows.

Rena wanted to sink through the floor. "Just take it."

"Smile like you love each other."

Axel hugged Rena to him, and his body heat warmed her all over. Stella seemed to be taking a long time to snap a few photos. Then she had the nerve to grab Rena's phone and take a few more shots.

Axel leaned down to whisper, "This does not count as a date, you know."

She turned to stare up at him. "It doesn't?"

"No."

Stella chose that moment to hand her back her phone. "Great shots, Rena."

Axel didn't look at anyone but Rena. "I would like to take you to dinner Wednesday night. Anywhere you would like to go."

"Dinner, huh?" Dinner was safe. In a public place, where she, one, wouldn't have to cook, and two, might get another chance to get to know Axel. And just maybe she'd get another kiss if she were lucky. "Okay. But you pick."

"Is there anything you don't like?"

"Hmm. I'm not big on seafood. Not sure why, but I've never liked fish."

"No seafood. Everything else works?"

She nodded.

He smiled. "I'll pick you up at six, okay?"

"Wait. Let me check my calendar." She scrolled through her phone. "Oh, that works. I'm actually done at five if you wanted to come earlier."

"*Ja.* Five-thirty. I'll get you from here. Okay?"

She nodded and held out a hand. "Our second and final date."

He gripped her hand, but instead of shaking it, he watched her as he brought her hand to his lips. Then he opened her fingers and kissed the center of her palm.

For some wacky reason, that gave her the shivers.

"See you then." He left her standing there, gaping after him.

She followed him into the outer room and saw him wave at

Tommie and one of the ladies still waiting with a magazine before he left. Of Cara, she saw no sign.

When the door swung closed behind him, Tommie turned to her with wide eyes. "Was that man real, or did Thor suddenly come to life and just leave with one kickass haircut?"

Stella grinned. "Rena, you *have* to put that picture of him and you on Instagram. He is hot, you're amazing, and you look great together."

"Oh, let me see," Tommie insisted.

Stella grabbed Rena's phone and showed the pictures to her, her client, and the lady still waiting.

But Rena's attention had been caught by Cara, outside leaning against Axel's truck, smiling as if she had a secret while striking a pose.

♥ ♥ ♥

Axel did his best to get himself under control. Being around Rena always turned him on to some degree, but having her breasts brush against his back, her scent surrounding him, so close while she touched and stroked him, made his blood pressure rise and stay risen. Like other, *harder* parts of him.

He let the cold outside calm him down. By the time he felt like himself again, he'd crossed the lot to his truck. Only to see a woman standing against it. She'd been getting her hair done by the cute stylist with the neon-pink eye makeup when he'd walked in.

The woman leaning against his truck was pretty enough, voluptuous, and knew how to look her best. The stylist had done a pretty decent job on her, cutting her hair so that it seemed to float over her shoulders, the dark ends curling over breasts tightly wrapped in a dress meant for summer. The woman wore a thick jacket over it, but she left it open. To better showcase her assets, he imagined.

"Hel-lo, sexy." She looked him up and down.

"Hi." He waited for her to move, feeling someone watching him. He turned to see what looked like movement behind Rena's shop door, though with the dark-paned glass, it was hard to tell.

"You want to grab something to drink, maybe come back to my place later?"

"I'm sorry. I have to get home."

She reached out and stroked inch-long nails in a leopard print down his arm. Good God, how could she function with nails that long? "Oh now, come on. Wouldn't you like to nibble on some of this?" She waved a hand down her body.

Not surprisingly, she left him cold. He'd long since passed the age where sexual conquest was the end-all. He didn't want meaningless sex and never had. Axel prized emotion and connection over physical satisfaction. Before he'd become enamored with Rena, his past lovers had been women he'd known and liked, long-term sexual partners he'd enjoyed for companionship as well as sex.

But the moment he'd seen Rena, he'd ceased being with other women. Busy with work and family, he'd at first found that the lack of sex hadn't mattered. He'd been hooked on Rena anyway. And then his mother had died, and he hadn't done more than grieve. When not grieving, he only wanted one woman.

And it wasn't this one.

He didn't answer, just stared at her until she moved out of his way. She didn't turn to watch him go, either, but hot-footed it to her sporty little coupe. Axel waved at the salon then got in his truck and left.

A new worry popped into his head. He had one more date to convince Rena to agree to see a hell of a lot more of him. Where the heck should they go? Should it be fancy or casual? Fun or more serious?

Would she be insulted if he took her somewhere she didn't consider date-worthy?

Hell. What to do? Once at home, he mulled over the list Del had given him of Rena's likes and dislikes. And he thought about Rena and all he knew about her. He was in for the long haul, but he needed something huge to grab her interest and hold it.

Time to go big…and hope it was enough.

♥ ♥ ♥

When Rena arrived home, she found her cousins waiting on her doorstep, both wearing wide, ugly grins.

"Oh, man." She groaned. "Come on in." She let herself into the townhome she used to share with Del before her cousin had married Mike. Rena appreciated having her own space for a while, but eventually she'd have a roommate again. "Have I told you how much I hate that you left me?"

Del nodded. "Ever since I moved out. But, hey, keep complaining every time I come over if it makes you feel better."

"It does." Rena grabbed a juice for herself and gave one each to her cousins.

Del looked around. "It's emptier without me, isn't it?"

"What's with you and Heller?" J.T. asked, no preamble. "Sam forwarded me the photo you sent to Lou."

"J.T. sent it to me too," Del added.

"Well, that was fast." Freakin' Stella must have shared the photo when she'd had Rena's phone. "I gave him a haircut. Didn't it turn out great?"

"I'll say." Del grinned. "He looks pretty chummy with his arm around you."

"Oh stop." Rena's cheeks felt hot. "It was a haircut. That's all."

"From an artistic perspective, I'd have to agree that you did a great job. The camera loves him." J.T. grimaced. "But don't tell him I said that."

"Ditto," Del agreed. "I like that he and I don't get along. It's the natural order of things."

Rena had had a long day. She still didn't know how she felt about Axel giving Cara the brush-off. Good and bad, because now she felt like he thought they had a thing going. Which they didn't, not yet, really. But she wanted to, and that bothered her. She liked him a lot. Maybe more than he liked her? Did he just want her for sex? And if so, would that be a bad thing? She wanted to try him on for size, for sure. But did she want more than that? She—

"Oh my God." Del groaned. "Her brain is doing that squirrelly thing where it runs and runs and never stops. Like a hamster on the wheel. J.T., smack her on the head so it stops."

Rena shot her cousins *the look,* and they cracked up laughing.

"Sorry." J.T. pulled her in for a hug. "Del made me come over to give you shit. You're a great stylist, honey. Seriously, Axel looked amazing in the picture. I guarantee you're going to have a ton of clients coming your way because of it."

"Thanks, J.T." Such pleasure from a simple compliment.

"Yeah, you're amazing," Del agreed. "And speaking of which, I need you to cut Colin next week if you can. He's getting so hairy he's scary."

"My little guy? Sure." Rena loved him. She glanced at Del's belly and felt a sudden yearning. Heck, she'd turned thirty-three not so long ago. When would she need to stop dreaming about having babies? Granted, women had them in their forties and later, but the risk for health problems went up as a woman aged. Oh no, what if she didn't find anyone in time and her eggs shriveled up and fell off her ovary tree?

"What's that look?" Del asked, leaning in.

Rena repeated what she'd been thinking.

J.T. ran a hand down his face.

Del tried to bite back a grin.

"It's not funny," Rena snapped, feeling emotional and tired. She tried to laugh with her cousin at the absurdity of an ovary tree then broke down in tears.

"Hey now." J.T. looked at his sister and back at Rena, worried. "We were just teasing you."

"I know. I just… I want to get married, have babies, be in love. I know more about romance than both of you put together!" She waved at the bookcases lining the living room, shelves filled with books about love from A to Z. "Why am I still single?" For some reason she wanted to lash out at Axel of all people.

"I shouldn't go out with him anymore," she mumbled to herself. "I don't have time to waste."

"What?" Del frowned. "Are you talking to us?"

"To herself, I think." J.T. sighed and picked Rena up as if she weighed nothing. He cuddled with her on the couch, the way he always did to make her feel better. "Rena, your time is coming. Now quit thinking so hard. Love comes when you least expect it. Hell, if Del could get lucky, you sure as hell can."

"Thanks a lot." Del shot him a sour look. "But he's right. Don't look for it and I swear Cupid will knock you sideways."

"But I can't stop myself from looking. I try to forget I want a boyfriend, a lover, a friend who'll put me first. But that desire for love is always there. You guys don't understand. I… Heck. I should stop messing around with Axel and get serious about finding a guy. I'll be thirty-four this April! God!" She rose from J.T.'s lap. "Sorry. I'm super tired. It's been a stressful day. You guys go home and tell Mike, Colin, and Hope hi from me. I'm going to bed early." She left them before she broke down in stupid tears again.

After a visit to the bathroom, she cried even harder and felt cramps set in. *Of course* she had to be overly emotional, on her period, and still single.

After settling into bed, she was surprised to drift right into sleep.

But damned if she didn't dream about an endless walk around Green Lake with a mute Axel. And in it, she aged into an old crone step by step while nearby, trees dropped green, baby-like leaves that withered and crumbled to dust, swept away by the wind.

CHAPTER FIVE

Axel stared at the front door of Rena's townhome, not sure if he'd made the right call by showing up unannounced. After the haircut Monday, he'd thought they were on track for a date tonight, but she'd called yesterday to cancel. "You're nice, Axel, but we'd never work as a couple. Thanks. I hope you understand," she'd said and hung up before he could respond.

He had no idea what he'd done or said to cause such a turnabout in attitude. From what he'd seen, Rena liked him well enough. First off, that kiss at Ray's had proven they had chemistry. So he had that going for him. Plus she'd given him a lot of interested looks in her salon, leading him to think the kisses hadn't been a fluke. So what the hell had changed her mind?

Damn it. He'd been too slow for too long. Then when he made his move, she rejected him without a reason? What about Ray's? Had their connection in the closet meant nothing to her?

He'd punched a heavy bag in his garage for a long time last night, enough to bruise his knuckles. He must have worn his mood at work because the guys had given him space. Even Rylan kept that big trap of his shut.

Stewing and irritated because he didn't stew, or at least he didn't like to think he did, Axel made a command decision. If Rena wanted to tell him to get lost, she could do it to his face. He'd accept her rejection with dignity, no whiny fool and too proud to beg. But damn it all, she should have the guts to give him a rational reason why—he intimidated her, he was too blond, too tall, too ugly, too stupid. Something more than a lame "we'd never work as a couple."

He left his truck and strode up the walkway to her door with purpose. Then he knocked. Firmly.

"Hold on," he heard her yell through the door and hated that his heart beat faster.

After a pause, in which he hoped she'd been checking on his identity through her peephole, she opened the door. "Axel?" Her girlish squeak made him want to smile. Her hand went immediately to the scarf hiding her hair. Then she frowned, dropped her hand, and growled, "What are you doing here? I told you the date was off."

He drank her in, starting at the top of her head wrapped in a pretty scarlet-and-yellow scarf, down to her face free of makeup and even more beautiful because of it, to the fuzzy lemon-yellow sweatshirt and matching bunny pajama pants she wore. On her feet she had thick orange socks. She looked tired, yet the sudden glint in her eyes warned him not to mention the fact or that he'd found her in her comfy clothes.

So he did anyway. "I like your pants."

She looked down at them and sighed. "It's pajama night."

"Okay." He stood there, staring at her, and all thought left him, the need to kiss those plump lips almost more than he could stand.

She cleared her throat, a soft look of embarrassment crossing her features. "Um, did you need something? Because it's been a long day and I'm in for the night."

Without him.

He frowned. "Tell me what I did. Why did you cancel our date? I'll go, I promise. I just want to know why."

She blinked. "You came over here to hear me tell you why I broke off the date?"

"Why you reneged on our bet, *ja.*" Annoyance replaced his adoration for the woman. "I was promised two dates."

"I, that's... What does it matter?"

"It matters," he muttered.

She stared at him, and he could see the nice person inside her wrestling with the bothered woman standing in front of him. Nice won out. "Oh hell. You want a second date? Fine. Come in." She turned on her heel, giving him a glimpse of her lovely ass bedecked by smiling cartoon bunnies.

"Thank you, *Häschen,*" he said, unable to stop a grin. "I am overjoyed to be invited into your lovely home."

She harrumphed and flopped back onto her couch, pointedly not looking at him. "I'm in real mode. This is me." She pointed to herself. A few golden curls escaped the scarf to frame her face, highlighting her delicate features, the warm brown of her cheeks. He wanted to tell her how pretty she looked, but she said, "I know I look like a hag. If you're smart, you'll shut up about it."

He had no idea what she was talking about. He preferred real to fake any day, and she had true beauty inside and out. Makeup only enhanced what was already there. But in her current frame of mind, she'd accuse him of being sarcastic if he told her the truth. Then she'd kick him out. So he remained silent and turned to study her home instead.

He couldn't believe she'd allowed him inside and hurried to get a better glimpse into the snarly little rabbit burrowing into her blanket.

The home looked lived in, the furniture comfortable and colorful, the wooden floor old and scarred and needing a new finish. Stairs to the left of the front door headed upstairs, and the hallway past the kitchen likely led to a bathroom or set of rooms farther back.

In her surprisingly spacious living room, on a dark-red couch, throw pillows in various colors were scattered, some on the floor, moved out of place by Rena's lounging. A blemished wooden coffee table and side table framed the couch, and two ratty red-and-tan patterned chairs sat on either end of the coffee table. The sectioned-off kitchen had an L shape with a dining area large enough for a table and six chairs but which currently had four. In the kitchen, a few dirty dishes littered the counters and sink.

The home felt like Rena, inviting, warm, and, he thought with amusement, a bit scattered. Unlike his own residence where everything had its place.

Rena also had a lot of photos of friends and family, with a sea of pictures on a side table in addition to the mantel over a fake fireplace. He saw her cousins and uncle, a woman who had to be either her sister or mother, they looked that much alike, the guys at Ray's, the gang at Webster's Garage, and a few more of Rena with people she obviously considered close.

And there, taking up the entire back wall of the living room, shelves teemed with row upon row of books.

Paperbacks filled four floor-to-ceiling bookcases. On closer inspection, he saw she'd organized them by genre then alphabetical order—according to the sticky note tags separating sections. He felt as if he'd walked into a bookstore, seeing some covers facing out, others with just their spines. Almost all of the books had couples or shirtless men on the covers. Just like the three books she had stacked on her coffee table in front of her.

A surreptitious glance showed buff, half-naked, long-haired men holding women in their arms. He blinked and leaned closer but only caught one title before she turned over the books, covers down.

"*Storm Lords: The Viking Who Loved Me*…?"

She kept her gaze on the TV. "Look, Axel. This is as good as it gets for me on a weeknight. I'm watching Lifetime, eating ice cream, and reading."

"All at the same time?"

"Yes, as a matter of fact." She finally looked up at him and arched a brow. "Is that a problem for you?"

"Depends." He nodded to the large tub of ice cream near the books. "What kind are you eating?"

"Vanilla creamsicle. Why?"

"My favorite." Before she had a chance to respond, he scooped her up and sat with her in his lap in one smooth move. While he adjusted the blanket back over them, she tried to scoot away.

She gasped and shoved, unsuccessfully, at his chest. "What are you doing?"

"I am getting comfortable. What do you think?"

"With me on your lap? Seriously?"

"*Ja.* You're warm. Must be the bunny pajamas."

She smiled before she could stop herself then scowled up at him, her eyes bright. "You're still wearing your jacket, doofus. How comfy can you be?"

He chuckled and shrugged out of the coat, tossing it behind him to the floor. "Ah, the love words. I knew they'd come."

"Idiot." She sighed and rested her head against his chest. "You're pretty warm yourself. Like a giant heater."

"Who has an amazing haircut." He wondered if she could hear his heart racing through his shirt.

She chuckled. "Yes, you do. You look great, by the way."

"I know."

She laughed again.

"So why did you"—*break my heart, ruin me for any other woman*—"cancel our date?"

She mumbled something against his chest he couldn't understand. He leaned back and looked down to see her eyes shiny.

"Rena?" He brushed her chin, aware of how rough his fingers felt against such soft skin. Damn, there went the rest of his body tensing up when he'd been trying so hard to be all friendly and nonthreatening, acting as if he didn't want to rip her clothes off and fuck her right here, right now.

But he wasn't an animal. And her tears bothered the hell out of him, so he willed his body to at least try to behave.

"I'm sorry." She sniffed.

"Stop." He hugged her close, ignoring her brief tension and reveling in the fact she relaxed and snuggled closer. "*Ja,* you just be easy, *Häschen*. I'll take care of you."

"What did you call me?"

"Little rabbit." He smiled. "It's actually a nice thing to say in German. Like a pet name."

"Pet. Ha." She grumbled something but didn't try to leave his embrace. "I shouldn't have canceled our date. A bet's a bet."

"So why did you?" He stroked her shoulders and back, offering comfort, nothing more.

She sniffed again. "Because I want to fall in love and have babies and in-laws and I'm thirty-three already. I haven't dated in a year, and no one flirts with me anymore."

He actually liked hearing no one flirted with her anymore, but he didn't think she had a clue that J.T. had put out the word to keep a distance, seconded by Ray, Axel, and the mechanics at Del's. People who all cared that the softhearted bartender deserved better than most of the clientele at Ray's.

But he stayed quiet and let her get it all out.

"And when I do date, it's all the wrong guys. We date, they seem nice, act like they want more than just a roll in bed. Then they're either too boring or they lie. They have girlfriends. They want money, a place to stay, free drinks at Ray's." She rambled some more, ending with, "It's the lies I can't take."

He considered all that she'd said. "You give free beers to your boyfriends?" That would have been an added bonus.

She pinched him.

"Ow." Or not.

"No. I do *not* give free beers at Ray's." She pulled away to glare up at him then squashed her head back to his chest. "I just want what Del has. What J.T. has. What everybody I know has." She pressed harder against his chest, and he had a feeling she was drying her tears, which hurt him more than he'd have expected. "I'm going to get a cat."

A random statement he had no idea what to do with, so he said what was in his heart, censored a bit. "Rena, you are the most lovable woman I know." *I think I love you. I want to marry you and have babies with you.* "You just need time to find the right man." *Me.*

She sighed. "Yeah, I've been hearing that over half my life. But when is the right man going to find me? When I'm eighty?" Her breath hitched. "I'm sorry for unloading on you. But you wanted to know why I canceled our date."

"I'm still waiting."

"Did you not just hear me tell you I want a man? For babies, marriage, for life?"

"*Ja.* And?"

She stilled against him. "Are you volunteering?"

Hell yes. He cleared his throat. "I think you go too fast. You must start small. With someone who is a good kisser, maybe."

She said nothing but didn't shake off the hand on her back.

"Then you go on some dates. You see what you have in common." Uh-oh. Not smart. What did he and she have in common? "What do you like to do?"

"I like to read."

"I like to read." Auto parts magazines and some old porn forums, but he could fake it, he was sure.

"Yeah? Romance books?" She sounded amused, no longer crying. That was good.

"Well, no, but I would try one. What else do you like to do?"

"I like babysitting Colin." She paused then started crying again. "I have no hobbies. No life. I work all the time, and now I realize I don't have anything I like to do except talk to people and pour drinks. I actually did like working at Ray's, but not as much as I love having my salon."

He let her cry it out, hearing some words he understood, though most he did not. *Single forever, old maid, dried up and done.* The gist of being single forever.

She did have a flare for the dramatic.

As she spoke, her ice cream melted, and the sitcom she'd been watching changed to a drama with potential. He stroked her back and hugged her tight, semi-aroused the whole while. Though he did his best to pay attention to her whispered ranting, he soon grew embroiled in a kidnapping that ended in a shootout and a huge kiss between the leads that didn't make much sense but that he found he liked. The credits rolled at the end, and he realized Rena had fallen asleep on his chest.

Holding her felt so right. He just sat there, keeping her close. She mumbled something in her sleep.

"Rena, sweetheart, you okay?"

"Axel, will you be my valentine?"

He froze, wondering if she was aware of what she'd asked. "Rena?"

She didn't answer, and he knew she probably wouldn't remember it come the morning. But he would.

"Yes, *Liebling*." He kissed the top of her head. "I am yours. Time to make sure you know you're mine."

When Rena woke in her own bed the next morning, she blinked up at the darkness. A glance at her phone showed it hadn't yet reached six, so she had a few more minutes to sleep in before she got a fresh start on the day. She stretched and moaned, feeling a few pops of relief.

Then she froze.

How did I get here?

The events of the previous night came rushing back at her, and she covered her face with a pillow, mortified that Axel had seen her in her bunny PJs while she'd been whining and crying about not having a man.

God. Can my life get any worse?

She sucked in a breath and darted for the bathroom. *Yes, my life can get worse.* She groaned again. There, out for anyone to see, six different hair products, a sludge of toothpaste on the counter she'd meant to clean up last week, an open box of tampons, and, on the floor, the dirty clothes she'd worn yesterday as well as the towel she planned to wash when she did laundry. She looked like a slob. She could only pray Axel hadn't needed to use the bathroom. Then again, if she'd been in his place and he'd been passed out, would she have snooped?

Yep. Totally.

She covered her burning cheeks and said out loud, needing to hear the truth, "Well, it's not like he can think worse of me than he already does."

Needing to clear her mind, she hurried into workout tights and some layers, donned a headband and her walking shoes, and set out for some early morning exercise. She knew this neighborhood in Rainier and felt comfortable walking with only her keys and pepper spray for protection, just in case. Rena was no fool.

No, not when it comes to protecting your body from a would-be mugger. But God forbid you not let on to the sexiest man alive how pathetic and needy you are.

Fortunately the chill air hadn't affected the dry sidewalks, so she didn't fear slipping. A good thing, because her walk grew faster as, in her haste to recall last night, she remembered everything she'd told him. Yet as she moved, she realized something else. Axel hadn't made fun of her. He'd listened. He'd called her the most lovable woman he knew. He'd held her close and hugged her when she'd cried. Her heart skipped a beat recalling that.

Such compassion from the big, strong bruiser.

Yet for all that he'd listened, he hadn't volunteered to be her Mr. Right, had he?

She would have sighed if she could catch a breath. Instead, she warmed up to a light jog, motivated to run off her embarrassment.

Half an hour later, she returned home and went into the kitchen to grab some water, glad she'd worked up a sweat despite the winter cold.

At the sight of a single red rose lying on the dining table, she froze. Had someone broken in while she'd been gone? Before panic could set in, the note by the flower held her transfixed.

She saw Axel's name scrawled at the bottom.

Rena stroked the pretty red petals and stared at the note. In strong, bold caps, he'd written:

HÄSCHEN, I AM GLAD YOU GOT SOME MUCH NEEDED SLEEP. YOU ARE MORE LOVELY THAN YOU KNOW. EVERYONE BUT YOU CAN SEE IT. THIS FLOWER DOES NOT DO YOU JUSTICE, BUT I WANTED YOU TO KNOW YOU DESERVE BEAUTY IN YOUR LIFE. I DID TELL YOU I WAS LEAVING WHEN I TUCKED YOU INTO BED, BUT I DO NOT THINK YOU HEARD ME. I WILL SEE YOU FRIDAY NIGHT FOR OUR NEXT DATE. (BECAUSE TONIGHT DID NOT COUNT)

HAVE SOME FAITH THAT YOUR MR. RIGHT IS WAITING FOR YOU. YOU NEED TO BE PATIENT.

AND DON'T EVEN TRY WIGGLING OUT OF FRIDAY.

XO AXEL

She fanned her face, hot and bothered by all the emotions she was feeling. She'd never had such a romantic note in her life. He called her lovely? A flower didn't do her justice? She lifted the rose and smelled its sweet perfume, then read the note over and over again.

One thing troubled her. Nowhere did Axel claim to be or want to be her Mr. Right. Was that a sign he was humoring her until he got her into bed? Did he want the date to show her he really liked her—he wanted her to wait for him? Or was he just being kind, wanting something casual and helping her to see her potential?

Or, as she'd often been accused, was she overthinking things?

I should just appreciate the flower and that I have a date Friday night.

She grew giddy and danced her way up the stairs to her room before settling down. She folded the note and tucked it away in a box where she kept her most prized possessions: two torn pictures of her father, her first valentine from a little boy in kindergarten, a child's locket with her initials on it (a gift from her mother), and a photo of her and Del when they'd signed a lease together for the townhouse. For now, Axel's note would join the items she treasured.

She sniffed the rose again and left it on the bathroom counter while she showered, singing Seal's "Kiss from a Rose" and sighing to herself, imagining her perfect HEA in which she kissed Axel and their four kids goodbye as they left for school…

The day passed in a blur, her clients happy, her stylists happy, and Rena's mood buoyant for no reason at all. She'd kept the rose at home except for one petal, which she'd tucked into the front pocket of her jeans.

As she finished sweeping, Tommie came up to her looking suspicious. All the clients had left for the day, with just the stylists remaining behind.

"What?" Rena asked, humming to herself as she turned to straighten up the wash station. She noticed Stella and Nicky watching.

"So did you get laid or what?" Tommie asked, blunt to a fault.

Rena paused. "Excuse me?"

Stella grinned, and Nicky gave her a thumbs-up and mouthed *You go, girl.*

"You had sex. It's been, what, six years?" Tommie snickered.

"Very funny." Rena had to laugh. "More like a year and a half, but who's counting?"

"So you didn't have sex?"

"Why are you asking?"

"Because you've been practically bouncy and cheerful all day," Stella answered. "I mean, you're normally happy, but not this happy."

Rena blinked. "You think I'm happier?"

"Yep." All three of them nodded.

"I did not have sex, not that it's any of your business." Although… she gossiped with them about their lives and the lives of others. It would only be right to share.

Tommie and Nicky handed Stella money, distracting her.

Rena frowned. "Wait. You bet against me?"

Stella nodded. "I'm a good judge of character, and you're a romantic. Since you haven't had a boyfriend in a while, I just don't see you jumping into bed with some guy. Even if Axel is hotter than the sun."

Rena felt her cheeks heat.

Tommie hooted. "She's embarrassed! I can tell."

"Because she's hot for the plundering Viking," Nicky said, nodding.

"Well, who wouldn't be?" Rena retorted.

"She's got us there." Stella grinned. "Hey, I'm happy for you. We're all happy for you. But we'd be happier if you'd share what the hell happened to get you so happy. If it's not sex, then is it almost-sex?"

"Oral?" Tommie offered.

"A hand job?" Nicky asked.

Stella frowned. "Why would giving him a hand job make her so happy?"

"I meant for her," Nicky clarified. "Well, what do you call it when a guy gets you off with his hands?"

Tommie pursed her lips. "Hmm. That's a great question. In the spirit of equality, I'd go with hand job."

"More like finger job," Stella mused. "I mean, the whole hand might be a bit much. A knuckle job?"

The three of them cracked up laughing while Rena wondered if they'd been drinking.

Tommie wiped her eyes. "Sorry. But that was funny. So if it's not a finger job, oral, or sex, what happened?"

Rena relayed to them her mortifying ordeal, which garnered her some much-appreciated compassion.

Stella stared at her in awe. "You are *so* lucky. Axel Heller, the Viking god who walked in here the other day, saw you without makeup, your hair undone, and in pajamas. He hugged you until you fell asleep, tucked you into bed, and left you a rose? He didn't bring flowers with him, did he?"

"Not that I saw."

"So that means he left, went out to buy you a rose, then came back to give it to you. And he left you a note that is even making me all fluttery, and I'm not the romance kind."

Rena nodded.

"I want to be you," Nicky gushed. "If my boyfriend would do anything that nice for me, I'd be his willing maid, cook, and love slave for life." She sighed. "I don't get love notes, but I settle for the occasional foot rub, some decent sex, and the 'no, that dress does not make you look fat' lie when I ask him." At the girls' commiserating looks, she added, "He's got a job and is good to my kids."

Stella nodded. "A keeper."

"But, well..." Rena needed advice. "I came across as kind of needy."

"*Kind of?*" Stella snorted.

Rena glared at her before adding, "And while he was sweet and nice and supportive, he didn't say he wanted to be *my* Mr. Right. Just that if I was patient I'd find him. What if he just wants sex?"

They all looked at her.

"Of course he wants sex," Stella said slowly, as if explaining to someone not so bright.

Tommie frowned. "That's a bad thing? Hey, if you don't want him, I'll take him."

"No, no." Rena sighed. "I just mean I want more, and he's confusing me."

"He's a man, that's what they do," Stella said bluntly. "Instead of just coming out and saying"—she added in a deep voice with a bad German accent—"'Rena, you are the love of my life, ya, ya, be my wife and have my many giant babies,' he tells you you're pretty and is encouraging without being obvious about wanting more than a date. Yeah, he's a guy. He definitely wants sex. But what else, who knows?"

The others nodded.

"But a date is a positive step in the right direction if you want a relationship," Tommie said. "I mean, he could have stuck around and pressured you into sex. See what he does Friday night. You are going out with him, right?"

"Yes."

"Good. So, like he said, be patient. Let him fuck up on his own. Don't rush him there."

"So encouraging, Tommie," Stella said dryly.

"I try."

Rena left last, locking up behind her, and paused when a sleek little sports car pulled into the back lot. Away from the street.

Oh, hell.

A cherry-red Mustang rolled next to her. The window slid down, and a familiar face smiled up at her. Nothing good ever came from that smile. "That's right. You're going to follow me home or I'll kick your ass into next week. It's time you stopped avoiding me. Time we talked."

Rena swallowed down her nerves, forced a smile, and said, "Yes, Mom."

CHAPTER SIX

Rena trailed her mother home, more than glad her mom hadn't actually followed through on moving in when Del had moved out. That would have been a disaster. Instead, Caroline Jackson had kept her nice little cottage in South Seattle, close to the VA hospital where she worked as a nurse.

Growing up with Caroline for a mother had been…interesting. Caroline was loving, sweet, and generous. She loved nothing more than showering Rena with kisses, always telling Rena she could do anything she set her mind to. Caroline had shown by example, having put herself through nursing school and working hard to raise her daughter without much help. Though Caroline had never considered family help.

Rena had always had proper support and a loving family. Of course, Aunt Bridget had passed when Rena was just a baby, so Uncle Liam had stepped in in a big way. Rena often wondered if her search for the perfect man had been colored by her affection for her uncle—by all accounts a diamond in the rough. All through her childhood, Rena had heard her mother talk about Uncle Liam a lot. The man swore, wore threadbare clothes with pride, and worked to keep food on the table and his hoodlum children from jail.

He'd done a stellar job, because Del and J.T. were awesome people who'd become super successful in life and in love.

Rena's own mom, on the other hand…

Rena dragged her feet as she left her car in her mother's driveway and accepted her mom's hug. It wasn't that Rena didn't love her mother. She truly did. She appreciated her mother's efforts to raise her right. What she didn't love were her mother's many—

"Oh, good. Dave, honey," Caroline said to the man who'd opened her front door. "Come on out and meet my baby girl. Rena, this is Dave. My boyfriend."

Crap. Rena pasted a smile on her face and turned to see the latest in her mother's long, never-ending string of loser men. She would have felt bad about putting him in the loser column, except she caught the once-over he gave her. And with her standing right freakin' next to her own mother.

So, yes, Rena had been putting off her biweekly dinners with her mother because she'd heard from Del that Aunt Caroline had a new boyfriend. According to Del, this guy might be worse than the last one, who'd stolen a few hundred bucks from her mom on his way out the door. Del couldn't read the guy; he was slick.

"Hi, Rena." Dave came out to shake her hand then wrapped an arm around her mother and gave her a big, wet kiss.

Gross. "Hi. Nice to meet you."

Caroline smiled at her new beau, a tall, muscular man with good looks and dark-brown skin. Just the way her mother liked them. Even better, this one wore an expensive-looking watch, nice slacks, and a button-up shirt. His hair looked styled, and he wore glasses. Rena thought he probably had money. Interesting. Because her mother usually liked them pretty, broke, and dysfunctional.

Dave looked from Caroline to Rena and shook his head. "Damn if you don't look more like sisters."

Caroline beamed.

Rena knew they looked alike, though she'd always considered her mother beautiful and herself just cute. Caroline had gotten pregnant at fifteen, and twenty-four-year-old Martin Bennett hadn't stuck around to help raise his baby. Hell, Rena had only two photos of a handsome man with skin a shade darker than hers to remind her she'd actually had a father.

But, hey, at least he'd been smart enough not to stick around and face possible statutory rape charges. That was if her deadbeat grandparents would have pressed any.

Just thinking about all the problems in her mother's past threatened to ruin the evening…if Dave didn't do it first. Rena caught him still looking at her, and when he saw her notice, he winked.

She hastened into the house, her mother and Dave behind her. To her relief, she found Uncle Liam and Sophie sitting in the living room.

"Well now, there she is." Her uncle beamed at her, his bright-gray eyes shining. "Our small-business owner and hair ar-teest." He stood to enfold her in a hug.

Sophie grinned. "You have such a way with words, Liam." Petite compared to Liam's overwhelming strength—the man had muscles as big as J.T.'s and looked decades younger than his early sixties—Sophie Aster looked his youthful equal, her black hair streaked with minimal gray, her green eyes full of life. "How is work treating you, Rena?" Sophie stood and gently tugged Liam away to hug her.

Rena hugged her back, pleased for the moral support. "Work is great. It's only been a few days, but I know this business is going to do well."

"That's the spirit." Uncle Liam gave her a playful tap to the arm.

"It's been more than a few days," her mother corrected her from the dining room. "You started last month, right, honey?"

"True, but now I'm down to just one paycheck. The salon is it." She turned with Sophie and Liam and joined her mother and Dave in the dining room. The table had been set, glasses filled with water, and a green glass bottle sat in a wine bucket.

"Your mom was telling me about your business," Dave was saying as he sat, not offering to help her mother with anything.

"Mom, you need any help?" Rena mentally castigated her mother's new man. Aside from being good-looking and likely wealthy, Dave didn't seem to have any socially redeeming qualities. But Rena told herself to give him a chance. She'd just met him. Axel would probably look as bad upon first greeting. A big man who said little and stared at everyone around him as if contemplating how to kill and bury the bodies.

And why am I thinking of Axel now?

"I'm good, sweetie," her mother called from the kitchen. "You talk to Dave and your uncle and Sophie."

Dave kicked back, his arms behind his head. "Yep. I tried helping and got told if I didn't stay out of her kitchen, she'd pop me on the behind with a wooden spoon."

Liam laughed. "She's done that to me before."

"Well, I'm learning my lesson from you two," Sophie said.

Rena grudgingly admitted to herself she might have misjudged Dave. Maybe.

"It's great to finally meet you," he was saying. "Caroline has been telling me how proud she is of you."

"That's nice." She did her best to pretend to be enthused. "How did you and Mom meet?"

"At the hospital. I'm a government contractor and retired Army.

Went in for a checkup and ran into the prettiest lady I've ever seen." He turned to Sophie. "Well, I hadn't seen you yet, Sophie."

Sophie chuckled. "Oh, you're smooth, Dave. I'll give you that."

Liam snorted. "Like a pig in grease."

Rena couldn't help laughing at that, but to her surprise, Dave laughed as well.

"Sorry. Can't help it. But that doesn't mean I don't know my manners." He winked at Rena. "I've been wanting to meet you all before now, but Caroline wanted to wait. I figured four months was long enough."

Rena gaped. "You've been dating for four months?" And her mother hadn't said a word.

Caroline entered carrying a large casserole and set it down on the trivet in the middle of the table. "That's right. Dave and I have been taking things slow."

"Well, he does have a job at least," Liam muttered, saying exactly what Rena had been thinking.

Sophie smacked him on the arm. "Liam Webster. You be nice."

Rena coughed so she wouldn't be caught laughing.

Dave didn't seem to mind. "Your mother isn't used to a good man in her life. I'm here to change that."

"I've heard that before," Rena couldn't help adding.

He shrugged. "Truth is in the doing. Come by for the next family dinner and see."

Caroline glared at Rena and Liam. "You two, behave." She sat and fluffed her hair. "Now, let's eat."

Dinner passed in a surreal haze of laughter, good-natured teasing, and an amazing beef casserole—which was no surprise. Caroline Jackson could cook her tail off when she chose to.

Rena didn't know what to make of it all. But if they could get through a meal without her mother having a hissy over something Dave did or didn't do, she'd be impressed.

When Dave stood to clear the table, insisting everyone else sit and talk, she didn't believe the show of good manners was sincere. A nice act, was all she could think. He returned a moment after he'd cleared the table and apologized for having to leave. "I'm so sorry, but I have to get to work. We have a situation on a current contract I'm in charge of." Apparently Dave worked for a tech company with contracts to the U.S. Army. He leaned down to kiss Caroline then nodded at everyone, his smile wide. "It was a pleasure to meet you all. I hope to see you again." Rena thought his gaze settled on her while saying that.

When her mother stood to walk him to the door, he shook his head. "No, honey. You stay and catch up with everyone. I'm so sorry about this. I'd love to stay, but I can't."

"Okay. Well, good luck. I'll talk to you later." Caroline kissed him, and Rena saw a tender look on her face, something totally out of character. Her mother usually only looked at Rena, J.T., or Del like that.

"Well, Caroline," Sophie said after the door had closed behind him, "Dave seems like a real catch."

Caroline beamed. "I know. He's such a sweetheart. So sincere." She stood. "Let me get the coffee and dessert going."

"Oh, let me help," Sophie insisted. "This isn't dinner. It's okay to get help with coffee."

Caroline laughed. "Good point."

The two chatted while Rena and her uncle sat together.

"Dave is a mistake," she whispered.

"I don't know," he answered as quietly. "He was different than the others. More respectable. Less…"

"Obvious conman?"

"Yeah." Liam blew out a breath. "Your mother confuses the hell out of me. She's got money, a great kid—"

"Yep."

He grinned. "And she's prettier than a golden goose."

"Weird, but okay."

"So why does she pick such sorry-ass men?"

Rena had a sudden thought. "Hey, how come you and Mom never hooked up? Or did you?"

He'd been taking a sip of water when she asked and choked on it.

"Sorry."

"No, you're not, you little snot." Liam wiped his mouth with a huge hand scarred from too many hot engines and hot grease spills. "For your information, your aunt was it for me until Sophie. Not saying I was a monk, but I never could see anyone in that light. I just had casual girlfriends."

"You mean strippers and hos."

"Rena. Minerva. Jackson. Watch your mouth."

She bit back a grin. "Hey, I'm just repeating what Del says."

"My daughter is not too pregnant to spank," he muttered. "But that was a long time ago. I've matured since then. I love Sophie."

She sighed. "I know you do. You're getting married on Valentine's Day. That's so awesome." She put her elbow on the table, her chin in her hand, and pestered him for details about his wedding in just a few short weeks.

Liam looked thrilled about his pending nuptials. Rena felt so happy for him. She couldn't imagine mourning a man for more than thirty years, the way he'd grieved his wife. Now *that* was a love written about in the books. She just wanted to find someone she could like for more than a few months.

A lie. She wanted a true love like his, but at this point she was settling for a date with Axel.

And again I'm thinking of him. What is wrong with me?

"What's that look?" her uncle asked.

Saved from answering by the return of her mother and Sophie carrying a tray of coffee and cake, she let her mother ramble about how wonderful Dave was. But it was what her mother didn't say that made Rena take notice. A glance at Uncle Liam showed he'd caught the same slip.

"So let me get this straight, Mom. Dave has an income from his retirement in addition to his contractor job. You met him at the hospital, where he wasn't coming off a high or from being in a fight?"

Her mother scowled. "Rena."

"And he isn't currently living here?" Rena waited for the other shoe to drop. With her mother, it always did. Now came her mama-drama.

"Rena, I would say that's insulting, but I know I've given you just cause in the past." Her mom sighed.

Liam stared, his eyes narrowed. "Who are you, and what have you done with Caroline Jackson?"

Sophie covered her eyes. "I can dress him up, but I can't take him out."

Rena snickered and met her uncle's amused gaze. "That's the truth, but he's got a point. Mom, I don't mean to make you feel bad. I'm just surprised. Dave seems nice." Much nicer than he'd been at first impression. He didn't seem to have any flaws, unless… "Is he married?"

Her mother glanced away and back again. "Technically—"

Rena groaned. "Oh, Mom. You know this never ends well."

Liam shot Sophie a look as if to say *I told you so.*

Caroline leaned forward and pointed at all three of them. "If you must know, Dave is legally separated. We met when he was separated, so don't accuse me of breaking up a marriage."

"Mom, how do you know he's no longer with his wife? She might think they're still happily married."

Her mother raised her chin. "It's called trust, young lady. Dave isn't scamming me for money, a place to live, or to get into my pants."

"Nice, Mom." God, her mother still talked about sex. And she knew her mom had to be having it. Ew.

"My point, Ms. Virgin Ears, is that Dave and I have been honest with each other. We're friends first, and neither of us is rushing into this relationship."

Just like you haven't rushed into any of the other relationships with married, divorced, or damaged men in your life. Rena felt sad for her mother, a woman who wanted so desperately to be loved that she often took anyone who expressed an interest.

And that, right there, was why Rena always tried so hard to find men who weren't like that. They had jobs. They didn't have girlfriends or wives. They didn't do drugs or drink to excess.

Well, she *tried* to find good ones. But she must have inherited the boy-trouble gene from her mother because her past boyfriends had been one mistake after another. Oh, they weren't all bad. A few had had potential, but for one reason or another, the relationships fizzled.

Which made her wonder just what she thought she was doing with Axel. He had trouble written all over him. In big letters in black ink. She'd seen him fight men his size, two and three at a time, and walk away unscathed. Violence surrounded the guy who'd watched her for nearly a year without ever asking her out.

Yet the same guy had finagled a date out of a bet and kissed her senseless.

He'd also held her when she cried and called her beautiful.

What the heck should she make of all that? Talk about confusing… But at least he wasn't married.

She saw her mother frowning at her.

"What?"

"You're pretty judgmental for someone who can't find a man."

"Whoa," Uncle Liam cut in. "That's a little rough, isn't it, Caroline?"

"I think my daughter and I need to talk."

Sophie gave Rena a worried look. She must have heard from Uncle Liam how Caroline could go off the rails. But Uncle Liam knew Rena could take care of herself. He'd raised her to be strong, after all.

Liam stood. "Come on, Sophie. Time for us to take off." They left after kissing Caroline and Rena goodbye.

Rena waited for her mother to turn into a raving shrew. Sadly, that too was part of her mother's MO. To instigate a fight and rant until Rena couldn't take the drama anymore and walked away.

How was it possible Rena loved her mom so dearly yet also pitied and disliked her at the same time?

"You shouldn't talk to me that way in front of your uncle and Sophie." Her mother fumed.

"Why not? I wasn't disrespectful. I was honest."

"You have no idea what it's like to fall in love and lose a man."

"Oh?"

"Because you never let yourself love," her mother ended, looking at Rena as if *she* should be the one feeling pity. "I admit I have issues with men. It all started with your father. I was too young and stupid to know better."

You got that right.

"But at least I loved him."

"And the ones after?" Rena asked with a lot more politeness than she felt.

"You watch that mouth, baby girl." Her mother's eyes snapped with anger. "I know I've dated a lot. I wanted to feel loved, and it probably goes back to your grandparents not giving a shit about me."

Whoa. Mom's breaking out the cuss words. Here we go… Rena waited for the fury to spill from a woman done wrong, scorned, ignored. Her mother had more self-pity than anyone Rena had ever met. Which made it worse when Rena herself fell into that same *woe is me* state. Oh boy. She really needed to apologize to Axel for witnessing her breakdown.

Caroline continued, "I thought sex would bring me happiness. And in a way it did. It brought me you."

Rena watched her mom warily, but Caroline didn't seem to be paying much attention to her, more introspective than Rena had ever seen her.

"My sister found what I always wanted. She didn't get to keep it long enough though, poor Bridget. Your uncle is a good man. I don't know why it's been so hard for me to find my own Liam, but I try. And I keep on tryin'. I'm working on myself now." Rena didn't know what that meant exactly, but she kept quiet, listening. "I'm trying to do better. I haven't shown you the best way a man and a woman can love, but that's changing." That was as close as her mother had ever come to apologizing for having had so many boyfriends. "And you're grown enough to set your own example anyway."

"Um, that's all fine. I'm not asking for anything from you, Mom." Rena deliberately gentled her tone, not wanting to cause a fight. "I just love you, and I worry about you."

Her mother watched her for a moment then sighed. "I know. I love you too."

"Dave seems nice. I just want you to find someone who treats you right. You're such a good person. You don't deserve to be somebody's rent check or provider." *You don't need a man to be happy*, she wanted to say. But she knew the hypocrisy of that considering she wanted a man to make herself happy.

Rena wished she could just enjoy being single. To love her friends and family and not want what they had. But with all her family coupled up, she constantly felt on the outside looking in. She missed the happily ever after she read about in her books. Despite knowing it was all scripted, she wanted to write her own ending, one in which a man found her desirable and worthy of being loved.

God, "worthy." I am *my mother's daughter, needing a man to feel fulfilled.* Ashamed for being so weak yet honest enough to admit she'd been built that way, she struggled to find that balance she'd sought so hard.

Her mother opened up her arms, and Rena went into them, wondering why she'd said anything in the first place. If there was one thing she knew, it was that her mother would do what she wanted and the consequences be damned.

All Rena had accomplished tonight was to make herself feel worse.

She stood in her mother's arms, some small part of her comparing the comfort from Axel's hug to the warm homecoming of her mother's.

And found she preferred her Viking's arms after all.

CHAPTER SEVEN

On Friday morning, Axel found himself behind his shop, peering into the bushes around the corner. He'd come out to throw some trash in the dumpster and been distracted by an old friend. He looked around for the gentle meowing he'd heard on and off the last year, hoping the little one would show herself this time.

"Come here, little kitty," he crooned in German. The cat seemed to prefer German to English. "Come and I will give you your favorite—tuna."

Though he'd been overseas as much as home the past few months, he'd instructed the guys to set out cat food near the small house he'd built for her. He could never get her to trust him enough to let him take her inside, but she'd enjoyed the small house he'd made.

And there, inside it on the ratty blanket, he saw her and smiled. "Ah, kitty. How are you feeling?"

To his shock, she waddled out of the house and rubbed her face against his hand, as if they were old friends.

"Well, now. You've got yourself a boyfriend, eh?" He saw her distended belly and too-skinny frame and couldn't in good conscience leave her to fend for herself any longer. "Time to see the vet." He took her in his arms slowly, but she did nothing more than purr and settle against him.

"Wish all my lady friends were this easy." He snorted at the thought of Rena snuggled up in his arms. She had fallen asleep against him. Then again, he hoped for a little more than sleep from the woman.

Axel sighed and walked back inside. The familiar smell of paint and clearcoat, the sounds of ribald teasing, rock music, the power sander, and the paint gun. Business as usual. Except for the purring and occasional meow from his little friend.

He took her into his office, worried the noise and smells might scare her. But the cat didn't appear bothered in the slightest. So odd. He set her on his desk, and she walked around the clear surface before settling into a sphinxlike pose next to his laptop, curling her paws and tail around her while she watched him.

Dirty, a bit scrawny for being pregnant, and rather small in size, the calico stray looked right at home in his office. Had Axel been an animal person he might have kept her. But he was always working, never at home long enough to give a pet the attention it deserved.

A knock on the doorframe turned his attention.

"Yo, Boss, what do… Is that a cat?" Rylan stared at the feline blinking back at him.

"No, it's a bear." Stupid question.

Rylan shot him a look before leaving. The equipment turned off. Smitty and Mateo returned with him, gathered at the doorway.

"Oh wow, she's pregnant," Mateo whispered.

"I think she knows," Smitty said. "No need to whisper."

Mateo glared at him. "I don't want to scare her."

"If she can handle being that close to Heller, I'm sure you won't bother her," Rylan said, his voice as hushed.

Axel sighed and in a normal voice said, "You three have never seen a cat before?"

"This is the one we've been putting the food out for." Smitty entered and held his hand out for the cat to sniff before petting her. When she let him, he smiled. "Aw, she's a cutie, aren't you?"

Mateo soon joined him, not crowding the cat but letting her adjust to a new scent before stroking her between the ears. "She looks just like my mom's cat. Except smaller. She's pretty tiny." He smiled at her. "You poor thing. Knocked up and deserted by that pitiful man of yours. We'll take care of you."

Everyone looked at Axel, who felt put on the spot. "*Nein.* I'm going to take her to a shelter. She can't hang around here. The paint would not be good for her health."

Smitty and Mateo no longer looked so pleased. Smitty cleared his throat. "Good point."

"I guess." Mateo left the office.

Rylan remained, his gaze fixed to Smitty petting the cat. "You sure? I mean, she could always sleep outside or just hang in your office. It's not like she has access to the paint rooms."

Axel just stared, reminding Rylan who ran the shop.

Rylan took another glance at the cat. "Just sayin'."

Smitty slung an arm around Rylan's shoulders. "Don't worry, kid. I'll work on the big man. We'll have a shop cat before you know it."

"Kid?" Rylan smiled at him, then his face froze, as if he suddenly realized Smitty stood so close. He ducked from under Smitty's arm and hurried away, yelling for Mateo to turn up the music.

Axel studied the interaction, curious as to the look on Smitty's face. A wondering kind of expression.

"You think to change my mind?" he asked Smitty.

Smitty sat across from Axel's desk, making himself at home. "Please. You already made up your mind. She's yours."

"What? No. That's not right."

"Uh-huh." Smitty grinned at him. "You built her a fuckin' house. You fed her, and you had us feeding her when you weren't here. Lie to yourself all you want. But you, my friend, have a cat."

"Shit."

"Exactly."

The cat just blinked at him, as if to say *Yes, feeble human. Accept your master.*

Axel glared at her, and she just kept purring.

To change the subject, he asked, "What's going on with Rylan? Is he doing his job well?"

"Well enough." Smitty shrugged. "I think something's bothering him though. He seems tense around me, but not around Mateo. Then again, Mateo's about as threatening as a flea."

Axel absently scratched the back of his hand and glared at the cat again. Damn it. He'd need to get her to the vet sooner than later. Kittens, fleas, and she'd need shots, he was sure.

"I need to go somewhere for a few hours," he muttered.

Smitty smirked at him and the cat. "Sure thing. I'll watch the phones. We've got parts coming in today, so we should be able to prep the fender for the Buick. Mateo's still sanding Mrs. Parker's Acura. Should be done in a few more days, no problems so far. Lou called, said he's coming in to talk to a client about a special paint job at four. Something custom."

"The Charger?" Axel nodded. "*Gut.*" Then he turned to the cat. "You will come with me and give me no trouble, *ja?*"

Her tail twitched.

"I'm thinking you should put her in a box so she doesn't freak out at the vet's," Smitty advised. "There's a good vet I know of." Smitty pulled out his phone. "I'll text you the clinic's info."

"I never said I was going to the vet."

"And you don't have a cat. Yeah, I got it." Smitty left the office, whistling.

Three hours later and a few hundred dollars poorer, Axel returned to the office sans an unhappy, pregnant cat. He had to go back the following day after the cat had gotten a thorough checkup. The poor little thing had been shaky and scared, and he hadn't liked leaving her there. But Smitty had been right. The veterinarian had been careful and patient. *She* hadn't been clawed or bitten.

He studied the wounds on his hands, annoyed he'd let the cat gouge him.

Last time I'm nice to snarling felines.

The thought reminded him of a snarling little rabbit he'd recently petted, and he grinned as he got back to work. The day passed too slowly, not enough things to keep his mind from the fact he had a date with Rena in another few hours. He'd texted her a reminder, and they'd settled on him picking her up at seven from her house.

He still had no idea what to do besides dinner and perhaps a movie. Bending her over a couch would probably not qualify as romance.

He sighed.

An hour later, the new client arrived to talk to Lou about what he wanted done to his Charger. They sat in the small meeting room designed to impress. Black cement flooring, crisp white walls, a round glass tabletop, and chrome chairs with black leather cushions gave it a motorhead-meets-modern look, something he'd borrowed from his father's knowledge of sales. The guy was an ass, but he knew how to sell himself.

A large television monitor mounted to the wall showcased a slideshow of their many paint jobs, some just detail work, others custom paints. And on the other walls Axel had hung framed photos of the staff, their tricked-out cars, and the original building from 1972. He liked seeing the old place, liked knowing how far the building—and he—had come since opening the shop seven years ago.

He sat in on the meeting, as he normally did with high-end jobs, wondering when they could fit this one in. On his laptop, he reviewed their already full schedule. Between the shop's glowing reputation and Lou's skills, demand for their services had been booming. In fact, Axel did his best not to have to turn people away.

Bringing Rylan on as temporary help while Kelly was away might very well turn into a permanent position—if Rylan stayed on the straight and narrow. Smitty was keeping an eye on the guy, but Axel knew how easy it could be to screw up a good work environment. He'd worked for several places before opening his own, and it still amazed him how just one shitty employee could ruin a good thing.

The meeting wrapped up with an appointment scheduled in a month and a half. The client left happy, and Lou continued to tinker with design ideas. "What do you think of this? Something a little less cartoony, more daredevil inspired. Not the comic, a daredevil attitude, I mean." Lou turned the sketchbook to face him.

"Not bad. I'd suggest cleaner lines though."

Lou shot him an injured look. "Hey, it's a sketch, man. I'll polish it up before my final draft."

Axel grunted. Artists could be so touchy. He stretched out his legs and arms, reaching up to loosen his shoulders.

"So," Lou said.

"So."

"You're going out with Rena tonight, eh?"

"How do you know this?" Had Rena been talking to Lou? Her friends at the garage, perhaps?

"Hello, my sister works at her salon."

"Oh, right."

"Stella happened to mention how cute it is you're rattling her boss."

"Rattling, eh?" Axel leaned closer to Lou. "What else did she say?"

Lou smirked. "What's it worth to you?"

Axel just stared.

After a moment, Lou's smirk faded, and he made the sign of the cross. "Quit freaking me out, Satan, and I'll talk."

Satisfied, Axel leaned back and waited. He considered Lou a friend. The man had five sisters and more than two dozen female relatives all living close enough to visit. "*A ladies' man in the womb,*" Axel had heard Lou's mother say. But Lou was a stand-up guy. He'd fallen hard for a shy florist and her son, and he knew how to romance a woman. He also had insider knowledge about Rena and wouldn't give him the third degree like her cousins.

Lou gave him a thumbs-up. "I heard all about you leaving her a rose and some sweet note that went with it. Finally. I have high hopes for you, man."

"She liked it?" He brightened. "*Gut.*" How to ask Lou what he wanted to know without coming across as pathetic. Or desperate. Or just lame.

"Now, Heller, if I could offer you some advice..."

Ah, he'd get help whether he asked for it or not. He waited.

"Rena's everyone's sweetheart. Not one person I know has a grudge against her, and that's saying something. *Stella* likes her."

"She is easy to like." And love.

"But you, not many I know like you."

"Is that supposed to hurt me?" Frankly, he couldn't care less what anyone thought about him. Except for Rena, of course.

"No, but I'm telling you the thought of you and Rena is like oil and water. Salty and sweet. Or, wait. Salty and sweet works."

"You have a point?"

Lou grimaced. "I had one somewhere. What I'm trying to say is she's known for being kind, and you're not. She loves romance. You don't seem to have a romantic bone in your body. *But* maybe you do, because you left her a flower. And a note. And she's acting all dreamy, according to Stella. You laid some decent foundation."

"*Ja.* This I know."

"Where are you going tonight?"

Axel sighed. "To dinner. After that, I don't know."

Lou blinked. "Ah, okay. What does Rena like to do?"

"She likes to read."

"That's true." Lou grinned. "She has my fiancée hooked on some books. And, boy, have they made our nights at home special." Lou and his fiancée acted like honeymooners, and they hadn't even gotten married yet. Axel saw their gooey-eyed looks at each other and wondered if he would ever share that with Rena. Or if he'd be the only one looking so foolish.

He recalled everything he'd learned about her in the time he'd been coming in to Ray's. "She seems to like television and staying home. I know she likes R&B music, slow songs, and animals. She's a big animal lover." He should totally tell her about the pregnant cat. "She's not a bad cook, likes milk chocolate over dark, and loves painting her nails different colors. She loves her family and thinks friends are important.

She's always loyal and apparently very into romance." And so fucking beautiful she made his heart stop.

"Jesus, you have it bad." Lou shook his head. "We all know you've been moping over the woman forever. Valentine's Day is coming up. Maybe you should ramp up your efforts into that."

"My plan centers around that stupid holiday. But first I have to get through tonight. I wish I knew what her favorite foods are." The things he'd jotted down from Del at the garage had been sparse. Roses and chocolates. Check. He needed more.

"Hold on." Lou dialed a number on his phone and hit speaker.

Unfortunately, Del answered.

Axel cringed. He appreciated that Rena's cousins had tried to put in a good word for him, but if it became known he had no game and needed their help to make Rena fall for him, he'd become a laughingstock and be forced to break bones in order to salvage his tattered rep.

He shook his head, but Lou held up a hand and mouthed *Relax*. "Yo, Del."

"Lou, what—hold on." She swore at Sam to pick up his stupid tools before she came back. "Sorry. What do you need?"

"I want to put twenty down on Heller by V-Day. I love the guy, but he's pathetic when it comes to Rena and needs all the time he can get. Another five weeks should do it."

Axel glared.

"Say, what's Rena's favorite food?" Lou asked her.

"I want to help you, I do. But I bet against him. As much as I'd love for the pair to work, he's gonna blow it. I mean, it's Heller."

He barely contained a growl.

"You should do it for Rena," Lou argued. "She likes him. Don't you want her to be happy?"

"I do, which is why I'm going to introduce her to my doctor buddy next week. Heller is great and all, but he's too wild. And honestly, I don't think he could romance his way out of a kissing booth."

"Real nice, Del." Lou shook his head fiercely when Axel would have commented.

"Okay, gotta go. And don't even think of hitting up my brother or dad about this. I'll know," she growled and hung up.

"What the fuck, Lou?"

"Heller, just trust me on this. And if you blow it, you cover my twenty."

Axel didn't like it, but when Lou got through to Liam and started getting information Axel could use, he figured he wouldn't hold Lou's comments against him. Much. Now Del, on the other hand…

Del held up a hand, and the garage quieted. With her mechanics stood her husband Mike and his son Colin, who'd stopped by the garage to pick her up. "That was Lou. Odds just went up Heller bites it before V-Day."

The guys started reconsidering their bets, and Colin scribbled down their new dates on the betting board J.T. had set up months ago.

Mike kissed her on the cheek and rubbed her back. "I hope you put us down for double or nothing on February 17th."

"Why that date?"

"Because we know Heller's a guy. He can't possibly live up to your cousin's ideal of romance. So he'll screw up on Valentine's Day. I'm giving him three days to get his act together and make things right."

"You think he's going to win her over?" Del had her doubts. Though she secretly liked Axel, and she loved him pounding the crap out of the guys who'd bothered her cousin, she didn't know if he had it in him to be what Rena needed.

Mike smiled at her and put a hand over her belly. "I saw him at Rena's going-away party. He's got it bad for your cute cousin. And she didn't look at him just as much as he didn't look at her."

"Huh?"

"Trust me. I know things. We McCauleys are good about falling in love."

"You're kidding, right? Took you long enough to find me."

He laughed. "But that's because I had to find a whip and chains first so I could keep you in line. And speaking of which, tonight's date night. Colin has a sleepover. So don't wear panties to bed."

She blushed; she couldn't help it.

Colin looked over, saw them hugging, and gagged. "Ech. Kissing is so gross."

"You got that right." Foley crossed his eyes, and Colin laughed. "But while we're talking about kissing, put me down for first kiss in public on the 27th." Foley handed Colin a five-dollar bill. "Closest to that date without going past it wins the smaller pot."

Colin nodded. "No cheating, Sam."

Sam scowled. "Del, what are you telling this kid about me?"

Colin held his own. "It was Johnny, Sam. He told me to look out for you. But not when it came to darts, because he said you suck at darts."

Sam took off after Johnny, who laughed and ran down the hallway shouting, "The boy lies. But not about the darts."

Foley leaned closer and handed Colin a bill the kid pocketed. Foley whispered something, and Colin nodded and wrote another date on the calendar.

Del sighed. “I am so proud of that little scammer.”

“Of Johnny for messing with Sam’s head?” Mike asked.

“No, of Colin for taking Foley’s money. I guarantee that kid gets Rena some insider information that changes a few dates on the board.”

Mike frowned. “Guess I’d better put my money down now then. And remind my mini-me that if he doesn’t help out his daddy in the pool, he’s got some early bedtimes coming his way.”

“Good move, Mike.” Del grinned. She thought it so cute that she was slowly corrupting her rule-abiding husband. Those goody-goody McCauleys had no idea how much their world needed Del in the mix. Mike liked to tell her she wasn’t as bad as she thought she was, and he sure the hell wasn’t as good. Especially when it came to being naughty between the sheets.

Thanking whatever stars had aligned to give her this wonderful life with people she loved, she shared a thumbs-up with the devious little schemer hunched over the betting board.

And Colin too, of course.

Rena hadn’t known how to dress for her date with Axel. But she figured she couldn’t go wrong in a form-fitting red sweater, black tea-length skirt, and knee-high leather boots. She felt feminine yet tough, a no-nonsense woman ready to meet a man who made her insides flutter.

With excitement or nerves, she didn’t yet know. Memories of that kiss they’d shared resurfaced, as did the notion her time of the month had ended. She technically had no reason to discourage some heavy petting should the date go well.

She flushed, wishing she could stop thinking about sex for two seconds, but Axel’s image had been ingrained in her brain, and the big, sexy man turned her on. Plus, that rose, that note. Handsome was one thing, but handsome *and* romantic? She felt like a swoony maiden in a romance novel. She wondered if her favorite author would consider writing a Viking romance in the future.

She fiddled with her jacket and purse as she hovered by her front door.

Her phone rang, and she checked it, wondering if Axel called. Another random number she ignored. She'd gotten a few hang-ups at work today as well and one call from a familiar voice asking if her heater was running. She'd recognized Colin and answered that it was.

"Then you'd better go catch it!" he'd yelled before giggling hysterically and hanging up.

Which made her laugh as well and reminded her to keep an eye on the scamp. He'd called her twice, once with that silly joke, the other to wish her well on *her date*. Hell, did everyone in Seattle know and care what Rena did in her spare time?

A big black truck pulled up in her driveway, and she left the house.

She was just locking up when a large shadow blocked her light. She turned to see Axel frowning down at her. Just the sight of him had her pulse pounding. Man, she'd made a huge mistake giving him that haircut because she kept envisioning him with an ax and a loincloth then wearing nothing at all as he marauded all over her.

"I was coming to get you."

"Like a gentleman?" She raised a brow.

"Well, kind of." He smiled. "Like a man excited to see a pretty woman."

She swallowed a sigh and reminded herself that tonight was a test. A special night, whether he knew it or not. She'd wait him out, sure he'd show his true colors. Then she'd either dump him or date him again.

She let him take her hand, and he surprised her by kissing the back of it. Wow. Tingles ran from her hand throughout her body. From a hand kiss.

"You look stunning." He clearly approved.

She'd pinned her hair back but left the curls at her temples dangling. The sweater she wore framed her figure nicely, and the skirt warmed her yet also allowed for movement. But her boots *made* the outfit, giving her a kickass feel while also allowing her to feel feminine and sexy.

Axel had yet to look away from her. She lost herself in his dark-blue eyes, hoping the night would go well. She didn't want to feel the disappointment that inevitably came when a potential good guy turned bad.

"I would like to take you to dinner," he said, his voice impossibly deep.

"Y-yes. That would be nice."

He escorted her to his truck, but instead of helping her step up into it, he lifted her by the waist with an easy strength and placed her gently on the seat. She felt his large hands around her waist even after he'd let go.

The inside of the truck was warm and smelled like his cologne. God, he was getting to her without even trying. A good thing she was sitting because her knees felt weak. Especially when he stood by her side and leaned in, at eye level.

"I have to," he whispered, his gaze lowered to her mouth.

"Okay," she whispered back, breathless. *Okay? Okay to what?*

Then he kissed her, a press of his lips that didn't linger long enough.

It was only as he pulled away that she opened eyes she hadn't remembered closing. She had a sudden urge to smack that gratified look off his face. Either that or pull him closer to finish what he'd started.

"You taste good, *Häschen.*" He stroked her cheek, and it did her a world of good to imagine his fingers trembled.

They drove with only the radio breaking the silence between them. Axel had an R&B station on, and John Legend put her in a more mellow mood. An unfortunate choice, in hindsight, because the silky tone of Legend's voice wrapped around her and made her want another taste of the big, silent man sitting next to her.

She watched the lights of the city pass by, a few couples walking arm in arm, packs of singles heading somewhere they'd find a party. Axel cut over from Rainier to Beacon Avenue and continued north.

"Where are we going exactly?"

"You'll see. It's a surprise."

She liked surprises. "Okay, but it had better be good."

"*Ja,* I'm hoping so," he murmured.

They continued past the North Beacon Hill nightlife and off onto a quiet street. The area looked a little rundown, older homes being renovated, a place where middle-class hardworking people took care of their property and land as best they could. She'd never been in the area before and looked around with curiosity.

When Axel pulled into the driveway of a cute corner house on a hill and parked, she had a burning desire to know where, exactly, he'd brought them.

"So, this is where we'll be having our date?" Though it was dark, she could make out a trimmed lawn, some boxwoods along the front of the brick two-story house, and a double-car garage. The house needed fresh paint and some rail work, but it looked nice enough.

He turned to her with a shy smile. "Welcome, Rena, to my home."

CHAPTER EIGHT

Axel prayed he hadn't made a huge mistake in inviting Rena to his house for dinner. But he'd done it all up. The house was always clean; he didn't believe in making messes. He'd ordered her favorite food and laid out some Valentine's swag that, according to Del's list, would make Rena very happy.

Axel didn't consider himself a romantic kind of guy—at all—but he liked flowers, and he knew Rena had loved his rose. Having a buddy whose girlfriend worked as a florist had helped as well. Lou's girlfriend had made him some beautiful bouquets *and* given him a discount.

He walked around the truck to help Rena exit. He loved holding her. She didn't weigh a thing, and he admitted he felt strong and manly lifting her with ease. He set her down and took her hand in his.

That she let him made him want to sigh and stare into her eyes all night. Not cool, he knew. But something about Rena hit him right in the heart. He just wished he knew how to handle the feeling.

She squeezed his hand and smiled up at him, and he smiled back as he led her up the steps of the landing to his front door. After letting them in, he stepped back and toed off his boots. She followed suit, unfortunately stepping out of those sexy black boots.

"You can keep them on if you like," he offered.

"No. I want to help keep your floor clean. I do that at my house too."

He hadn't known that. Next time he'd make sure to take his shoes off.

If he could get a next time.

He took her coat from her, inhaling the warm, sultry perfume she wore, and grew immediately hard. With a suppressed groan, he hung up their jackets and tried to will away his excitement. When he turned around, he saw her studying his home.

They walked past a small formal room he rarely used and turned toward the living area. The dark leather furniture and wooden tables had crisp lines. They served his needs yet also had a minimalist, modern style he appreciated. The large screen television got plenty of use, mounted to the wall over a gas fireplace, done in jet-black tile. When he'd bought the place, he'd known a more modern open floor plan wouldn't work unless he knocked through a lot of walls. But with time and money not his to command, he'd done his best by putting in hardwood floors and giving the interior a fresh coat of paint. Light-gray walls provided a neutral enough palette against his darker furniture and mahogany hardwood.

The living area and dining room were one, and he'd done up the rectangular dining table with white plates and two bouquets of red roses decked with baby's breath and fresh greenery, both in his mother's favorite crystal vases. On the coffee table in the living room, he'd left a wrapped box of chocolates and a card—putting everything on the line within a pink envelope.

"Axel, this is beautiful. I love the flowers." Rena looked impressed.

He gave her a relieved smile. "*Gut.* They are for you." He paused.

"But not the vases, I am afraid." A stupid detail he'd overlooked. "They were my mother's."

She put a hand on his forearm, and he felt how tense he'd become. "They're beautiful. I bet your mom would love knowing you used her crystal to hold such pretty flowers."

"*Ja.*" He cleared his throat. "She would like knowing I got you roses. They match the color of your sweater." *Match the color of your sweater? Oh man, I am dying here.*

She blinked at the comparison and gave him a shy smile. "They do."

He blew out a breath, pleased she hadn't called him on being an idiot. "Would you like to see the house?"

"That's only fair since you already saw mine." She gave him a look. "You looked around, didn't you?"

"I did not… Okay, I did," he confessed.

She laughed. "I totally would have if I'd been you. So show me around."

He took her through the doorway into the kitchen, which he'd upgraded. Darker gray cabinets, stainless-steel appliances, a white marble countertop, and a black-based kitchen island kept everything simple and uncluttered with plenty of space for storage.

They continued the tour down the hall to the two guest bedrooms and guest bath before hitting the master.

"Do you want to see my room?"

She bit her lip.

"What?"

"Are you trying to get me into your bedroom, Axel?"

He felt himself blush, even harder when she laughed. "Would it work?"

"I don't know. Depends on what's for dinner," she teased, and he realized he hadn't messed up. Yet.

Careful, so careful, he made himself go slowly with her, teasing but not too much. Always keeping aware of his size to not make sudden movements or scare her into thinking he might take advantage.

Axel usually spent a lot of time being less than he was in an effort not to scare his dates. But with Rena, he worked doubly hard because he wanted more than anything for her to like him.

She didn't say much about his king-size bed or plain black furniture. His walk-in closet wasn't anything special, though he considered the master bath the crowning glory of the home. The large walk-in shower fit him, with an overhead rain showerhead which hadn't been cheap to install. And the large tub could comfortably fit him as well.

Being six foot six had its share of advantages, but when it came to furniture and plain old living, he had a tough time getting anything to fit him correctly.

They returned to the dining area, and he sat her at the table at a spot right next to his at the end.

He returned moments later with her favorite drink, a Virgil's root beer, and a plate of lemon butter angel hair pasta over spinach and pine nuts. Then he brought himself a beer and a plate of the same. She'd poured her drink into the glass by her plate, so he did as well, forgoing a bottle in favor of a pilsner glass.

"Is the food from Vicente?" she asked.

"*Ja.*"

"It's my favorite," she confessed, her voice soft. "Thank you for doing this. It's lovely."

For you, Rena. Anything. He waited for her to take a bite before he ate, ignoring the nerves that threatened to turn him inside out. Tonight had to be *perfect*. "I'll be right back." He hurried to put on some music, a contemporary jazz station he preferred. "Do you enjoy this music? I can change it to something else if you want."

"You know, I like it." She smiled. Then she held up her glass. "To a fabulous dinner, and to my handsome host."

He hated that she kept making his cheeks burn. "And to my beautiful dinner date. May she find the night better than an evening of Lifetime, ice cream, and books."

Rena chuckled. "Smartass."

"Takes one to know one."

They clinked glasses and locked gazes. And something passed between them. At least, he felt it, a sizzle of attraction and something much deeper.

Then she took a sip, and he could see nothing more than those lips hugging glass.

And once again, he wanted her more than breath itself.

♥ ♥ ♥

Rena sipped, unable to look away as Axel devoured her with his eyes. God, how the hell did a woman resist a man who not only got her flowers and knew her favorite foods but looked at her as if she really was his world?

It was too soon to feel so close to him, wasn't it? But she could certainly appreciate his efforts.

"So whose idea was a dinner date at home?" she asked. "My money's on J.T. He's good like that."

Axel smiled but didn't answer, stuffing his mouth full of noodles. Everything about him seemed restrained. She couldn't put her finger on it, but he seemed to be extremely careful with her. Not that he ever set out to harm her or be rough, but Axel was hesitant before saying or doing anything tonight.

She didn't know if she liked such care. She wanted to know Axel Heller the man. The real body and soul behind the giant. So how to put him at ease?

"Axel, tell me about your home." There. That seemed simple enough. Nonthreatening and something he could talk about that had nothing to do with sex or would give her sexy thoughts. Like the ones she'd been having since he'd picked her up wearing dark jeans and a button-up shirt that did nothing but promise a peek at his strong neck and glorious pecs. Or the thoughts she'd had upon spying his big, broad bed, imagining lying on top of him while he gripped her by the hips and—

"...seven years ago," he was saying, and she prayed she hadn't looked as if she'd been zoning out. "Right after the shop, I wanted something to call mine. I had been renting, but the opportunity to buy this house, a foreclosure, came up. I did a lot of work on it, and it still needs more." He described what he'd done to fix it up, and she realized she hadn't seen the basement yet.

Watching him talk about his project, seeing him so animated, made her forget all about her discomfort with her attraction. She wanted to hear more. "So what about your shop? What prompted you to open an auto body and paint store?"

His expression darkened as he chewed more of his dinner, making her wonder what had brought on the shift in mood. But it passed, and he said, "It's kind of a family business. My father has a chain of auto parts stores in Germany and a few here on the West Coast. My brother owns several car dealerships. I wanted to do something with cars as well, but I've always loved color."

She glanced around. "Really?"

He blushed, as he'd been doing tonight. She loved making the big man a little uncomfortable. It put her on even footing; she'd been off her game since she'd met him.

"I like my house neutral because I do much relaxing here. When I think, in my office downstairs or at work, there is more color."

"Do you draw?" she asked, not having considered there might be an artistic side to Axel.

"Not like J.T. or Lou." He shrugged. "I'm not bad. But I am better at knowing what works than creating it from scratch. And there is an art to bodywork, to fixing what is broken."

"I agree." She drank the rest of her root beer, not having expected him to fetch her another right away. "Um, thanks. Were you ever a waiter?"

"I am good with personal service." He winked.

Her face felt super hot, and he must have noticed because he chuckled.

"I'm like you in that way," she said, not sure why he looked so happy about the fact.

"We have much in common."

"Well, I don't know about much, but—"

"*Ja.* We both like Italian food. We love your haircuts. We like to read."

"About that—"

"And we love art. You are artistic with your hair salon, me with my shop."

"Oh, well, yes, then I guess we do have a lot in common." She pushed aside her plate, too full to eat the rest. "What kind of movies or TV do you like? Do you even like movies?"

"I have found I like dramas. Your movie the other night. It was *gut.*"

She frowned. "What movie? Wait. Do you mean you watched Lifetime?"

He shrugged. "It was entertaining. Why are you laughing at me?"

She tried not to but found the thought of big, strong Axel enjoying a channel usually watched by women amusing. "Um, well, it's usually a channel women watch."

"That makes sense. I didn't actually understand all the kissing at the end of the kidnapping, but it wasn't so bad."

She laughed. "You're a funny guy. It's surprising because you look all tough, but you're a softie at heart, aren't you?"

The look he shot her made her girl parts stand up and take notice.

"Not always so soft," he muttered.

Her mind went straight to the gutter.

"I was hard on Rylan, one of my new guys. He's not a bad man, but he's been screwing up a lot lately."

Of course he meant "not always so soft" in reference to work, not his dick, Rena!

"Oh, that's too bad."

"What about you? How are the ladies who work for you?"

"They're good. I'm sure we'll have issues at some point. But I really like our dynamic. And they're all good at different things, from color to nails to updos, so we have specialties that overlap."

He nodded. "You are busy at work, yes?"

"Yeah. It's exciting and scary at the same time. I love working for myself though. I miss the guys at Ray's, but not working those hours."

"The guys?" he asked.

She rolled her eyes, ignoring a tingle of warmth at his jealousy.

He sighed. "Well, you can always go back for a beer with me if you want."

"Only with you?"

Axel shifted in his seat. "I meant I'd go with you. If you wanted. You don't have to go with me, of course."

She grinned. "Relax. I'm giving you a hard time on purpose."

"Minx."

She started. "Did you just call me a minx? Have the 1940s come back when I wasn't looking?"

"*Was?*" he asked in German.

"That means 'what,' right?"

"Yes. I make a German out of you yet." He chuckled and murmured something in German she didn't understand.

"What did you say?"

"You'll just have to learn enough to find out." He stood and cleared their plates. "No, no. You sit. You are a guest."

"If you keep spoiling me, I'll never leave." It surprised her to learn she meant it.

Though she'd been attracted to Axel for a long time, she never could have guessed he'd be fun and charming. Or that he could talk so much! They'd been having real conversations, so much more than the one or two sentences he'd share at Ray's. Even better, his conversation had been personal, not just about sports or the weather. Thank God.

He returned to her with a glass of wine. "This is a nice after-dinner wine to go with a present for you."

She warmed. "You didn't have to get me anything."

"*Ja.* I did." He walked to the coffee table and brought back a pink envelope and a box that looked suspiciously like chocolates. "Open this, *bitte.*"

Rena loved gifts and always had. But she tried not to show it because she didn't want to be seen as mercenary. Her cousins had teased her mercilessly while growing up about her addiction to wrapping paper. Heck, Axel could have gotten her a roll of toilet paper. It was the unveiling of the surprise that triggered her happy place.

She started for the card, but he pushed the package at her.

"That first."

Happy to oblige, she opened the box to find a twenty-eight-piece box of truffles from one of her favorite chocolate shops in Queen Anne—Chocolopolis. And they weren't cheap. "Oh, Axel. This is amazing. You shouldn't have."

He looked anxious. "You like this?"

"Yes, I do." She reached across the table to take his hand and squeeze. "Thank you. Do you want one?"

"Maybe after." He swallowed, and she realized he was nervous. "Open this one."

She frowned at the envelope, wondering why he seemed so anxious. Not wasting any time, she opened and read the card. It had hearts all over the front. "You make my heart glow," she read and smiled at him. "Cute. I love the hearts." Then she opened it up. It was blank but for one line: *Be My Valentine.*

"Axel?"

"I mean this. I want you to be mine." He paused. "My valentine."

Her heart sped up, confusion, longing, and more confusion setting in. "What does this mean?"

"It means I would like us to date. I want you to be mine," he repeated.

"For how long?" That was a pushy question, but she needed to know.

He shrugged. The king of noncommittal.

"But…I don't…" *I'm making too big a deal about this. Didn't I want a valentine this year? Now it looks like I can have one.* "Is this so I'll sleep with you?" she blurted, not understanding the romantic gesture, especially coming from Axel. The man had a whole five weeks before Valentine's Day.

"No. I mean, *ja,* I want that." The look he shot her seared her to the bone. "But this is for you. For romance. Because you deserve it."

"You sure say all the right things."

He cocked his head. "I do not understand. You're angry?"

"No! I'm…not sure how to feel. You make me like you a lot. But I don't know why you did all this."

He smiled, the expression kind, not calculating, and on Axel, the word *beautiful* totally fit. "Because you like romance, and you deserve flowers every day." He left the chair to bring her to her feet. "I feel something for you, Rena Jackson. I have for a long time. I just do not want to ruin it."

"Ruin what?" She stared up into his face, unaware she'd been tugging him down to meet her kiss until his lips pressed against her mouth. "Open, baby," she murmured against his closed mouth.

Startled when he groaned and opened up for her, she suddenly found herself in his arms, his hands on her waist as the kiss grew more intense.

Her panties felt damp, and she sure as heck felt something massive in his pants against her belly. She ran her hands up his chest and cupped his cheeks, and he growled something at her.

She broke free, breathing hard, and realized *her feet weren't touching the ground.* "Axel?"

"I—I do not want—" He said something in German she didn't understand, but she heard his frustration, feeling it all the same.

"You don't want me?" She'd find that hard to believe. *Hard* being the key word.

"*Nein.*" He carried her to the couch and sat down, spreading her knees on either side of his lap. "Rena, I don't want to scare you away. You are precious."

Wow. He was good. "So you don't want sex?"

He closed his eyes and grumbled under his breath. When he opened his eyes, they were so dark they looked black. "Do you?"

Looking down at his handsome features, the taut strain of need on his face, she wanted to say *hell yes,* she wanted him. But she worried that then it would all be over, and to her surprise she wanted another date with the big guy. "I do, but—"

"*Ja.* See? You want, but you don't want. It has to be perfect."

"And this isn't perfect?" she asked, knowing the answer.

"Not yet. But I can help you with the *I do* part."

"What?"

Then he was gripping her hips, the way she'd imagined him holding her in that big bed of his. "You tell me no if you want me to stop. Okay?" He looked concerned.

"Yes."

"I mean it. Just say no."

"I will." Never, ever, not as long as those big hands kept creeping up her legs, pushing her skirt higher.

He stared into her eyes as he moved his hands over her bare thighs and cupped her ass. Over her panties, but still.

"*Oh.*"

"I love your ass," he said, his voice thick. "And your legs, your belly, your arms, your breasts." One hand left her leg to slide up her stomach and cup her breast.

She couldn't help arching into his touch.

"Oh, yes. You feel so full, so good in my hand." He squeezed, and she felt way too aroused. On the verge of an orgasm from a little nipple action? God, she needed help.

Then he roamed. He kneaded her ass and slipped a hand under her thigh, his fingers moving under her panties to the heat of her, all while he watched her coming apart.

"So hot and wet," he murmured. "So slick for me."

"God, Axel." Rena couldn't take much more. Embarrassingly, she knew she'd come pretty soon if he didn't stop. And she didn't want him to stop.

"So beautiful." His eyes shone like deep sapphires, glittering with desire. "I want to be inside you more than anything, *Liebling.* I'm so hard for you."

"Yes," she breathed, wanting to feel him deep inside. She kissed him, unable to be apart any longer.

Axel moaned and slid his fingers past her folds and into her.

The intrusion of his thick finger shocked her into a gasp, and he froze. But she didn't want that, so she encouraged more, kissing him, stroking his tongue the way she wanted her body to glove him, touch him.

He worked her with his fingers, finding the taut nub that threatened to undo her with so much pleasure. She pulled her mouth away, moaning his name. He played her, fucking her with his fingers and hand, bringing her to the brink in a shocking, sudden climax that made her scream.

He rocked with her, locked beneath her in passion, in need. Then he pulled his hand away, and she sagged against him, both of them panting.

Rena rained kisses over his face, mouth, and neck. Everywhere she could reach. "Axel, oh, honey. That was so good." And something he hadn't yet experienced, as evidenced by the bulge between his legs and his hiss of pained pleasure when she rocked against him.

She reached between them, wanting to ease him as well, but he stopped her.

"Axel?"

"*Nein,* not for me. For you," he managed, sounding strangled. "I wanted this for you. Okay?"

"Whatever you want," she said, not sure what had just happened. "You do want me though, right?"

"*Ja,*" he said, loudly. "More than I can say. I want to fuck you. To have you come all over me," he growled, the hunger on his face stirring her once more. "I want to lay you back and take you, over and over, hear you scream my name."

She was close to it now. Man, was he good at the sex talk.

"And I will kiss you again, right between your legs, and lap you up. All that sweet cream just for me." He brought her head down for another kiss, one that left her in no doubt of how much he wanted her. He rubbed up against her, his erection impossible to miss. "And I will fill you all up, *Häschen.* Both of us joined together." He let her go, closed his eyes, and leaned back.

She stared down at male perfection. Awash in an almost surreal feeling of lust and affection and trust. Awareness came back, that she was wet between her legs, her skirt hiked up, his hands on her thighs. Jazz played on speakers around them, and the scent of roses mixed with the scent of sex and Axel's heady cologne.

He opened his eyes, the need searing her. "We will make love when you are ready. And you will tell me this."

"I will?" came out in a croak.

"*Ja.* When I make you my valentine." He smiled.

"You mean I have to wait another month?"

He chuckled. "No. Unless that's what you want. I'll prove to you that I am a man worth being by your side. And you will know that I can be trusted to keep you safe."

"I do know that."

"Not yet, but you will."

She didn't understand him. "Well, if you say so." She stood on her knees and stretched, feeling languid. How long had it been since she'd had an orgasm without having to do all the work?

She looked down and saw the strain on his face. "Poor Axel." She kissed his firm lips, enjoying the contrast of such softness on such a hard man. "You sure you don't want me to help you out?"

He groaned. "Stop tempting me. If you get your hands on me, I might lose my purpose."

"Purpose?"

"You must trust me first. To know me." He nodded, and she felt a strange spark of more than affection fill her, a confusing mix of amusement and warmth.

"I look forward to getting to know you."

"As do I." He grimaced. "Now, please, get off me and give me a few minutes to calm down."

"Oh, sorry." She left him sitting there. "I'll just use the bathroom."

He waved toward the hallway. "Down there."

She returned, all cleaned up, and saw him standing with a paper grocery bag for her. In it she saw both bouquets of flowers, wrapped, and her chocolates.

"Is the card in there too?"

"Yes."

"Good." A Valentine's Day card. Her first in years. She planned on adding it to her keepsake box. "I guess it's time for me to go home, huh?"

"I think it best."

Tonight had colored her view of Axel for sure. Though he'd never offered to be her Mr. Right, he'd offered to be her valentine. And she could concede he was right. Waiting to make love—not fuck or have sex, she noted the difference—was smart. She'd have a clearer understanding about the man she was coming to like *a lot.* And now it wouldn't feel weird when she saw him again because they would take their relationship slowly.

That was if she could remember not to jump him the next time she saw him.

"You know, that haircut I gave you is a real turn-on."

"You think?"

"Yes. I keep wondering about that beard and mustache."

He leaned down to rub his face against hers, and she marveled at the soft feel combined with a scratchy texture, both of which made her hungry to have him all over again.

Her voice sounded breathy when she asked, "You're using that cream I used on you, aren't you?"

"I learn from the expert. You like it, yes?"

"I do," she confessed as he walked her out to his truck.

They chatted about her roses and about Del and Mike's growing family on the way home. Axel surprised her by mentioning his mother and what an avid gardener she'd been.

"My mom likes lilies," she told him. "But she can't tell the difference between a dandelion and lettuce."

He laughed. "At least her daughter can. You like the roses?"

"My favorites."

He seemed happy to hear that. They pulled in front of her townhome all too soon.

"Well, I guess we'll have to have a third date to see if you can do any better," she teased.

"I don't know. Tonight seemed pretty perfect to me." He stroked her cheek. "You are so very, very lovely."

"Axel." She blushed. "Stop. You'll give me a big head."

"It cannot get bigger. Or is that because of your hair?"

She gaped. "You did not just make fun of my hair."

He nodded, more playful than she'd ever seen him. "I did. Your curls are the envy of women everywhere. You need a great man like myself to remind you that you are human and not the goddess you appear."

"Oh my God, just stop before I have an eargasm. That voice, those words. Ack!" She leaned over to give him a peck on the lips before hopping out, too fast for him to stop her.

"Rena," he said before she closed the door on him.

She hurried to her house and unlocked the door. "Bye!" she yelled before slamming it closed. She leaned back against it, wondering if she'd dreamt up the whole thing.

Axel couldn't possibly be that amazing, could he?

CHAPTER NINE

Apparently, Friday night had been a fluke.

When Rena learned Axel had joined Del's betting pool to see if and when they'd have sex and/or become a couple, she'd grown livid. "That horse's ass!"

Tommie paused in the art of snipping her client, a big biker who liked to gossip more than Rena did. "Hey, George, gimme a sec."

He flipped through a *People* magazine. "Go ahead. Sounds like issues with my old lady can wait. What flipped Rena's switch?"

Rena swore under her breath and sequestered herself in the nails room, currently empty of people until Stella's next client arrived for her appointment.

"Yo, Rena. What's up?" Tommie asked.

"Shut the door," she snarled.

Tommie's eyes, highlighted today in neon purple, widened. She shut the door.

"Did you know about a betting pool going on, about me and Heller hooking up?" She only ever called him Axel. But today, he was a Heller. A hell of an asshole, a hell of a dickhead, a hell of an ex-almost-lover.

"Sure. We all put money down."

"*What?*"

Tommie took a step back. "You didn't know? Rena, Del's the one who organized it. Yell at her, not me." Tommie darted out of the room and closed the door behind her.

Yell at Del? What a grand idea. Rena planned to do it in person.

She dialed Mike's cell and, before he could answer, asked, "Is your wife at home or at work?"

"Um, on her way home. Why?"

Rena hung up and left the office. "Sorry I yelled, Tommie. Nicky's in charge. I'll see you guys tomorrow."

Tommie gave a salute. George, her client, snickered. "Give 'em hell, Rena."

Nicky and her client waved.

Rena drove to Del's home in Queen Anne, a cute Craftsman with loads of charm. Del and Mike had a little boy, a baby on the way, and a big goofy dog named Jekyll to round out their family. That was if Rena didn't make Mike a widower.

Gah. It was lucky Del was pregnant.

Rena screeched to a halt at the curb outside Del's place just as Del pulled into the driveway in her '69 GTO. Rena left her car and raced to Del, who pulled herself out of the car with effort.

The front door opened, and Colin started to step outside, but Mike yanked him back in.

"No, Son. We do not want to see this."

"But Aunt Rena is going to pound Mom."

"Yep. Let's let them fight it out."

"Ten bucks on Mom."

"You," Rena poked her cousin in the chest. "Teaching that innocent boy to bet. What is wrong with you?"

She heard Colin ask, "Who is she calling innocent, Dad?"

"I have no idea, Son."

The door shut.

Del had the grace to wince. "So, ah, you heard about the pool?"

"*Heard* about it? My stylists, my nonexistent boyfriend, and half of Seattle has apparently heard about it!"

"Don't be such a drama queen." Del tried to shrug her off, but Rena got right up in Del's face. It wasn't often they argued. Rarely, in fact. But when Rena got mad, she got Caroline Jackson crazy. "Um, I'm pregnant, you know."

"Which is why I'm not killing you right now!"

When Rena poked her again, Del apologized. "Okay, I'm sorry. Who knew you'd be so testy? Come on, Cuz. You know the guys bet on everything from darts to how many times Johnny says 'I love you' every time he talks to Lara on the phone. It's harmless."

"Not to me." Rena felt tears come to her eyes. "Axel bet on us."

"No, he didn't."

Her eyes widened. "Don't you dare lie to me, you blond bee-yatch." As big an insult as Rena could come up with for her cousin.

Del cringed. "Okay, just stop. If you're going to cuss me out, do it. *Bee-yatch* is so high school. And for the record, I never took a bet from Axel."

"Yes, you did."

"No, I did not. I know for a fact because I have the board in my back seat."

Rena pulled out the whiteboard before Del, in her unwieldy pregnant state, tried to bend over to do it. "See! Ha. There it is. Heller. He bet we'd…have sex and he'd ruin the relationship before Valentine's Day." Well, that didn't sound promising. Heck, he should have bet he'd ruin things, minus the sex, for January 14th because she was dumping his ass today! Winner winner!

"Read the notes." Del pointed at the board.

"What?"

"See the asterisk?" Del took the board out of Rena's hand and flipped it over. "That's a bet Mateo made. The Heller notation means it came from Heller Paint and Auto. Hence the Heller PA on the front." She flipped the board again and pointed to the PA after Heller's name. Del frowned. "Who told you Heller bet, anyway?"

Knowing he hadn't bet on their relationship eased the disappointment and tension she'd been carrying since she'd found out. "I got an anonymous tip."

"Seriously?" Del looked intrigued. She put a hand to her lower back. "Let's go in and talk about this new mystery."

Rena trudged next to her. "Sorry for blowing up at you."

"Sorry the best thing you can think to call me is bee-yatch. Damn, girl. I taught you better than that."

Rena flushed. "Ass."

"There you go."

They entered, ignoring the fact the front curtain swayed and Colin and Mike perched innocently on the couch, pretending to be engrossed in Mike's phone.

"Gimme a break," Del drawled. "You two are *so* not fooling anyone."

Colin scowled. "See, Dad? I told you to let me go back to my room as soon as they walked to the door."

"But then who'd cover for me?"

"Plebian." The eight-year-old sneered at his father before stalking back to his room.

"He gets that from Brodie," Mike grumbled, describing one of his brothers who could often be found instigating and cheating his way through cards and board games. Rena liked him, *and* he'd married her favorite romance author, so he got a bye with his shenanigans from her.

Del turned from him. "So, Rena, why did the possibility of Heller betting on you make you so mad? We bet on everything at the garage. You know that."

"Oh, so that's what got her in such a hissy." Mike nodded. "Makes sense. You're into the guy, and you think he's just hanging with you to make a buck. Not that the stone-faced killer you're dating would sink that low. But I *could* see him betting on killing someone and whether we'd ever find the body."

"See, I was thinking that same thing at dinner with my mother the other night."

"I don't even want to know." Del sighed and muttered under her breath as she headed down the hall, likely to the bathroom.

Mike patted the spot next to him, and Rena sat.

"Tell me what's wrong, Rena."

She blew out a breath. "Okay, but you can't tell Del."

He moved back so she could see the disbelief on his face.

"Well, not while I'm around. And pretend it's a big secret so she won't bring it up to me."

"That I can do."

"I think I like Axel. Like, I *really* like him. But I don't know him that well, and he's not that great at communicating, though he's getting better. My mother thinks I'm afraid to open myself up to fall in love, but I've had plenty of boyfriends before."

"Have you loved any of them?"

"Maybe. Yes. No. I don't know."

"Okay."

"And she's dating a married man, who's separated. I'm kind of dating Axel, a man I don't know much about. I don't think he's married."

"He's not. This I know because Del and Liam checked him out."

"Not J.T.?" she joked, not surprised her family would be so protective. It sometimes irked her, but their care also made her feel warm and loved.

"No, because he likes Heller. Says the guy is bananas for you."

She groaned. Maybe she shouldn't have left that ugly message on his voicemail earlier. "Well, I thought he'd been betting on us hooking up, which is lame even for high-schoolers."

"I agree." He patted her shoulder and put an arm around her.

She rested her head on his broad chest, wishing it was Axel's large frame. "I jumped to conclusions because some idiot at Del's garage wrote his name on the betting board, and another idiot called to tell me about it." She sighed. "I left an ugly message on Axel's cell phone. And he was so nice to me the other day." She quickly described the dinner but left out the sexy parts.

"Huh. Sounds like a pretty romantic night to me."

"I know. He pulled out all the stops."

"And Chocolopolis? Those truffles are expensive. Del likes them too." He groaned. "Don't tell her you got any or I'll be forced to show my dedication by getting them for her. Okay? And between you and me, she can't tell the difference between them and a Whitman's Sampler, so I try to keep to a budget."

"Deal." She pulled her head off his chest and scooted back, and he turned to face her. "So if you were me, how would you handle a nasty phone message?"

"I'd tell him to his face you're sorry. And if he hasn't listened to the message yet, which, if he's into you, he totally has, then tell him to delete it." Mike checked his phone. "It's not quite five. You think he's still at work?"

"Probably. He works long hours."

"I'd imagine. They've been getting a lot of business from Del and vice versa."

"He's pretty smart."

"And big and threatening. I'm sure people go in there and decide to stay because they're afraid to say no to the guy."

She snorted. "You should talk. But with you, it's because you're so handsome."

"Stop." He turned crimson, as she'd known he would. "Go away, evil woman."

"And my work is done." She stood and wiped her hands. "Tell Del I said sorry. I've gotta go grovel, on my knees if I have to."

"I'd be wary about the on your knees part. Heller's a guy, and a woman on her knees can send the wrong signal." Mike turned even redder. "Just sayin'."

Rena laughed and left, driving to Axel's without having to look up the directions. Though she'd never needed paint or auto body work for her car, she'd satiated her curiosity about where Axel worked a few days after they'd first been introduced.

His shop wasn't too far from Webster's Garage on Rainier. Axel's place was a little farther north. She passed a few parts stores and some industrial-type shops and parked in the lot behind the building. She saw his truck, fortunately, and three other vehicles as well. Likely his employees. She didn't see space for customers behind the building. In the front and to the side, several cars had been staged.

She parked next to his vehicle and tried the back door, surprised to find it open. Entering, she walked right into the meat of the shop.

The area felt cool but not cold, and someone blasted rock music in the large bay. She glanced around, seeing a few cars parked inside. There were two smaller bays, a long bench, tools, and machines stashed to the side, probably used for painting or sanding, banging, and hammering. However they fixed dents and dings.

A big white guy with a red Mohawk stood by the tools staring at her. He had a barrel chest, arms almost as big as Axel's, and sleeves of tattoos. "Hello." And a deep voice that managed to be pleasant. He smiled.

"Hello." She smiled back.

Another big man joined him, this one scowling, with ragged dark hair and an attitude she could see from clear across the bay. Her smile faded.

"Oh, don't mind Rylan," Mohawk said. "Is there something we can help you with?"

"I, ah, I'm looking for Axel Heller?"

Mohawk's smile grew even wider.

Rylan swore. "Damn it."

Another guy entered the bay from a side door. He wore a yellow protective suit and a mask he'd pushed up off his face. Cute and lean, he reminded her of a fox for some reason. Maybe it was the twitchy way he walked.

He saw her and stopped. "Who are you?"

Rude, but okay. "I'm Rena, and I'm looking for Axel Heller."

The man swore. "Damn it. I'm out twenty bucks!"

She narrowed her eyes. "Which one of you is Mateo?"

The twitchy guy suddenly remembered he had more work to do and darted away.

Mohawk man walked to her and held out a hand. "Hi. I'm Smitty. I do all the real work around here to make Heller look good. You met Mateo, and that's Rylan. The FNG."

She shook his hand and tried to hide a smile. "Ah. Nice to meet you. Rena Jackson."

Smitty walked her to a closed door bordered on either side by large panes of glass. She saw the back of Axel's head as he faced the bulletin board on the wall behind him. He was on the phone and swearing, his voice dark, mean. Sexy. *I mean, scary.*

"Uh-oh. Maybe not the best time to be here. Five to one says he's talking to his dad." Smitty looked down at her. "His dad's an ass."

"Oh." She should go, but then Axel turned around and froze in the middle of what he'd been saying, staring at her through the glass.

"Might as well face the lion in his den," Smitty murmured and opened the door while knocking. "Yo, Heller. Visitor for you. Me and the boys are taking off."

"*Ja.* Okay. See you tomorrow," he said absently, staring a hole through Rena's head.

"Good luck," Smitty whispered before pushing her gently inside and closing the door behind them.

She heard movement outside as Axel finished his phone call, with more harsh words, these not yelled so loudly, for the person to whom he spoke.

The outer doors banged closed. And then…

Mreow.

Rena blinked. She looked around and spotted a small doghouse. Or was that a cat house? It had the word *CAT* painted on a nameplate above the structure. Inside, a calico cat licked her paw and cleaned her face, sitting half in and half out of the house.

Rena squatted down to see the furry beast, astonished to see the cat was pregnant. "Oh my gosh. You are too cute."

She stood and found Axel right behind her, his phone on the desk. "Hello."

"Hi." She looked up at him. "Can we talk?"

He nodded and sat in one of the chairs across from his desk. He looked at the other one right next to it, so she sat and turned it to face him. "You have a cat?"

"Just until she has babies. Then I'll find them all homes."

She glanced again at the tiny house the cat had disappeared into. "Did you build that?"

His cheeks looked pink. "It's cold out."

"That's sweet." And just like him. She felt terrible. "I'm sorry."

His expression remained impassive.

"I got bad information and thought you were just using me for sex and money." Best just to lay it all out on the line.

His eyes widened. "*Was?*"

"Yeah, I know. Sounds silly now that I think about it. You're not like that." She explained about the betting board and her anonymous caller and could see his rage building.

"This betting makes you unhappy? I'll rip the board apart and make sure they all know to stay out of our business," he promised.

Visions of him tearing up Webster's Garage scared her. "No, no. Please don't."

He frowned. "You want them telling lies?"

"I like them caring enough to include us in their games. They do it to the rest of them too. About whether Liam will flip out over his wedding, when Johnny and Lara will tie the knot. They even bet when Del's baby will be born."

He relaxed a little. "Then why did you get so mad at the thought I might be betting?"

"Because the other night was magical," she admitted, relieved when his gaze softened on her. "And thinking it might not be so magical to you…hurt."

"Oh, *Häschen.* Come here."

She moved to him and let him tug her into his lap.

"I cannot wait to be with you again. You make me smile, Rena. We will have more dates, and you will trust me." He glanced at the clock on the wall and swore. "And tomorrow you will make sure no one ate the present I sent you for today to your shop. It is only for you."

"You sent me another present?" She wanted to clap but refrained. She wasn't three, after all.

"*Ja.* I plan to be your valentine, *Liebling*. But you see, you need trust. Proof I will not hurt you."

She cupped his cheeks and kissed him, loving his soft sigh. "Just promise me one thing."

"Anything."

"Don't lie to me. Men have lied to my mother for as long as I can remember. And too many have lied to me too. I want to trust you. And I hope I will. But the lies…I can't handle them."

"I swear." He held her hand against his heart.

And she felt something else. Something more than his heartbeat. Something stiff and prodding against her backside. She blinked up at him.

He flushed. "I'm sorry. I can't help it around you."

She felt super sexy all of a sudden. And she remembered in detail what he'd done for her Friday night. All for her, he'd said. She should have trusted him. Perhaps she could make things up to him…

She smiled.

He leaned back. "What? What did I do now?"

CHAPTER TEN

Axel didn't trust that sly smile on Rena's face. God, she'd crushed him earlier. Cutting things between them before he'd had a chance to show her what was in his heart had been devastating. Then to get a call from his father and learn that Jannik Heller and Maksim, Axel's older brother, would be coming for a visit? It had thrown him into a fit of anger.

This shop belonged to *him.* He didn't need his father or brother fucking with his life. And no matter what they said as an excuse to oversee the American stores his father owned, he knew they'd come to talk over matters of his mother's estate. One she wanted kept far from her louse of a husband.

But having Rena here, now, made all the hurt go away. The icy numbness followed by rage melted into warmth and caring.

He saw the affection in her amber eyes, knew the bliss of having her go liquid around him. He'd had to take himself in hand several times a day since then, thinking about her like that. So sexy and soft, post-orgasm.

But he hadn't seen this look before. Naughty mixed with fierce.

His heart raced.

"Axel, I'm so sorry." She ran her nails over his chest, scraping at the collar of his shirt, grazing the flesh of his neck.

He sucked in a breath. "No problem."

"I should make it up to you."

"You have nothing to apologize for."

She leaned in to whisper, "I remember Friday night, do you?"

He moaned, hard enough to bend steel. "*Ja.* Too much I remember."

She nipped his earlobe and licked his ear, and he couldn't help jerking under her, his entire body one taut snap away from crumbling.

"Did making me come make you feel good?"

"Rena, what are you doing to me?" he moaned, shocked when her hands ran down his chest to his stomach, and lower.

"Answer me." She kissed his cheek, his neck, and sucked.

He groaned, long and loud, uncaring if everyone had left. Though anyone could pass by and see them through the glass on either side of the door, he could barely think past the throbbing in his cock.

"*Ja.* Being with you makes me feel good. I sucked that finger clean, *Liebling.*" In German, he added, "And I want to fuck you. I want to slide my dick between your lips, want to eat you out. Feel you come over my tongue. I want to take you, everywhere. Rena, I want you more than anything."

She kissed him to silence then unsnapped his jeans.

The sound was overly loud in the room. Nothing to be heard but the ticking clock and his zipper moving slowly down.

"You're so big," she said. "You'll be a tight fit, won't you? *Liebling,*" she teased. Then she kissed him again.

She slid her hand inside his underwear, and her fingers moved past his slick tip, spreading that moisture over the rest of him.

He wanted to tell her to stop, to wait, that she didn't have to do any of it. But his body had other ideas.

"Rena. Fuck. I want you."

"So big and hot," she whispered and kissed him as she stroked, her small hand holding his cock then pumping him as she licked and nibbled at his mouth. Her tongue slid against his, and he was pushing into her hand, unable to keep still, seducing her with every kiss even as she made him mindless with desire.

He swam in her scent and touch. They kissed, the woman more than arousing, especially because her little moans of pleasure made everything so much hotter. As she moaned his name and ground against him, ordering him to come, he lost it.

He leaned his head back and swore, coming so hard he saw stars.

She continued to pump him, kissing his cheeks and mouth. And still he came, so gone he couldn't reason.

When he finally rejoined his body, she was wiping her hand over his belly, using the underside of his shirt to clean herself.

Her smile was wide, her satisfaction impossible to miss. "You came a lot, baby."

"Rena, Jesus." He sagged back, done in.

"If that's some of what you have to offer, I think you're gonna make one hell of a valentine." She stood. "Where's your restroom?"

He nodded in the general direction of the area out front.

"Be right back."

He sat there, his dick out, his shirt covered with cum, and stared blankly at the wall. When he heard footsteps again, he took his shirt off and used it to clean up. Man, she hadn't been kidding. He'd made a mess.

After cleaning up and zipping up, he tossed his shirt to the floor and sought a spare tee from his bottom drawer. In a shop where things often got messy, he always kept a spare set of clothes.

Rena came in and gaped. "Oh my God. You are seriously cut!"

He grinned. "You see what you will be getting? An even better valentine, *ja*?" Now if only she'd whip off her shirt and show him those beautiful breasts. Feeling them had been amazing, but he wanted to suckle as well.

"You have tattoos." She walked right up to him and ran her hands over the right side of his chest, his shoulder and arm. "Why not the left side as well?"

"I'm planning on it." Something with rabbits and golden-eyed beauties would do.

"Well, let me know when you go because I want to watch." She gave him a naughty smile. "Now I know what you felt Friday night."

"*Nein.* You don't know how many times I've made myself come, thinking of you. How many times I've imagined licking you up between your legs." He moved closer and ran his beard over her cheek. "Between your legs, *Häschen.* Won't that feel nice?"

"Damn. You are lethal." She fanned herself.

He put his shirt on and laughed. "No more than you. I came so hard I nearly passed out. And I'm getting hard again. Come. Let me walk you out before I bend you over my desk," he muttered, aware his body might make a mess of this courtship before he could again engage his brain.

But then she stopped him, a hand to his chest, engaging his heart. "Axel, I really am sorry."

"Ah, sweetheart, I know. Me too."

"For what?"

"For waiting ten months and two weeks to finally ask you out. I'm an idiot." He'd turned her speechless, he saw with some amusement.

At her car, he waited until she'd belted in then signaled her to roll down her window.

"Yes, *Herr* Idiot?"

"Very funny." Actually, it was. He chuckled. "I will make you mine by Valentine's Day, Rena. This I promise." And he'd have a nice talk with the pregnant she-wolf as well. He didn't appreciate anyone upsetting his woman.

"Yeah?" Her eyes sparkled, and he wanted to capture this moment of having her all to himself, happy and tender and loving. "So you think you can win me over by Valentine's Day?"

"*Ja.*"

"Well, I think it might take you a little longer than that." She smiled, but she didn't sound so sure.

"Until our next date, *Häschen*."

"Until then, big guy." She motioned him to come closer then kissed him cross-eyed. "Now sleep on that."

Rena spent the next day smiling. Everyone commented on it, but she didn't care. She'd been so amazingly sexy and take-charge. She liked a playful relationship, but Axel wasn't the playful type. Yet he seemed to be thawing. He smiled at her a lot, and he talked now.

He'd texted her a good morning with a goofy bunny emoji that made her laugh. Unfortunately, she'd had to tell him that only a wrapper remained outside her shop when she'd arrived that morning. Someone had stolen the present he'd left for her. He hadn't seemed too bothered, though he promised to leave her gifts (gifts!) inside from now on.

Work passed by in a blur, her friends cheerful and gossiping, sharing the what and who about everyone. Rena loved it.

Tommie broke her train of thought with a customer requesting Rena's services, so she stopped restocking the bottles on the shelves and met a grungy-looking guy with hard eyes. He had really short, uneven hair that needed help.

"You Rena Jackson?" he rasped.

She didn't like the way he looked at her, but she couldn't put her finger on why. He didn't leer or anything, but she had a weird feeling. "Yes, I'm Rena."

The man smiled. "I'm Daryl. I was told you're the go-to person for haircuts." He rubbed his hand over his shorn scalp, and she saw dirt under his fingernails. "I know it's short, but it already feels too long to me."

"Sure. I can fit you in." She had an appointment in another hour and a half, but his cut wouldn't take long at all. "Come on over."

He sat in the back in the chair not occupied by Nicky's client. Nicky and Martin would chat from the time the guy sat down to the time he left.

Rena draped a cape over Daryl and buttoned it at his nape. She looked up and met his gaze in the mirror. "So, do you know what number they used on you last time? The size guard?" she asked, referring to the size of the guard on the clippers used to shear his head.

"I think a three on top and a one on the sides. I like it short." He smiled at her. "Kinda like a skinhead."

His smile wasn't kind. It creeped her out. But as a businesswoman, she knew she'd have to work with strange people sometimes. "I'm sorry. A skinhead?"

"You know, those white douchebags with the bald heads, all that *Heil Hitler* shit?" He chuckled. "I ain't heil-ing nothing." He laughed again.

She exchanged a glance with Nicky, and Martin raised a brow, but they kept talking. And since Daryl hadn't acted as if he too hated anyone darker than his own skin color, she tried to ignore his remarks and reached for her clippers.

She gave as many haircuts to men as to women, so the barbering side of doing hair came naturally. And despite being black in a city dominated by white people, she wasn't inundated with African American clients. Rena worked on a mix of races, genders, and sexualities. And she liked that.

But sometimes, when a guy like this one showed up, she had to wonder if she had more racist clients than she knew. Because he might not like skinheads, but she had a feeling he didn't like her either.

"So who told you about me?" she asked as she started at the base of his hairline on his neck and worked her way up.

"Oh, I've heard your name a lot. Used to go to Ray's."

"That explains it." She smiled at him in the mirror.

He didn't smile back, just looked at her. "So, you cut a lot of hair, huh?"

Not a great conversationalist, but she'd roll with it. "Yes. I love it. I like making people look nice and feel better about themselves. Take you, for example."

"Yeah?" He sounded suspicious.

She continued to work, focused on his hair. "You have a head that's perfect for this kind of cut. Your shape is round, no need to hide yourself with a lot of hair."

"Huh. Yeah, I do look good like this." He started to nod and she stopped him, holding his head straight.

"Sorry. Don't move. I don't want to mess up your fade."

"The last fuckhead who did my hair totally gave me a line. I looked like I had a bowl cut for a week."

"Oh, that's tough. I won't to do that to you." She kept trimming then switched to a number three guard to get the top. "We'll keep this slightly longer, okay? I really like your color. It's a rich, dark brown."

"Thanks." He cleared his throat. "So, uh, do you like it here better than Ray's?"

"I love styling hair. Better than pouring beers? Oh, yeah. But I miss the people at Ray's."

"You didn't find them too stupid or poor? Too 'beneath you'?"

She paused. "What? Beneath me? Where did that come from?"

He looked at her in the mirror. "I dunno. Heard you thought you were better than everyone."

She gripped the clippers tightly, ready to shove them down his throat.

Better than? She'd give *his* better-than white ass a—

"But I don't see that at all. You're kinda nice." He sounded surprised, and she saw him blush. "I mean, you're doin' a great job on my hair and all."

"Hmm."

"Hey now. I'm just sayin' what I heard. Me? I'm gonna tell my friends you do good work. Maybe send more business your way."

She continued trimming his hair, praying he wouldn't tell anyone he knew to visit.

"So, uh, are you dating anyone?"

She nearly slipped but held the clippers steady at the last instant. "Yes, as a matter of fact." *He's huge and could crush you with one fist, so back off.* "A great guy."

"Oh." He sounded disappointed. "I mean, I get it. You're pretty for a..." He stopped himself. "For a girl not much older than me," he mumbled.

Yep, she'd been due. So many great friends and customers who didn't give a hoot about skin color. Of course she'd have to get a few rotten ones. It probably would have bothered her more if he'd been someone she cared about. As it was, she just wanted him gone.

She gave him a bright smile and chattered about the coming winter festival downtown. When she asked him about his plans for the day, he told her he worked down at the docks. Then he continued by complaining about everyone who didn't work as hard as he did and who couldn't see his value as a fuck-tastic, amazin' employee.

That value must be buried deep, deep down.

She finished up his hair in record time and dusted off the excess. Then she used a bit of product to cause the front of his short hair to spike up until she thought he looked less grungy and more cool-slash-funky, wearing the crusty clothes as if a fashion statement and not that he didn't believe in a washing machine.

"Wow." He turned his head in the mirror while she drew away his cape. "I look good. This is much better than what Milton does."

"I'm glad you like it." She gently encouraged him toward the front of the shop. She didn't offer him the Ray's discount and instead charged him full price, though he didn't seem to realize it. Maybe if she were too expensive he wouldn't come back.

"Huh. Kind of pricey."

"Well, we're a boutique, so you do pay more, but you get better service."

"You got that right," Tommie said as she put more foils in her client's hair.

Daryl handed her two twenties, and when she gave him his change, he pocketed it all. So, no tip then. She mentally sighed. "Have a great day."

"Don't you want your tip?" He leaned closer, staring, and said in a low voice, "Don't stay late here alone. It ain't safe." He fingered his hair then turned and left.

Feeling scared for the first time in a long time, Rena watched him go.

"What the hell was that?" Tommie demanded. "What did he say? I didn't hear him."

The salon grew so quiet only the low background music could be heard.

"Oh, nothing." Rena brushed it off, not wanting any drama in her shop that didn't involve lighthearted gossip or laughter. "He asked if I had a boyfriend, and I told him yes."

"Woot woot!" Nicky yelled from the back room, only to hear Martin add, "So she's off her no-men streak? Wow. Never thought I'd live to see that happen."

"Martin, I can hear you." Rena ignored the coughing that didn't quite hide laughter from the back.

"She hears everything," Nicky said. "And through that thick hair. It's a mystery."

"I heard that too!"

"See?"

The rest of the day passed without incident, but Rena couldn't get Daryl's warning out of her mind. She wanted to ask Nicky to stay to help her clean up, but she didn't want to kowtow to some racist schlub. Why give him any power over her?

But she was angry as well as scared because he'd made her feel unsafe in her shop.

She finished closing up and double-checked that all the doors were locked. But as she made to leave through the back, she heard something outside. And froze.

Something was being dragged. Then some weird rustling.

She had her ear to the door but couldn't see anything because there were no windows in the back. She didn't want to be the stupid teenager in a horror movie who went outside by herself. Although the hour had grown late and the sky dark, the overhead streetlight illuminated the back parking lot. She quietly unlocked the door and opened it a crack.

She didn't see movement, but she heard something. She opened the door wider, and the movement stopped. Her heart racing, she gripped her keys and her pepper spray and threatened, "My boyfriend is on his way, and I have a gun."

Silence greeted her. She felt like she stood still forever, but maybe a minute had gone by. Then, feeling foolish, she stepped outside, the back door still open behind her.

She saw what had been dragged and blinked. It wasn't a body, thank God. And yes, she'd really gone there. Too many Lifetime movies, unfortunately, combined with Daryl's warning. No body, but a crumpled bag of caramel corn with pieces strewn around it. And a few pieces led into the bushes by the side. They were too small to hide a man. But not too small that a rabid raccoon couldn't be waiting to jump out at her.

Rena slowly approached and heard a high-pitched growl. A dog, maybe?

"Hey, it's okay. Come on out. I won't hurt you," she crooned and knelt. Looking around, she spied more popcorn and grabbed some, then tossed a few pieces at the bush. "Come on out."

She shivered, and she had a jacket on. She could only imagine the poor creature hiding in the bushes.

A tiny muzzle peeked through, followed by what couldn't be more than three pounds of skin and bones. It bared its teeth at her even as it trembled.

"Oh, sweetie. It's okay." Her heart melted, and she put a few pieces of caramel corn on the ground near it, not wanting to throw the treat and scare the dog away. The dog, likely a Chihuahua, had a Doberman's coloring. She hadn't known they could look like that. It had spots of fur missing and a cloudy left eye. Part of its left ear had been torn, and it had to be freezing its little butt off.

She just sat there, watching with compassion, and it crept slowly closer.

"You need a buddy, don't you? You're so tiny. I mean, geez. I could probably hold you with two fingers." She kept her voice soft. "You haven't had an easy time of it, have you?"

No way this dog had recently run away from its owner. It wore no collar and looked starved. She could count its little ribs. But she hadn't seen the tiny guy?—gal?—before because she would have done something about it.

She smiled, realizing she and Axel had another thing in common. Stray pets hanging around their businesses.

As long as nothing else hung around. Daryl's words churned in her thoughts.

The sudden silence, but for the wind and a phantom beep or screech of tires, felt oppressive. She wanted to get in her car and go home. But she couldn't leave the dog.

"Can you come with me?" She moved closer.

The dog growled and showed sharp teeth.

A car drove by, slowly.

Rena wasn't waiting. She lunged at the dog and held it in her arms as she hurried back into the shop to lock up, then through to her car, praying the dog wouldn't bite her. It was shivering too hard to do much damage. And once inside her vehicle, its pitiful barking turned to whimpering.

So small and uncared-for. Her eyes teared. She felt bad for the stray. *Don't worry, I'll take care of you.* She locked her car door and sat there, breathing hard. The dog grew still.

She cuddled it closer against her jacket and stroked its head. At this point, if it bit her, it bit her. She felt nothing but relief, safe and sheltered from the wind—and everything else—outside.

"Well, little guy, let's go home. And please, don't pee or poop before we get there."

She made it home only half successful, her jacket wet with dog urine. It just figured the dog had left a mess before hiding in the back seat. It took her forever to get him out and into her house, but he didn't once bite her.

She wasn't allowed to have pets in her townhome, but who would know? At least she had time to find this guy—and it was a male—a good home.

"Let's get you cleaned up a little." She had no idea if the dog would welcome a bath. Afraid to put the Chihuahua down and lose him when and not if he bolted, she took him upstairs and into her bathroom before locking them both inside.

The moment she set him down, he barked at her and ran around, trying to find a place to hide. He ended up cowering behind the toilet. Which made her tear up again.

"Whoever did this to you should be beaten, given the worst haircut known to man, and tossed to Axel." She understood her Viking better than he thought she did.

In all the time she'd known him, he'd never once picked on anyone smaller than himself or gone out of his way to make trouble. Trouble usually found him, true enough, but his fights involved standing up to bullies or stepping in when someone picked on someone weaker. And the man owned a wooden shelter for a pregnant cat he said he didn't plan on keeping.

She chuckled. "Okay, little fella, I'm going to find you some food and water and see if we can't clean you up. Don't worry. Everything will be okay."

Everything was not okay. The chihuahua had gotten over his fear enough to eat the shaved ham and drink a bit of the water she'd given him after she'd left him alone to eat it. But when she'd spent time with him, he seemed scared, preferring the space alone. A bath had not been in his immediate future, or so he'd convinced her each time she'd tried to rub a warm washcloth over him.

Apparently, he didn't like the bathroom because he barked. *A lot.* Ear-piercing yips from a tiny dog burrowed into her brain throughout the night. But she'd kept him in there because she didn't want to give him free rein in her home, not sure of what kind of damage—or vermin—he might spread.

In the morning, she found him sleeping, curled on the bathroom rug by the sink. He'd also left her a tiny poop in the tub, though she had no idea how he'd gotten in there.

Tired but amused at the stray's spirit, she could only be glad she didn't work until noon and left the bathroom to text Nicky. Nicky texted back right away that she'd open the shop that morning. One problem solved.

Then Rena called Axel, hoping he'd be awake at…six in the morning. Whoops.

"*Ja?*" came his gritty voice over the phone. "Rena?"

"Hi, Axel. Sorry. I didn't realize it was so early." The dog heard her voice and yipped.

"What was that?"

"That is the reason I'm calling so early." She explained about the dog and its behavior, and Axel laughed at her.

"I must see this dog."

"He needs a vet, so I was wondering if you could give me the name of the one you used."

"I can take you there, if you like."

"Oh. That would be nice."

"And we can have breakfast together. Okay?"

"Sure." Another date with Axel. She shivered, and not from the cold.

"I'll swing by to get you in an hour. The vet opens at eight, so it will give us time to get him in or at least schedule an early appointment. Will that work?"

"How about an hour and a half?" She had to do her hair and dress...after cleaning the tub with bleach.

"Okay. See you soon, *Häschen*."

A bunny, a possessed Chihuahua, and a pregnant cat walk into a bar together... She had to find a way to make that joke work.

She entered the bathroom, shutting the door behind her, and squatted to look the dog in the eye, well, his good eye. He had hidden behind the toilet once more, but he poked his face out now and then when he barked at her.

Today, though, he didn't sound angry or scared, but chatty.

"Okay, little guy. I'm going to clean up your mess, shower, then fix myself up. And you're going to the vet for a checkup." She smiled. "Don't be a pain about it, okay?"

He stared at the finger she held out for him to sniff. Slowly, he crept forward, sniffed, then walked even closer and sniffed her whole hand.

She stroked the top of his head once. Twice. Before he jerked back and hid behind the toilet.

"It's okay, I—"

He started barking.

"Yep. You're gonna be a pain."

CHAPTER ELEVEN

Axel would never have guessed a tiny beast would frazzle Rena Jackson. The woman charmed everyone she met. But she had no idea how to handle the squirmy dog in her arms.

"It's okay, sweetie. Just relax." She saw Axel watching her and grimaced. "At least he hasn't peed on me yet today."

He tried to bite back a smile. She stood in her doorway looking irritated, and so damn sweet. He kissed her, ignoring the squirmy canine starting to growl, and pulled back regretfully. "Give him to me."

"Are you sure?" She gave him a dubious once-over. "No offense, Axel, but you're a lot more threatening than I am."

"Give me the *hund*."

The exchange didn't go so smoothly. The dog had sharp teeth that sank into his thumb, and it kept growling and squirming in his arms. But he cradled it and spoke softly, in German, to soothe the creature.

In seconds, it stilled, then went limp and let go of his now--bleeding thumb.

"How did you do that?" Rena gaped at him. "You're the Chihuahua whisperer."

"Would you get me a bandage?" He held his bloody thumb out.

"That has to hurt, you poor thing. Hold on." She ran back inside.

He used that time to carry the dog to the back seat of his truck and put him into the crate he'd once used for the cat. In fact, he had the same blanket in there the cat had laid upon, so he hoped the dog didn't mind it. The fierce Chihuahua that thought itself a Doberman sniffed all around then lay down and put his head on his paws.

"It'll be fine, boy. Don't you worry," Axel said in German. Animals seemed to respond to that language better, he'd found. And his deep voice soothed. Perhaps that was why Rena had warmed up to him. He'd started talking to her, and his voice had done the trick.

He doubted it had been anything else. His good mood deserted him, reminders of his dreams causing him to rethink and doubt himself. He'd been doing so well lately that he'd forgotten he didn't actually deserve happiness, something his father would be only too happy to remind him of when he arrived.

In two weeks.

"Axel, I'm coming," Rena called out, and he forced himself to ignore his father's impending visit and his bad dreams, the ones where he hurt his mother, the way his father had hurt her all too often.

Rena came around the truck and stopped. "Hey, you okay?"

"Oh, yes, fine." He wanted to pull back, to stop the ugly stain of his life from tainting hers. Then he told himself to stop the melodrama and live in the now. Any man who would turn away the angel in front of him in favor of self-denial was a fucking fool. "Sorry. My thumb hurts."

It stung a little, now that he thought about it. But not that much.

"Axel. Oh, honey." She fussed over him, cleaning, medicating, and patching his torn thumb. Her care soothed all his aches and started a new one he had no business thinking about with so much to do today.

Just because he thought about sex with Rena every waking moment didn't mean she did.

Except… He glanced at her hand, remembering how it had felt wrapped around him.

She looked at her hand as well then back up at him. "You're making this weird."

He had to laugh. "I'm sorry. I can't help remembering everything about you that I—" *love* "—like."

"Is my hand the only thing that you like?" she asked in challenge.

"*Nein.* Look at you. Your smile always makes me feel good in here." He thumped his chest.

She gave him a shy smile, and he fell in love with her all over again. "You are *really* good with words. Why don't you use them more often?"

"I am trying with you." He drew her to the passenger side and lifted her inside. "I love picking you up, holding you."

"You make me feel like I'm light as a feather."

She was in a teasing mode, so he answered in kind, "I wouldn't say a feather."

She laughed. "Okay, smarty-pants. What would you say?"

"More like a mound of gold."

"Gold is heavy." She frowned.

"Is it now?" He grinned.

Her lips curled, but she tried to hide it. "Well, you're no Viking dreamboat."

"Yes, I am. We should sail away together. You can be the sexy Valkyrie who brings me mead."

"Well, I was a bartender."

Enthralled with how much fun it was to spar with her, he said, "See? It fits. You should always wait on me."

"You know what else fits? Your foot and your mouth."

They teased each other all the way to the vet, and Axel felt like he could move mountains, high on life and laughter. On Rena.

She made him feel worthy, the way his mother had. With Rena, he could talk and smile. She never called him names or made him feel as if he didn't matter, as if he'd never be or do anything of value in his life. His nightmares held no sway in the light of her smile.

That joy in life, that goodness, so reminded him of Ilse Heller, it was as if he could feel her with them in the truck, giving her approval for this woman he wanted to call his own.

"Hey, Axel, are you okay?" They'd been sitting in the vet's parking lot while he stared at her. "What's that look?" She stroked his hand gripping the steering wheel.

"I..." He cleared his throat. "I think my mother would like you very much." His eyes felt scratchy, a ball of emotion suddenly making it hard to breathe. "I'll get the dog and meet you in the lobby." He tore out of the truck before he made a fool of himself.

By the time he met Rena inside, he'd put a lid on his emotions and ignored the questioning look she'd shot him. He waited while Rena signed some paperwork and explained the situation with the stray to one of the techs.

"Okay, we'll have a look at him." The vet started to take the dog away, and it started barking like crazy inside its cage.

In German, Axel said, "Calm down. We'll be back. Relax, little fellow."

And like that, the dog went quiet. The assistant grinned at Rena's shock. "He's magical. When he came in the other day with his cat, the minute he spoke, all the animals stopped talking and looked at him."

Axel felt his cheeks heat. "She's saying that to get me to volunteer with the animals."

"You totally should," Rena agreed.

"We must go." He hurried her out of there before he said yes to make her happy. With so much else going on in his life, he just didn't have the time to devote to anyone else. "And it's not my cat."

Rena buckled herself into the truck and gave him a smug look. "Uh-huh. Sure."

Why does no one believe me when I say this?

He took her to breakfast at the NorthStar Diner in Greenwood, and she settled into the booth, looking pleased. "I haven't been here in forever. Good choice."

He grunted, starving. "It's been a while for me too. I get so busy with work I usually get something on the way."

She looked him over. "You shouldn't get fast food. With that big body, you need real nutrition."

He gave a mock sigh, not looking at her as he studied the menu. "If only I had someone to cook for me. Or serve me. The way my favorite bartender used to."

"Ha ha. Laugh it up, but with those big feet, you know you have a lot of belly to fill."

"Are you saying I have a big stomach?" He patted his abs.

"Oh stop. You know your stomach is like a washboard," she muttered and shoved her nose in the menu. "It's like a six-pack and a twelve-pack had a baby and made your abs."

"*Ja.* I am so strong, like ox," he said, his accent deliberately thick.

She snickered.

"This breakfast for us, I'm paying."

She looked as if she wanted to argue, but he gave her his stern look, the one that said he wasn't budging. "Fine. You want to pay? Next meal is on me."

"Deal." And people thought he wasn't good with women. He'd just gotten yet another date out of her without trying.

They ordered, and the waiter brought them both coffee. Rena took hers black, which surprised him as he doctored his with cream and sugar. He would have thought someone with a sweet tooth like hers would want something to ease the bitter taste.

She snorted. "Wuss. A real woman drinks her coffee black."

"Then it's good I'm not a real woman."

She crossed her eyes at him. "So how do you do the animal thing?"

"What?"

"You're an animal charmer. Why don't you volunteer at shelters or with the vet?"

He sighed. "I like animals, and I'd like to help. But I am so busy with work I have no time."

"I understand that." She sighed with him. "I've been working my tail off to open my own salon. I'm so happy to have it, but I worry a lot. Stress over bills, over clients, over weird noises in the parking lot." She grinned. "That dog took years off my life last night. I think he's the one who ate your gift, by the way. That's if you gave me caramel corn, which can't be good for his teeth."

He frowned. "You went out in the parking lot by yourself last night? Alone?"

"I have pepper spray."

"It's not safe."

"Axel, I—"

"Tonight, I'll walk you out. When are you done?"

She studied him, and he wondered what she saw. But her smile, when it came, warmed him from the inside out. "You care about me, don't you?"

Was the woman serious? "*Ja,*" he said slowly. "Is there some reason you think I do not?"

Her smile widened, taking up her face. "You're really working on being my valentine, aren't you?"

Which reminded him. He reached into his pocket and pulled out a small box. "For you."

She lit up, a fan of presents as her uncle had mentioned. Axel planned to get her something every day until February 14th.

She opened it up and stared. "Wow. Um. This is great." She gave him a weird smile. "What is it?"

He leaned over to stroke its neon-orange hair. "It's a troll, to bring you luck." He'd found the tiny doll in a kitschy store downtown and thought she might like it.

"Good luck. Cool." She smiled. "Thank you."

"*Kein Problem.*"

"Huh?"

"No problem."

"Oh. You need to teach me how to speak German."

"Then how can I say naughty things about you that you won't understand?"

"Axel."

"Rena." He loved teasing her because she smiled so prettily when he did.

The waiter brought their food, and as they ate, she told him about dinner with her mother the previous week, something that had been weighing on her.

"I don't know if telling her what I felt was wrong or right. I love my mother, but she has the worst taste in men."

"Unlike her daughter," he had to slip in.

She just looked at him.

"*Was?*"

She ignored what he'd said. "I mean, this guy Dave looked different from the slick guys she usually brings home. But he's married."

"You said separated."

"It's the same thing."

"Is it? He's not hiding his marriage from your mother."

"No, he's not. But he's also not divorced. I wonder if he's stringing her along."

He speared eggs and cheese and chewed, thinking. "He could be. But your mother is her own person. She has to make her own choices," he said, remembering Ilse's poor decisions. "Nothing you can say or do will change her mind. Just be there to help her if she falls."

"More like *when* she falls, but you have a point." She sipped her coffee, accepting the waiter's offer to top it off, and spoke once the man had gone to a new table. "It's so weird because my mom is smart and pretty. In all other areas of her life but her dating life, she's amazing. But then you add a guy to the mix, and she's a hot mess," she said bluntly.

Axel watched her, seeing the thoughts his Rena did not say. "You worry you are like her."

"I am." She met his gaze, direct. "That's why I tried to break it off with you before. I want a man to stick around, to be honest with me. I want to get married and have babies with someone I can love." She lowered her voice. "Not a guy who'll ditch me after sex or treat me like I don't matter. I'm worth more than that."

"You are worth everything," he said quietly, hearing her inner pain, her past sorrows. "You should have a man who will protect you, help you, support you when you need it. A man who would never lay a hand on you in violence or hurt your feelings. And he should like your friends and your family." He paused. "My mother never had any of that, and it hurt me to see her in pain."

Rena's eyes widened. "Is that why you don't get along with your father?"

"Yes, and many other reasons." Jannik Heller was an abusive and controlling asshole. "I think your mother should know what you told me."

"I tried to tell her that already."

"Did you?"

She paused and took another sip of coffee. "Maybe not in those words."

"Then tell her in those words. Not the hot mess part, but that she is so amazing, you think she should have someone who treats her that way." He reached across the table and put his hands over hers, his heart in his eyes. "She deserves to be treated like a queen."

The world around them stopped.

He stared into her eyes, and she stared back.

After a charged moment, Rena slid her hands back. "Like a queen." She nodded, her voice hoarse. "I'll definitely tell her that." She stared at him. "Would you like to meet her?"

He felt them taking a step closer to that relationship he desperately wanted. "Meet your mother?"

"*Ja,*" she teased.

He chuckled. "I would, very much."

"I'll tell her. She's a mean cook."

"Like you?"

"I'm not bad. My mom can make a tin can taste good."

"Then by all means, we should meet her for dinner."

Rena shook her finger at him. "Just remember, she's my mom, even if she looks more like my prettier older sister."

Axel didn't like hearing that. How could Rena not realize how beautiful she was to him? "*Nein.* No one is prettier than you."

"Oh stop." But he could see the compliment pleased her. "Not to change the subject, but about your cat..."

He groaned. "It's not my cat."

"What are you going to name her?"

"She's not mine to name."

"How about Lady, since she's the lady of the house you got her?" She gave him a smirk. "Or did you make it? Because it's wooden and not something plastic you might get at the store." She laughed. "Ha. I can see you blushing."

"I'm not blushing."

"You totally are." That dimple winked at him.

"It's not fair that you get cuter when you're smug. You should be hideous and harpy-like so I can banish you to the underworld."

She blinked. "Did you say *underworld*?"

"I like fantasy movies." And the Viking romance book he'd borrowed from her collection last week had been written with a touch of fantasy and used the word *underworld*—which struck a chord. Almost as big a lure as all the wild, unprotected sex the characters had gotten up to. He needed to read the sequel and wondered if she owned it.

More, he wondered if she'd be up for recreating the many sexual positions and acts the characters had performed.

"What is *that* look for?" she asked, leaning back.

He tried to clear the lust from his expression. "Look?"

"Never mind." She glanced away and said half under her breath, "I know exactly what that look meant."

"Did I—"

"Oh my God. *It's him.*" A young woman stood next to the table, staring at him.

"Jenna, it is!" Her friend stared as well.

"Can we help you ladies?" Rena asked in a more polite tone than he would have used.

"Yeah. Can we take some selfies with him?"

"Selfies?" Rena looked confused.

The starstruck girls looked to be of college age.

He frowned. "What do you want those for?"

Jenna shivered. "And he's got *that voice*. I am so posting this." She leaned forward and put an arm around him, shocking him to stillness. Then she put her phone out in front of them and snapped a picture.

"Oh, me next," her friend said.

"Wait, wait." Axel tried to stop her, but the girl moved behind him, her head on top of his in the booth she'd climbed into. Her girlfriend snapped a picture.

"Thanks so much!"

They left in a hurry, giggling to themselves as they looked at Jenna's phone.

"What was that about?" Rena asked him.

"I have no idea." He shrugged. "A college prank?"

"Maybe."

Once they finished, he paid the check and took her back home. He walked her inside and wondered how to say what he needed to without scaring her away.

"Go ahead and spill." Rena stood in her living room, her hands on her hips, waiting. "You have that 'something is preying on my tiny mind' look."

The teasing. He loved that she felt comfortable with him. "I…I want you to know that I will not use you for sex, or lie to you, or do things so you won't trust me." He held a hand over his heart, his pledge solemn. "And the truth is…" *I love you.*

She looked ready to bolt.

"I am always wanting you. You are beautiful, and you make me smile. I want sex. A lot. But I am waiting for you to want me back." He cleared his throat, hoping she wouldn't make too much out of the huge erection he couldn't hide.

Her eyes widened as she looked at it before she whipped her gaze back to his face.

"I don't want you to be with other men. Only me. We should just date together."

"Date together?" She sounded breathless.

"Just you and me. We date only each other."

"No other women."

"*Ja.*"

"Exclusive."

"Exclusive." Exactly.

She stepped in his direction and stopped. "And you want me to make the first move?"

"I want you to tell me what you want, and I want to give it to you. But for the sex, I have to know you trust me."

She frowned. "You mean like not wearing condoms or something?"

"*Nein.*" He was frustrated—and more than physically. "I want you to know you can count on me not to hurt you. Ever."

"But that's a little unrealistic, isn't it? I mean, people in relationships argue all the time. And feelings can get hurt."

"But I won't try to hurt you. And I won't like it if I do."

She studied him. "This is really important to you, isn't it?"

"Yes. I…it is."

"Okay."

He blinked. "That's it?"

"Sure. You want me to tell you when we can make love, right?"

He nodded, unsure of everything. Rena definitely kept him off-balance.

"You want me to trust you and believe in you. That's what you're saying. And to know that you're interested in me for more than sex."

He nodded again. "Exactly. Yes, this."

She ripped off her jacket, toed off her shoes, and proceeded to get naked in the middle of her living room.

"So how about now?"

CHAPTER TWELVE

Axel stood there, not saying anything, more still than she'd ever seen him.

Hmm, maybe she should have thought this through.

But he was so dang sweet, standing there looking so sincere, wanting her to trust him and believe in him while he sported one huge erection.

A woman would have to be stupid or gay not to want a piece of Axel Heller.

She'd been in lust with the man for a long time, but lately her affection had started to deepen into something more. Perhaps her mother had a point about her keeping a distance because Axel said and did everything right, yet she held a part of herself back. Maybe because it was hard to believe he could be as perfect as he acted.

Then again, she thought with amusement, he had given her an ugly little troll doll as a present. A definite miss in the gift department, though his intentions had been heartfelt.

When he continued to stand there without doing or saying anything, she grew self-conscious. Though she'd shaved her legs and lady-scaped earlier that morning, she hadn't paid strict attention to her body, not anticipating she'd strip down in front of anyone.

Perhaps he—

She jumped when he came at her like a battering ram. He drew her into his arms and kissed her until she couldn't breathe, consumed with devouring her.

Before she knew it, he'd lifted her in his arms and carried her upstairs into her bedroom.

He placed her gently on the bed and began tearing off his clothes. When he got down to his boxers, he stopped.

Nooo. Not now! I was so close to seeing all of you!

"I don't have any condoms."

His deep voice sent shivers through her. "I do." She turned over to reach into her nightstand and had just grabbed a box when the bed dipped and he pressed himself, naked, against the back of her.

The heat he generated was insane, as was the feel of a huge cock against her ass and lower back.

"I have wanted you for a very long time, *Häschen,*" he said softly, more a growl than a purr. "And I will have you today and every day after."

Lost in his touch, she nodded then moaned as his hand stroked her back and curled under, cupping her breast. He kept his weight off her, propped on his side, a good thing considering how much bigger than her he was.

"I love your breasts. So full." He rubbed her nipple then slid his hand across to tease the other one. "I want to bury my head between them. I want to fuck them," he said, his voice harsh.

He squeezed, and she arched back, grinding against that hard body.

"In me," she said. "I want you to make love to me."

He groaned and slid his hand down her belly, kissing her shoulder, the side of her neck, nuzzling through her hair. That talented hand moved down, over her belly and threading through the trim thatch of hair guarding her sex.

He slid a finger through her wet folds into her, and she whispered his name, lost.

He said something in German as he touched her, his stiff torso a tease, close but not close enough. He rocked against her, his cock thick, bruising.

She loved knowing he wanted her so much, and then he was gone. Before she could question where he'd gone, he flipped her to her back and settled between her legs, his mouth drawing her clit deep, flicking his tongue against the places she needed him most.

She ran her hands through his hair, keeping him close, her legs on either side of his head. And that's when she felt the tickle of his beard, his mustache one giant massage toy as he made her scream as she came.

Axel wouldn't stop, moaning against her, so good, so fucking fine.

Just as the sensation grew too much to bear, he eased off, kissing her thighs and his way up her stomach to her breasts. He paused to look down at her, his gaze both soft and satisfied.

"Mine," he said.

She couldn't think, so she nodded.

His mouth clamped over her nipple. He sucked, hard, and she felt her desire return in a rush. As his lips and teeth made her mindless, his facial hair like another set of hands caressing her skin, he molded her other breast with his hand, learning her shape.

"So big. I love your breasts." He slid his cock against her belly, and she felt moisture graze her stomach. "I want to fuck you so hard, Rena. I want to be gentle, to not bring anything but pleasure." He bit her nipple with enough sting to make her cry out for more. "But I don't know if I can be."

"Fuck gentle," she rasped. "I want you in me."

He blinked then smiled, a look of such sin she couldn't stop herself from taking charge. She pushed against his chest, and he eased away enough that she could flip him onto his back. She took a packet and ripped it open, grabbing the condom.

Then she took a good look at what she'd been missing.

"Oh my God. You are *huge.*"

"And so hard." He kept talking, switching to German, and caressed her breasts, looking up at her with such possession.

She eased back and looked her fill. The man had so much strength, so much muscle. The right half of his torso and arm from shoulder to biceps was covered in tattoos. His beard and mustache framed the lower half of his square jaw, and those dark-blue eyes gleamed with desire.

"I want you to sit on my face," he said, "so I can eat you again. You taste good, *Häschen.*"

"That is *it*! You are getting this on and getting inside me right now." She put the condom over him, stretching the latex over one fine dick. She rubbed his balls, and he spread his legs wider and moaned. "You need to come, baby?"

"Inside you, Rena. So hot." He had his hand between her legs and slid his finger inside her, pumping in and out. Damn, he was good at sex.

"Yes."

But before she could mount him, he turned the tables and had her on her back again, blanketed by his big, hot body.

"First time, let me be on top. To be easier," he said, his voice tight.

He looked wild, verging on growing out of control.

She'd never seen a more beautiful man in all her life.

"Come inside me, Axel. Just you and me."

He nudged her thighs wider and put the tip of himself inside her. Then he leaned on his elbows to keep his weight clear and slowly slid inside, inch by inch.

He just kept moving, until she didn't think she could take one centimeter more.

"You are perfect," he rasped, so still, so thick inside her.

His body trembled with the effort, and Rena wanted more. "So are you…if you'd just move." She wrapped her legs around his waist, pulling him deeper.

He groaned and withdrew, only to push back inside. He went slowly, not giving her what she needed.

"Axel, more. I won't break. Fuck me."

He leaned back and stared into her eyes as he withdrew all but the tip of himself. Then he slammed back into her.

She came on a shriek, gripping him tight, her nails leaving marks in his skin.

But he got the message. He fucked her like a man possessed and ravaged her into an even longer orgasm as he shouted her name and released.

He stayed there for a while, his climax powerful and so damn beautiful.

Rena rubbed the nape of his neck, dragging him down for more kisses once they'd both caught their breath.

When he drew back, he stared down at her in awe.

She smiled. "Was I worth waiting for?"

"*Ja.*" But he didn't smile back, and she started to fret. "I must go." He left before she could say anything, and she wondered what she'd done wrong. But he returned seconds later and grabbed another packet which he put into her hands.

"Now that the first one is over, we have time to make up for my hurried performance. I can do better."

She gaped. "Better? I nearly died."

"Twice." He smirked. "The little death, your orgasm. You're a screamer. I like that."

"Stop." She flushed. "You screamed too."

"Oh, so you want to see if I can come quietly? That I can do."

"Wanna bet?"

By noon she'd lost several times. But it was *so* worth it.

♥ ♥ ♥

As they walked into Ray's together, Axel glanced down and grinned. Axel loved contrasts. He especially loved the sight of Rena's lovely brown hand in his paler one. It reminded him of how perfect she'd looked juxtaposed against his naked body.

She tugged his head down and whispered, "Stop smiling. Everyone will know."

It was just two nights after sharing a heart-stopping intimacy he'd never felt with another. Because with Rena, his orgasms had been beyond good. They'd been almost spiritual. At least to him.

She had seemed a little spooked after they'd made love for several hours, so he'd given her space, letting her set the pace of their relationship, telling her he'd wait for her to invite him out again.

But he'd still given her Valentine's gifts, and he'd still walked her out to her car each evening. She had seemed pleased over the silk flowers and box of candy hearts. So he planned to continue his efforts to woo her through Valentine's Day.

She'd invited him to accompany her to Ray's, finally, and as they walked through the crowd, he saw friends and acquaintances, Del's mechanics with J.T. playing darts. Smitty, Mateo, and Rylan sitting at another table.

"What will they know?" he asked, his hand on her shoulder, feeling possessive. But now he felt he had a right to that feeling.

"You know." She tried to pull his hand away, but he stopped moving, halting her as well. She turned to face him. "Don't look all wounded. You big faker."

Yet he wasn't exactly pretending to feel hurt. "You don't want anyone to know we are together?"

She huffed and yanked his head down for a kiss that made him forget they were in Ray's. "There. Happy now?" Around them, people hooted and yelled at them to get a room or give the crowd a show.

Axel answered her in thick German, "I'd be happier if you'd let me bend you over the bar and fuck you raw."

A man nearby guffawed, understanding him, but quickly looked away from his stare.

"I don't even want to know what you just said. Now go be with your friends while I hang with mine for a while. Don't worry, I won't ignore you forever. But I need some time with my old peeps." She kissed him again before flouncing to the bar to see a bunch of her friends.

He looked over and saw Smitty waving to him. As he passed the dartboard, he heard Foley say, "Shit. I bet they'd hook up on Valentine's Day."

Sam toasted Axel and said, "Nah, man. I told you. It's us big tattooed freaks you have to watch out for."

J.T. grinned. "I'm still in the running."

Axel ignored them and sat with Smitty and the guys, keeping an eye on Rena.

"So." Smitty paused to swig from his bottle. "You've been mighty chipper since you came in to work late on Wednesday."

Only two and a half days had passed, but Axel felt as if his entire life had changed.

"Rena and I are now dating. Life is *gut.*"

Mateo said, grinning from ear to ear, "You cost me money, Boss, but you've been great at the shop. I like Rena."

"I do too." Rylan ran a hand over his hair. "Your girl gives a mean haircut." The style made him look rakish and more than appealing, or so Smitty had said to Axel yesterday when Rylan had arrived looking stylish. To Rylan he'd merely grunted then ordered him to help on a busted back fender.

"My girl is amazing." Axel smiled at her laughing with Sue and Josie. Ray came out to give her a hug, and she hugged him right back.

Ray glanced over to see Axel and waved.

Axel nodded back.

"So weird to see you smiling," Rylan muttered.

"Well, well, what do we have here?" Expecting trouble from that tone, Axel glanced over and relaxed, seeing Foley standing with a beer. "Yo, Heller, you up for a game of darts? We need one more. Sorry, guys, but the game demands a fourth."

Smitty shrugged. "Have him. He's too damn happy for my taste."

"Yeah." Rylan shook his head.

"I plead the fifth." Mateo held up a hand.

"Assholes." Axel tried not to smile at the finger Smitty shot him. "Sure. Why not?"

He played with Foley, Sam, and J.T., ignoring their razzing, and was winning by fifty points when trouble walked in the door. Big J, one of the bouncers, kept an eye on the trio of idiots who'd entered.

"Are you kidding me? Who decided Daryl and his fuckhead buddies were okay to come back to the bar?" Foley asked.

J.T. grimaced. "They like it here, though God knows why. We're not all Aryan white brothers." He paused. "No offense, Sam."

Sam chuckled. "Fuck off. And I think you meant that for Heller, anyway."

Axel gave him a look.

J.T. laughed.

"Oh yeah." Foley grinned. "Remember when we met, and I called you Adolf? I swore you were gonna rip my head off."

"I still might," Axel growled, his gaze darting from the racists to Rena.

She stood with her back to the group and seemed to be enjoying herself.

Since the three troublemakers kept to themselves at a table on the other side of the room, Axel relaxed with the guys once more.

He won soon enough, much to J.T.'s amusement. "Good thing we weren't playing for money."

Axel paused. "We weren't?"

"Nope."

"Not at all," Sam agreed, tucking away some bills that had been in the middle of the table.

Axel grunted. "You're all bad liars."

"Yeah. We miss Johnny." Foley sighed. "He's out for the weekend with Lara."

"Ah, young love." Sam knocked back his beer.

"Please. You were out last weekend with Ivy," Foley grumbled.

"And you live up your girlfriend's ass. Gimme a break," Sam said back.

"Up her ass? That's kind of personal, don't you think?" J.T. looked from Sam to Foley. "Then again, I hear you guys are pretty tight, so maybe you share a lot."

"What?" Foley's eyes widened.

Axel tried not to laugh at the hole J.T. kept digging himself into.

Sam choked on his beer.

"I meant you guys talk a lot and…oh forget it. If I have to explain the joke, it's not as funny."

"Wasn't funny to begin with," Axel had to say.

"Yeah." Foley glared. "For talking shit, you owe me a pitcher."

J.T. held his hands up in surrender. "Easy, Foley. I was just kidding."

The minute he walked away, Foley relaxed.

"Nice." Sam and he clinked glasses.

"Mr. Sensitive is buying more beer. What a great guy."

Realizing J.T. had been had, Axel shook his head, trying not to laugh. "I have to go save my girlfriend from the bar." Many of whose patrons had sidled up to talk to her. "You're both welcome for not shaking you down for the money you owe me. You guys are not very good at darts."

"Yeah, yeah." Sam grumbled, hiding a smile.

Foley shook his head, looking less than innocent. "Money? No idea what you're talking about."

Axel left them for Rena. But before he could get to her, he overheard Daryl say his name.

He turned and took a punch to the stomach that stole his breath because he hadn't been expecting it. But that had never stopped him from giving back what was owed.

♥ ♥ ♥

Rena watched from the bar with a sigh. They'd been doing so well tonight. Axel had been giving her the space she needed. She'd planted a big old kiss claiming him as hers—as much for her peace of mind as his, truth be told. She'd seen a few women eyeing him up the minute they'd entered. Because, yeah, her man was freakin' sexy as hell.

He'd been good, playing darts with friends. No fights for Axel tonight.

Until he'd been provoked.

"Why do people always start shit with him?" Sue asked. "I mean, I'm not into fighting, but even I can tell Heller can break most people in half. The guy is fucking huge."

"Oh, *is he?*" Josie asked, batting her lashes as she looked at Rena.

Who blushed. "Stop it, Josie."

"Ha! You fo-ho! I knew you had it in you." Josie giggled, sounding more like a teenager than a thirty-year-old. "Get it? *In you*?"

Fo-ho—Josie's way of complimenting someone for being a fortunate whore. Josie loved knowing Rena was finally getting "a hot piece of ass," as she liked to call Axel. Honestly, the girl was addicted to sex, but she was so nice and unassuming most guys had no idea she'd take them out back and bang them for nothing more than mutual pleasure.

Not one to judge, Rena nevertheless appreciated what she'd shared with Axel. In just one morning, he'd given her earth-shattering orgasms and scared her senseless. She had no idea if she could handle that much pleasure again, and though she wanted it, she also feared it had been a onetime shot. As in, she hadn't had sex in so long, she was overdue for major orgasms. She didn't want anything to mar the magical time she'd spent with him. Which was nutty, she knew.

How much sense did it make that a virtual stranger—Axel—would know just how to touch her to get her off? Or was the man just that good with women he could get them to have multiple O's the first time out?

She needed to be with him again and find out, praying she wouldn't be disappointed. She planned to have sex with him again once they left Ray's. But maybe not if he was going to spend so much time fighting. Though she really liked him, he scared her a little when he grew violent. She knew it wasn't his fault, but seeing him beat the crap out of people reminded her how strong and vicious he could be.

She started to go over to him when she felt someone watching her. She turned to see Daryl, the weirdo she'd given a haircut to, staring from a corner booth. And suddenly she felt unsafe, even surrounded by people she knew. Without realizing it, she looked for Axel, her safety in the storm.

Axel caught her gaze at that moment, having dispatched his attacker with a punch to the gut and a follow-up to the jaw that had put the man on his ass. He followed her gaze back to Daryl, though she hadn't meant to look back at him.

And Axel's expression turned blank.

Icy.

Mean.

"Uh-oh." She had a bad feeling, especially when Axel made a beeline for Daryl, who hadn't sensed his danger because he kept looking at her. By the time he understood he needed to run, Axel had him by the throat up against the wall.

The entire bar quieted. She noticed Big J and Earl watching with satisfaction, doing nothing to stop the altercation.

"What the fuck did you do to her?" Axel asked, his voice a low grumble but loud enough to be heard in the silent bar.

"Axel, I think we should go." Rena tried to cross to him.

J.T. stopped her. "No, Cuz. Let's see what Daryl has to say."

"You know him?" The two men sitting near Daryl cleared out fast.

"He's one of Fletcher's buddies."

That made it all worse. Much, much worse. Because Daryl's warning now had a weight it hadn't before.

"We will go outside and…talk. *Ja?*" Axel dragged him out the back. When a few people made ready to follow, Earl yelled that they should all mind their fucking business or be kicked out for the night. This time no one followed. Talk resumed, and the bar felt as bouncy as it had before, excitement stirring at the notion of a fight.

But Rena had a bad feeling about Axel getting in trouble.

"J.T.," she said to her cousin, "Daryl came into my shop for a haircut the other day."

"Shit. That's not good. He's a problem, Rena. And so are all his friends, who do whatever Fletcher tells them to. I know you don't like it, but Heller fought with Fletcher before because Fletcher was mouthing off about you."

"He shouldn't have done that." But he'd been protecting her. How could she not be crushing on the guy?

J.T. sighed. "Not all of it was racist bullshit. The guy wants you."

"I know. Axel and I are dating."

"No, not Axel. Fletcher. He's into you, *and* he seems to hate you. Excuse the expression, but he's one twisted fuck you need to stay far away from."

She cringed. "Fletcher? Ew."

"Yeah. I heard a few of the things he said, and I'm surprised Heller didn't give him more than a few bumps and bruises. I'd have ripped his nuts off."

"J.T."

"Sorry, but he's a dick. A dangerous one because he thinks he's untouchable."

She didn't like Axel being outside with Daryl by himself. "Is he?"

"I don't know. I don't think he's part of the white-power gangs in the city, but I'm not sure. He likes to talk a big game."

"Well, that's not good."

"I know."

"Daryl told me not to be by myself at night at my shop. That it could be dangerous."

"That piece of shit."

She grabbed his arm. "J.T., he said it so no one else could hear it. I don't think he was threatening me. I think he was warning me."

"You do?" He glanced around. "That's odd. The guys he was with are real assholes. I mean, alone they're easy to beat. But they have a habit of ganging up on people. They don't play by any rules. They see a black man and go hunting for a length of rope and a tree, you get me? And it's not any safer to be any shade of brown around them. They only tolerate whites, period. I don't know what Ray was thinking to let them back in here."

She looked around and frowned. "That's a good point. What was Ray thinking? And where did those guys disappear to? Because I don't see them in here anymore, do you?"

CHAPTER THIRTEEN

Axel had Daryl up against the wall out back, behind the bar, his hand around the guy's scrawny neck.

Daryl was fighting to get free, but Axel was furious.

"No. Not to…hurt her." Daryl struggled in Axel's hands. "Trying…to…warn her."

What he said filtered through, but Axel didn't immediately believe the shithead. He dropped him and watched as Daryl scrabbled to stand, clutching his throat. "Fletcher…insane. Watching…her."

"Shit."

Daryl's eyes widened over Axel's shoulder, giving Axel the warning he needed to avoid a lead pipe to the back of the head. Instead, the hit glanced off his shoulder. It still hurt, but not as much as it would have had he not moved.

Daryl took off, so Axel focused on the two assholes in front of him. Scott and a guy they called Rabies because he acted like a mangy, crazy dog in a fight approached wearing ugly smiles.

"Oh, look, Heller wants to play." Rabies flipped him off. "Want to get fucked up, shit for brains?"

Axel had been wanting to beat the crap out of Rabies for a while, but the opportunity hadn't presented itself. The guy was a bully, a racist, and a perverted pig. And still Axel preferred Rabies's company to Fletcher's. At least Rabies didn't hide what he was.

"We like your girlfriend," Scott added. "But don't you think she's a little dark for you? You're white, brother. Remember your blood." Scott had been trying to get Axel to join their little crew for a while. So had Fletcher, until Axel had kicked Fletcher's ass. But while Fletcher wanted to kill him, Scott still thought he could somehow turn Axel into a white supremacist.

Axel cracked his knuckles and smiled. "Let's get something straight. I am never going to join up with you inbred assholes. And my girlfriend is not a subject you should ever talk about."

Normally, Axel was cold. He fought without emotion, using skill and strategy. And he liked fighting. Not to hurt people but as a sport. He didn't have the right technique for boxing, but he'd been built to take a hit. And he knew how make an opponent go down and stay down. The challenge of it all sent his blood rushing and made him feel alive.

Kind of the way he always felt around Rena.

Scott tried to hit him with the pipe. Rabies waited, a cunning adversary and the stronger of his opponents. Axel threw Scott into Rabies, gratified when they got tangled up together. But Scott rebounded, only to take another hit to the face that knocked him off his feet. He swore and shoved himself up off the ground while Rabies stayed out of the way, just waiting for his chance to take a shot at Axel.

Rabies started insulting Rena, using the coarsest and most appalling words Axel had heard in some time. Then Scott chimed in, and they started on talking about what they'd do to her once they got her alone and how much their friend Fletcher wanted her all to himself.

Axel knew they wanted him off-balance, enraged, and not thinking straight. For the most part, their plan worked. But they'd made a grave mistake.

When he fought cold, he controlled himself. He didn't do more damage than he intended. That rage he kept inside, the stuff that came from his father's side of the family, festered and boiled. But now it had an outlet. He was fired up and ready to make people hurt.

It was personal.

Men who had every intention of hurting the woman he loved had threatened her. The thought of Rena ever looking the way his mother had, of seeing the pain that refused to fade in her eyes, snapped something inside him.

He took the hit from Scott's pipe then knocked the guy out with one punch. In doing so, he left himself open to the blow Rabies shot at his face. His head snapped back, but that didn't stop Axel from deflecting more of Rabies's attacks.

He fought in silence, burning with fury as he destroyed Fletcher's dickhead friends.

Rabies knew some kind of martial arts shit that worked. He landed kicks and punches, drew blood even. But with Scott down, there was no one for Rabies to hide behind. After more fighting, in which Rabies tried to shout him into submission—what the fuck?—when he saw his punches had little effect, a tired Rabies started to panic.

"I'm sorry, man," Rabies tried. Axel hit him again in the stomach and backed off, just watching with murderous intent. "Talk, you big asshole," he rasped, and groaned when Axel hit him again. And again. "Stop. Heller, enough," came out garbled, and then only the sounds of his moans and the thuds of contact filled the crisp air.

Lost in a haze, Axel continued to press on, to eliminate the threat, until someone tackled him and several guys held him back when he would have returned to finish Rabies off.

"Jesus, Heller, he's out," Sam said. "Enough."

Axel strained, needing to eliminate the danger to Rena.

"Is he still breathing?" Foley asked. "Heller, relax, man, it's us. Sam, hold him tighter."

"He almost took my head off," Sam growled. "Earl, grab his hand."

"I got it," Earl said. "Yeah, unfortunately, Rabies is breathing. That arm and his face look bad. Broke for sure, the nose, I mean. And that arm. Maybe some ribs."

Ray swore from behind them. "Motherfuckers. I didn't want this in my house. No trouble, they said. Those lying, mother-humping, shit-sucking…" He kept saying words that made no sense to Axel.

Or to anyone else apparently.

"I didn't know that was a word," Foley muttered.

"I told you letting them back in was going to be a problem," Earl said. "Heller, relax, man."

Axel didn't realize he'd been trying to get free, but still hopped up on adrenaline, he needed a minute to understand the threat had ended.

Ray groaned. "We're gonna have to call an ambulance. This is serious."

Big J whistled, now blocking the back door with his big body. "No way to avoid it unless you want the cops finding bodies in the parking lot."

Axel stared at the ground, taking pained breaths. Rabies must have bruised a few of his ribs. His cheek ached, as did his hands. And, yeah, his thigh hurt from being kicked a few times. *Should have broken his leg, not just his arm,* he thought darkly.

Sam said over his shoulder, "Hey, Big J, don't let Rena out here."

"Rena?" Axel felt his aches, but that name caused an even bigger one. *Oh shit. What did I do? She can't know I lost it.* A glance at his assailants showed them passed out and broken. Jesus. He felt a little queasy.

"Easy, she's inside. Safe," Sam said and patted Axel on the back. "Your work buddies are keeping a close eye on her. Smitty said he had her, and J.T.'s with her."

Axel liked J.T., but the man was a lover, not a fighter. Smitty, on the other hand, could handle himself and regularly did what needed to be done to keep the peace.

Sam continued, "Nice work, man. I think the only one somewhat okay—and I use that term loosely—is Scott. You must have knocked him out first."

Remembering what they'd all been saying about Rena started the anger back up. "They said—"

"No, hold on, hoss," Foley said. "We need to get you out of here. Ray, come up with something to tell the EMTs, who are no doubt going to report this to the police. Like, the guys beat each other up. Or someone jumped them all. We'll back you up, but you'd better think fast. Rabies doesn't look so good."

"Neither does Scott." Earl sounded impressed. "Fuck, Heller. Are those fists or anvils on the ends of those arms?"

"Gotta say, Sam, I think he'd have you beat in a one-on-one." Big J sounded apologetic.

"Yeah, maybe." Sam chuckled. "Want to try me, Heller?"

"I could kick your ass easily." Truth to tell, Sam knew how to fight. It would be an interesting match. Axel shifted his jaw and groaned because the action pulled at his cheek. That hurt. He straightened and shook off the arms holding him back from launching at someone. "I'm *gut. Danke.*" He glanced around. "Where did Daryl go?"

"Coward must have skated," Earl scoffed. "What a pussy. Too bad *we* missed the fight though."

"I bet it was something to see." Big J sounded wistful.

"Idiots," Sam muttered and ignored their dark looks. "Ray, I'm gonna take Heller home. Foley, you want to follow so you can bring me back here? Darts rematch, just you and me."

Foley grinned. "You're on."

"Wait." Ray frowned. "You can't leave. I need someone to back me if they bring in the cops."

Big J and Earl volunteered to stand as witnesses.

"Blame it all on Fletcher's gang," Axel told Ray. "A lot of racist talk. And do *not* let them come back," he warned.

"Yeah, Ray," Sam said. "Gotta say that wasn't cool."

Ray flushed. "I know. But they threatened to give me problems if I kept them out."

Big J gave him a dark smile. "Is that right? You should have told me. I know people. I'll take care of it."

"But I—"

Earl clapped Ray on the back. "Let him. Trust me, don't ask questions."

Foley said, "Maybe just keep it simple. Call in an anonymous tip from one of the burner phones we all know you have stashed in the bar."

Ray frowned, but Foley continued, "Someone found bodies in the back lot of your bar. No one saw anything. No one knows anything."

Ray lost his frown. "That's not a bad idea. I'll make an announcement."

Not that he'd have to. Axel knew that no one at Ray's would say a word to the cops about anything. Not if they wanted to be welcomed back. Or eat without using a straw, something Rabies and Scott wouldn't be able to do for a while.

Axel took two steps with Sam before he stopped. "Rena. I brought her. I need to—"

"Go home and sleep it off. Trust me. You really don't want her to see you like this. J.T. can take her home."

"*Ja.* I guess." He sighed, disappointed in himself and in the evening. He'd had a better night planned. He handed Sam a small card from his back pocket. "Can you give her this from me?"

"Sure. Hey, Foley," Sam said to his buddy. "Give this to Rena from Heller. And tell J.T. to take her home, okay?"

"Sure. Heller, gotta say, man. Nice work." Foley slapped him on the shoulder, and Axel barely bit back a growl and glared at him.

Foley laughed. "Sorry. Later."

He left. Sam ordered Axel to stay put, took his keys, and returned driving Axel's truck. Axel got in on his third attempt, his ribs and leg beginning to really hurt.

"Man, your face is already starting to bruise. Fucker hit you, but at least it's under the eye. How's the rest of you?"

"Hands are sore but okay. Shoulder hurts a little. But it's my leg and ribs that have the most damage." Annoyed he'd gone all berserker mode and hadn't protected himself better from Rabies, he huffed his disgust...and told himself not to do that again. Definitely bruised ribs, but he didn't think them broken. He'd had broken ribs before, and this didn't feel as bad. "Rabies and his kung fu shit." He muttered more insults in German.

Sam chuckled. "He won't be using his hands and feet anytime soon. You fucked him up good."

"He had it coming." Now more than ever Rena would need to

be careful at work, Axel worried. "Can you have J.T. stay with Rena tonight? Or have her go with him? I don't have a good feeling about this."

"Good point. Can you text him?"

Axel managed to get his phone out and called J.T. Unfortunately, Rena answered the phone.

Tonight was really not his night.

"Axel? Hello? Hey, are you okay?" Rena heard him breathing into the phone, but it took a second for him to respond. She swore he tried to sound upbeat, but she heard his pain.

"*Ja.* Rena, I am so sorry. I need to get home. I have a project early in the morning. Can you please stay with J.T. tonight? My talk with Daryl worried me. You need to be careful. I promise I'll make our date up to you."

"Sure. It's okay. I'm with J.T. right now." She paused because Foley had arrived and handed her a small envelope, what looked like the size of a gift card. He drew J.T. aside, said something, then darted away. "Foley just gave me something."

"Your valentine." He sucked in a breath and swore at Sam. "Sorry."

"Sam is with you?" She narrowed her eyes on her cousin.

J.T. shrugged. "Don't ask me. I've been in here with you all night."

"Ah, *ja.* Sam needs a ride somewhere. I will drop him off and am going home."

"You big liar. He's taking you home because you can't drive, isn't he?"

A large pause. "Now, *Liebling*, I—"

She disconnected. "You." She poked her cousin in the chest. "You're taking me to Axel's. Right now."

"Aw, Rena. You should really wait."

"Wait? I know something happened outside, and that it has to do with me. If Axel is hurt, there will be hell to pay."

J.T., wise man that he was, cringed. "Why me?" He sighed. "Come on."

On the drive to Axel's, she fumed while J.T. was mostly quiet.

"Fine," he growled. "Look, you need to know. Heller got into a fight. Daryl took off, but Heller ended up fighting Scott and Rabies."

"Those bullies?" They were Fletcher's friends. "This is because of me."

"Maybe. But it's also because Heller likes to fight," J.T. told her. "So don't go borrowing blame. Trust me. Axel Heller is no saint. He's a good guy, yes. And he's been crushing on you for months. But he's not the safest man to be around."

She pondered that as J.T. turned onto Axel's street. "Do you think he'd ever hurt me?"

"No, or I never would have let him take you out."

She thought that was sweet, even if Rena didn't need a hovering father figure and if J.T. thought he could prevent Axel from doing anything. Her cousin was a big man with a lot of friends, but Axel was Axel.

"He's made some enemies," J.T. continued. "I like the guy, but he's not Mr. Friendly. And he doesn't hide how he feels about jerks and racists." At that he smiled. "I hear he left Fletcher's crew in a world of hurt."

"And got himself hurt in the process."

"Well, yeah, but that's how it goes. When you care for someone, you have no problem putting yourself in harm's way to protect them. Heller will do what he feels is right to protect you. I like that."

"I don't need someone protecting me. I'm not a little girl. I can think and act on my own."

"I know that. But guys like Rabies don't care about the law or about doing the right thing. I don't want to see you hurt. Sure, go to the cops and manage to get a restraining order. You think that will stop him?"

"You're not making me feel any better."

"Sorry, but you know what I'm saying is true."

They pulled into Axel's driveway, where his truck sat next to Foley's car.

She turned to face him. "I love you, J.T., but if you don't want to get hurt, you'll get out of my way. I need to talk to my new boyfriend and tell him exactly what I think of all this macho BS."

J.T. groaned. "Rena, maybe you should—"

"Bye." She slammed out of his vehicle and stomped up the steps into Axel's house.

He was standing near Sam and Foley in his living room talking until he saw her and froze.

She swallowed down her gasp of surprise, not liking the purplish bruise under his eye that seemed to spread across the half of his face not covered by his beard. She pretended she didn't see the arm cradling his side slowly drop, as if he hadn't been hurt. He straightened, no longer putting most of his weight on one leg either.

"Gentlemen, thanks for helping Axel," she said. "I've got this now."

Sam and Foley looked at each other, at her, then at Axel, who said nothing. His face looked as if it could have been carved from granite.

Foley chuckled. "There. Now your girl is safe and sound with you, and you're safe and sound with her."

"Safe?" Sam shook his head and said to Axel, "You poor bastard."

They left, closing the door behind them.

Axel looked at her like a sulky little boy in a big man's body. "It's not so bad."

"Liar. And you know I hate liars." Worry and affection turned her ball of anxiety into anger that he'd put himself in danger. She stalked to him and poked him in the side.

He winced.

"Why did you try to fight two men at once and not come in for help?"

"Help?" He seemed confused. "Why?"

"You lied to me. You don't have a meeting tomorrow, do you?"

He at least looked shamefaced. "No."

"Then why did you say you did?"

"I didn't want you to worry."

"Well, I'm worrying," she shouted. "You're a moron. And what is this?" She waved the small envelope in his face.

"Your valentine."

She opened it and saw a Claire's gift card for $10. *What the hell?*

"Do you like it?" He looked hopeful, that battered face eager to see her joy. No matter that he stood there injured, a warrior fresh off the battlefield. He wanted her to be happy.

As a twelve-year-old wanting to shop for glittery earrings, costume jewelry, and Hello Kitty doodads, she would have loved it. As a thirty-three-year-old? Not so much. So she lied. "Yes, thank you."

He sighed. "*Gut.* I hoped you would. They have colorful jewelry in there."

"I know." What should she do with this man? "Come on. Let's get you fixed up."

He followed her meekly into his bathroom and did what she told him.

Once he'd gotten naked and she saw the myriad bruises on his body, she wanted to hit him for getting hurt. Her eyes welled.

"Ah, *Häschen,* don't cry. I have been hurt much worse than this. I'm okay. Just some bruises that will fade in a week or two."

"I don't like seeing you hurt, okay?" She wiped her eyes, annoyed she'd cried.

"But the hero must protect the heroine, yes? To prove his worth." He sounded teasing.

She frowned. "What are you talking about?"

He looked embarrassed all of a sudden. "That book you were reading when I came to your home. I borrowed it." He left and returned with it in hand.

She blinked. "So *that's* where it went. I looked all over the place for it!"

"I read it." He paused, his cheeks pink. "Do you have the next book, maybe?"

"Wait. You read *Storm Lords: The Viking Who Loved Me*?"

"I just said so," he said, sounding testy.

Which made her laugh. "Yes, I have the next one. You want to borrow it?"

"Maybe."

"You liked it, didn't you?"

"I just wanted to see what *you* like about it."

"So reading the next one will show you that?"

"*Ja.*" He sounded so worldly. "You love romance books, so I read them, and I learn that the hero saves the woman, and he gets hurt many times before she sees he's worthy of her."

"But you don't have to go pick fights, you big doofus." She started the bathwater, her belly fluttering and her heart thudding, wondering why his interest in what she loved made her feel so funny.

"I will always pick a fight to keep you safe, Rena."

She turned to see him smiling down at her, though the expression pulled at his bruised face and caused a slight wince.

She sighed, aware she was falling in love with the man, wondering if that would turn out to be a good or bad thing. Because this guy could seriously break her heart if he left. Or, worse, if he turned out to be the villain instead of the hero.

"Do you have any Epsom salts?" she asked.

He pointed to the cabinet under the sink.

She poured a bunch into the tub. "Oh, smells like eucalyptus."

"My mother always said it was good for soaking tired muscles. I have mint salts and milk-and-honey salts in there too."

"Nice." She adjusted the bath temperature. "This is more like a mini pool. Jeez, Axel, how long does it take to fill?"

"Not long."

She just looked at him, and though he had to be sore, he apparently couldn't help responding to her nearness. His cock thickened.

"Wow. You are just big all over," she whispered.

"Would you join me in the tub?"

He had plenty of room. "But I don't want to hurt you."

"You're hurting me now."

"I am?" She was confused.

He took himself in hand, his eyes dark with pleasure or pain, she couldn't tell which. "I am aching here, *Liebling*. I need release. Will you help me with that?"

"Maybe." She nibbled her lower lip, aware her body had grown soft and willing at just the sight of him. "But nothing that hurts you, okay?"

"Of course." He drew closer and kissed her, and his beard and mustache reminded her of how good they could feel against her skin. In other places…

"Rena, the only time I hurt is when I am not with you."

She crossed her eyes. "You and your words. Stop talking." Because he got to her with his bad presents and his big body and his soulful eyes. Those words, spoken from the heart, meant so much. In English or German.

She didn't understand when he spoke his native language and looked at her, but she understood the tenderness in his gaze, the ache in her heart from wanting what he promised. Or what she *hoped* he promised—a distinction that would kick her in the ass if she weren't careful.

"Okay, I'll take a bath with you. And to show you how much I care, I'm going to get my hair wet for you. But no comments if I look all droopy tomorrow."

His eyes crinkled. His smile grew wide. "As long as there is a tomorrow, *Häschen*, I do not care what you look like. Only that you are with me."

CHAPTER FOURTEEN

The bath felt good against his aches, and Axel eased into the water with a groan. The feel of it gloving his body aroused him even more because he imagined soon feeling a woman's wet warmth around him.

Rena stood naked, her full breasts, narrow waist, and womanly hips beckoning. He wanted to lick her up, to suckle between her legs and swallow her down.

She always smelled so good to him, a combination of honey and flowers and Rena.

"Do you wear perfume?" he asked. "Because you smell good all the time."

She smiled. "No. Well, I do have a nice lotion I like. It's good for my skin, and I use some stuff in my hair that might be what you're smelling."

He guided her down over him, conscious of his dick pressed against his belly, the front of her body keeping him in place. He leaned close and inhaled at the crook of her neck. "No. It's you. Not lotion or hair sprays. It's just you." He drew her head close to kiss her, so glad she'd followed him home tonight.

She shifted and hit his ribs, and he couldn't contain a small start, though he shrugged off the pain.

Unfortunately, she must have felt it because she drew back in a hurry. "I'm sorry, baby."

He *loved* her calling him that. "I'm fine."

"No, you're not." She pushed up on her knees, and he grabbed her hips and held her in place.

They both froze when his dick, now free in the water, notched between her legs.

He wanted so badly to bring her down over him that he could do nothing but remain frozen, caught in the most beautiful pleasure–pain between hope and the knowledge he couldn't have all of her. Not yet.

Rena stared into his eyes. "I want to feel you in me."

"Fuck. I want that more than anything. But…"

She eased down, bringing the head of his cock inside her but no more. He had to close his eyes, for fear that if he saw her nibbling her luscious lips for one more moment he'd take the choice from her.

"Hold on a sec, sweetie." She moved off him, and he sucked in a breath, missing her but glad she'd moved when she had. "Where are the con—"

"Top drawer to the left of the sink." He slowly, painfully, sat up out of the water, planting his ass on the edge of the tub, his lower legs still encased by warmth. Easier to put the condom on without the water in the way.

She came back looking like a mermaid, all slick and brown and curvy. He wanted to suck her breasts and finger her until she came. Then eat her out all over again.

"You keep looking at me like that and I won't last," she rasped.

"I don't care. I want you so much. I feel no pain but this." He gripped his cock.

"Oh, let me help you with that, you poor thing." She stepped into the tub with the condom, but instead of tearing open the packet, she held it and looked into his eyes. "Axel, I need to ask you something."

"Yes?" He released his grip on himself, worried he'd end up coming before she'd put the condom on.

"Do you always practice safe sex?"

"*Ja.* Although a few years ago, I had a woman, and we did not use condoms. We were together for a while, and she could not have children. But I have been tested since, and I'm healthy. No disease or anything. I am fine to wear the condom, *Häschen.*" He didn't want her to worry.

"When's the last time you had sex? Before me, I mean."

He flushed. His answer would be telling.

"Axel, tell me." She moved closer, her body just a breath away from his.

He swallowed. "Last year. Back in April, I think."

She blinked and smiled. "Before we met?"

He sighed. "You ruin me for other women."

"And men?"

He frowned. "What about men?"

"You've never been with a guy or anything? I don't care, I'm just curious."

He chuckled. "*Nein.* I like a beautiful set of breasts and a curvy ass. And I definitely love a warm, wet pussy."

"You sweet-talker." She sounded breathless, perhaps because he grazed her pert nipples with his knuckles. He continued to skim his hands over her body, barely touching, yet the contact remained. And then he reached between her legs and slid his finger inside her.

"You're wet for me, pretty Rena." He had a hard time breathing, wanting badly to fuck her.

She watched him, reached out a hand to cup his cheek, and he turned to rub against her palm.

She sighed. "You are killing me. I'm trying to be all sexy, and you're making me want to cuddle you."

He pressed into her belly, his dick stiff. "Cuddle away."

She chuckled. "Not what I had in mind. But let's see if you like this." She kissed him, and when he would have pulled her closer, she moved those kisses down his beard to his neck. Then she followed his tattoos down his right shoulder and arm and across to his nipples.

When she teethed him, he hissed, sensitive and on the verge of orgasm. His entire frame, even the bruised parts, felt like one giant nerve.

"I love your body," she murmured, kissing her way down.

His stomach tensed as she traced her way past his navel and lower.

"And this cock. Such a pretty man. Your balls are hard, baby."

He groaned and spread his legs, arching toward her when she cupped him, rubbing his sac.

"I see you all shiny and wet for me. See? Men are just like women that way. Wet when they're excited."

"*Ja, Liebling.* Lick me, suck me there."

"Oh, Axel wants a kiss, hmm?"

He looked down and saw her ripe lips parted over his cock. A sight that burned into his brain. "A kiss. *Please.*" He'd resorted to begging, her warm breath over his shaft making him tremble.

Then she put her mouth over him, and he closed his eyes and tilted his face up to the ceiling, thanking God and heaven for this treasure at his feet. "Rena, careful. I'm so close," he groaned. All his strength and size, done in by a woman he could lift with one hand.

She has totally ruined me for anyone else.

She moaned around his cock, drawing him in and out while she rubbed his balls and grazed her nails along the inside of his thighs.

"Fuck. Yes, more." He grunted. Groaned. Begged and swore. His orgasm threatened to tear from his body in a violent storm of love and need. Then Rena deep-throated him while her hands stroked him to heaven. "Pull away now. I'm coming," he warned, barely able to talk. But instead of pulling away, she bore down.

He couldn't stop himself. He shouted and tensed as he shot down her throat, the pleasure overwhelming as he poured all of himself into her.

The ecstasy drugged him, and he floated in a world where nothing hurt as she slowly eased away, sucking him hard at the end, so that a second, even more brutal orgasm swept over him.

He was groaning and praying when she stood.

"I didn't understand any of that," she said, and he realized he'd resorted to German. Thanking her, loving her, wanting her never to leave him. "But it sounds pretty good."

He just looked at her and opened his arms.

She came into them, and he shivered, still sensitive as his body came down from a major rush of endorphins.

I love you so much. He sighed against her neck and nuzzled her hair, so taken with the pretty swirls of gold and brown. "I am sorry."

She pulled back to look at him with a frown. "Sorry?"

"That we did not use the condom. Yet." He grinned, his heart light, his body not feeling any aches at all. "Now why don't you sit here, right at the edge of the tub, so I can apologize properly. And spread your legs wide, so I know when you accept."

She did as he said and gave him a wicked smile. "Oh, I don't know. I'm still pretty mad at you for getting hurt. And then not using that condom when I went to the trouble of leaving this warm bath to get it for you? That didn't help."

He knelt, ignoring a twinge from his ribs and thigh, the pain returning. "Ah, *Häschen.* Then let me show you how sorry I am."

♥ ♥ ♥

Rena succumbed to her first orgasm faster than he had. But it had been his fault. Blowing him was such a turn-on. She loved the act because she felt powerful, giving so much pleasure. And with Axel, she especially loved making him lose all control. She'd peek and see him lost in pleasure or looking at her as if he couldn't get enough of her. So, yes, she'd been close to her own climax after blowing him.

But he wouldn't stop. Insatiable, he licked her to orgasm then kissed her and stroked her all over, pushing her through one climax without respite into a steady rise toward another.

He turned her around, bent over, standing out of the water, while he plucked her nipples and ground against her lower back from behind.

She wanted to feel him inside her, skin to skin, but she also worried about the implied intimacy.

Which was nuts because he'd touched and kissed her almost everywhere already, so how much more intimate could they get? But still. She wasn't on any birth control, and as much as she wanted a baby, she wanted to be married first. That she kept imagining babies and a family with Axel scared her. She wanted it too much.

"Where is your head, little rabbit?" he crooned and smacked her ass, as he'd done a time or two before. Then the bastard would rub the sting away and play with her pussy until she wanted to scream.

"With you," she moaned. "God, Axel. Fuck me already."

He started with the German again, and she shivered, loving that deep voice saying all kinds of stuff she didn't understand. He could have been talking about the weather, and she'd melt under that sexy voice.

He switched back to English. "I want to take you hard, bent over like this." He leaned closer to whisper, "To fuck you so hard and jet inside your pussy. Leave you wet with my cum."

She groaned and leaned back against him, letting him take her weight as he pushed against her lower back and fingered her to the edge of climax. Then he stepped back.

"Axel, please."

He rustled behind her, then she felt him again, there between her legs, his thick shaft pushing past the swollen folds of her sex and into her. He lowered them both into the water, and as she sat facing away from him, she took the whole of him inside her.

"Ah, yes. So good," he moaned and forced her to ride him up and down then faster. A reverse cowboy that made him feel so fucking big inside her. "Touch yourself. Come *mit* me," he ordered.

She did, feeling her orgasm coming.

"Tell me. How do I feel inside you? Do you like my thick cock?" he murmured, going all in with the dirty talk. He said a few things that shocked—and intrigued—her, and then he was taking over all control, fucking her in earnest, the water in the tub sloshing all over.

She came, gripping him inside her, and she lost awareness as the orgasm took over. She felt him stiffen, his hands gripping her so hard, that forceful side of her lover so damn hot. He really was like a Viking warrior claiming his woman.

She smiled to herself, drifting in bliss.

He lifted her off him and turned her around.

She blinked as he hurried to fit himself back inside her, still hard, but now she would see him face-to-face.

"I wore a condom, don't worry."

"You are so sexy." She wrapped her arms around his massive shoulders and kissed him. But this time the kisses were languorous, soothing, sexy yet comforting.

"*Ich liebe dich.*" He'd been saying that on and off, and as much as she wanted to know what it meant, she just liked hearing it in his sexy voice. His mouth was made for sin. What he could do with that tongue between her legs was lethal.

"How are you so good at sex?"

"I am good, yes." A lot of male satisfaction in those dark eyes. "I like to know what pleases my partner. But with you, it's so easy. Everything about you is worth pleasing, and I want to take my time making love to you. Kissing you." He showed her just how much he liked kissing. "Touching you." He cupped her breasts, rubbing his thumbs over her nipples while he looked into her eyes. "Holding you." He sighed and kissed her again. "I never want to move."

"Sorry. But you're moving whether you want to or not." He slipped out of her, and she hurried to reach down and catch him. Then she pulled the condom off and placed it on the corner of the tub, folding it over itself so it wouldn't spill.

"So sad. A waste of so many fine swimmers." He didn't smile, so she didn't realize he'd been joking about what was in the condom at first. But when she did, she made a face.

"Sperm jokes are stupid."

"So why are you smiling?"

"I'm not." She was. "You are so much more than you seem." She let him cradle her against his chest and studied him, caressing his neck and arms, aware of yet another bruise forming over his shoulder.

"Oh?" He watched her, his gaze roaming her face, focused on her.

"When I first met you, all I saw was a big German guy who growled at people and scared most of Ray's customers."

"Did I scare you?"

"Not scared, maybe intimidated a little." She touched his jaw, wondering what he'd look like without the beard. Wondering if she could handle all that handsome without the facial hair. "You still had the words though. You said my hair was like sunlight. I remember."

"It is." He touched a stray curl. "I love the bounce."

She grinned. "I keep it natural, but I can do so much with it. Bouncy, straightened, combed, braided."

"I like it the way you like it."

"Good answer."

He smiled.

"Now when I see you, I see that smile. I see how you protect people. Me especially."

He shifted, now looking uncomfortable with her praise. "I don't like bullies."

"Me either." She kissed his cheek, and he sighed and curled his arms around her. "You're sweet and kind. You give me presents every day, which you don't have to, you know."

"*Ja.* I must. I am winning you over with trinkets to be your valentine."

She chuckled. "Oh that. Sure. You can be my valentine now, if you want."

"*Nein.* I must earn it."

"Sure, sure." She patted his chest. "Where was I?"

"I'm amazing and sweet and kind."

"I don't think I said amazing."

"You were working up to it."

She laughed. "Okay. You're amazing…when it comes to finding trouble."

He grew still, and she knew she'd hit a sore point—and not on his body.

"Axel, why are you always fighting? It's scary. I don't want you hurt."

"I would never hurt you," he said in a rush.

"I know that."

He sighed. "Rena, I… I have had a temper my whole life. And it's not good to be big and angry. You can hurt people without meaning to."

"I know you'd never hurt me."

"Never," he swore like an oath. "Once you do something like that, it stays with you. Something you never get over."

After a pause, she asked, "Did you hurt someone once, when you got angry?"

"To my shame, yes, I did. And it haunts me still." He grew silent then added, "I hurt her, badly."

She saw tears in his eyes. "Oh, Axel. I'm sure it was an accident."

"Yet the results were the same. She was hurt because of me. I never forget this. But I learned as well. It's not a bad thing when you fight to protect others."

He sounded as if he was reciting something he'd once memorized.

"No, I don't suppose it is bad if you're helping protect people," she said slowly. "But at some point you could get in trouble. With the law, with hurting someone who doesn't deserve it."

"*Nein.* I never start battles, and I do not hit those who don't deserve it. But I don't want you to see that." He blew out a breath.

"I've seen you fight plenty at Ray's."

"I know, and I'm sorry. I don't want you to think of me like that. I'm not a mindless machine. I don't actually like hurting people." He paused. "Well, I liked hurting Daryl, Rabies, and Scott. And I *really* want to hurt Fletcher," he growled. "But they are not good people. And if hurting them stops them from hurting others, it's good, *ja*?"

"I see your point. But you have to be careful."

"Believe it or not, I don't look for trouble," he said, humor in his voice. "But I'm tall and it always seems to find me. Hard to hide in a crowd."

She laughed. "I know. It's like being black around white people. I stand out."

"You stand out because you are beautiful, and everyone loves your laugh."

"Stop." She blushed.

"To be honest, the first thing I noticed about you was your hair." He threaded his fingers with hers.

She smiled.

"Then I saw your honey-colored eyes and, well…" He chuckled. "You have amazing breasts and an ass I want to write poetry about. And I don't write poetry."

"Stop it." She laughed, embarrassed, then said, "It *is* a nice ass, isn't it?"

"The best." He confessed, "Sometimes when you'd wait on my table, I'd drop things so you would bend over to pick them up."

"Axel Heller!"

He grinned, unrepentant. "I left you big tips."

"You did at that. And I just had a really big one twice." She wiggled against him.

"*Ja.* I came a lot for you. It's tough to be around you because I'm always hard." He let out a moan that made her want to try him on for size again. "I feel weak. And the water is getting cool. We should get out."

"You're right." But she'd never look at his bathtub the same again.

She got out and helped him to his feet. They dried off, and he scooted her out of the bathroom. As she dried off and looked for something of his to wear, she heard the toilet flush and the sink go on.

When he came out, he found her wearing one of his T-shirts that came to mid-thigh.

He blinked. "Will you stay with me?"

"Tonight? Sure. But I'll need to swing by my place to grab some things or my hair will be a mess tomorrow."

"You are never a mess."

"Because I have a routine. We stylists always take pains to look good, especially when we go out. The one time you don't, you run into a client. Swear to God."

He laughed and stepped into a pair of sweatpants. No underwear, she noticed. Hmm. Easy access later?

"I bet," he was saying. "So how about you stay tonight? I will run you home tomorrow to get your things. Then would you come back to be with me?"

"Wait. Be with you tomorrow and Sunday? Or leave tonight and stay tomorrow?"

He took her in his arms and brushed a tender kiss across her lips. "Spend the weekend with me. I will give you many orgasms, feed you, and give you more orgasms. And maybe, if you are lucky, I will watch Lifetime with you."

"*And* Hallmark?"

"*Ja.* That too." He smiled. "And we can read passages from your book to each other and act them out."

"Oh my God, yes. I mean, you had me at Lifetime, but yes."

With an itinerary like that, how could she refuse?

CHAPTER FIFTEEN

Sunday night, Axel stood holding hands with Rena on her mother's doorstep.

"You are sure she is fine with this so soon?"

"Yes, now stop fidgeting." Rena dusted a speck of something off his shirt.

She seemed to do that a lot. Personally, he thought she just liked touching his chest. He wondered if he might get away with doing the same to her. In private, of course.

"What's that grin for?" she asked.

He stared at her breasts. "I see lint there. Can I brush it off?"

She snickered. "Okay, I was feeling you up. Happy?"

"I would be if you hadn't stopped."

She opened her mouth to say something but her mother opened the door.

Rena and her mother embraced, chattered, and laughed as if they hadn't seen each other in ages.

Axel stared in surprise. Though he'd been warned, Rena hadn't been exaggerating. Her mother didn't look old enough to have a grown child. She had the same features and coloring as her daughter, though she wore her hair short and straight in a classic bob. He knew much about hairstyles since meeting Rena. He'd been studying all about hair and beauty to impress her.

Caroline Jackson wore a pretty brown sweater and jeans, and she was beautiful. Big gold eyes, full lips, those same cheekbones and dimple that had so attracted him to her daughter. They shared a similar build and had the same laugh.

But Rena was softer, her eyes a reflection of a pure spirit. Caroline had been through a lot. He could see it in her stare and feel it in the way she stood, defensively, at the door.

"Hello, Ms. Jackson. It is a pleasure to meet you."

"Call me Caroline, honey. Wow. What door did you run into? And did it survive your face?"

He grinned. "This is nothing. You should see the door."

Rena hastily cut in, "Mom, this is Axel." She paused. "My boyfriend."

He tried to hide his sheer delight in being called Rena's boyfriend, but he must not have been successful. Caroline lost some of her standoffishness and smiled. "Nice to meet you, Axel."

"The pleasure is all mine. Rena loves you very much, so you are special to me already."

Her mother's eyes widened. "Oh, he's good. And I love that accent."

"Yep. He's got all the words." Rena smiled at him.

God, he loved her so much.

Her mother coughed, and he realized he'd been mooning over Rena. He flushed. "Sorry. I don't meant to let the heat out."

They stepped inside, and she closed the door behind them. "Dave is inside. He made dinner tonight."

Axel sighed. "I had heard such stories about your ability to cook.

I am saddened by my loss." He thickened the accent. Women seemed to like it.

Her mother sure did.

Rena narrowed her eyes at him, but he ignored her.

"Oh, honey. No worries. I'll cook for you the next time you come."

"*Ja. Bitte.*" He took Caroline's hand and kissed the back of it.

Her mother tittered and made no move to take back her hand.

"Mom, you can have your hand back now." Rena sighed. "Easy on the charm, you big German Casanova."

He raised a brow but let her mother's hand go. When he saw Rena trying to hide a grin, he knew all was well.

"Oh, he is precious. And so…big." Caroline looked up at him. "Axel, how tall are you?"

"Six foot six."

"That must make things interesting," he thought he heard her murmur.

"*Mom.*"

He bit back a laugh and followed them into the kitchen, where a well-dressed man wearing glasses and rolled-up sleeves pulled something out of the oven.

"That smells great," Rena said.

The man turned. He saw Rena and gave her a big smile. His eyes widened when they settled on Axel. "Wow. You're not how I imagined Rena's 'little friend' would be." The man put the dish down, took off the oven mitts, and offered a hand. "Dave Wallace. Nice to meet you."

Axel grasped Dave's hand in a firm but not hard handshake. He let Dave set the pressure and responded. A subtle but telling way to take a man's measure. "Axel Heller. Nice to meet you too."

Dave seemed genuinely happy to see Rena again. During the meal,

Axel tried, but he didn't sense anything off about the guy. Dave acted respectful and loving toward Caroline. He didn't leer, as Rena had said he once had, nor did he ogle her at all. Not like Axel did.

"Quit staring at me," she whispered at one point during the dinner, when her mother and Dave were laughing together.

"Sorry. But that blue sweater is so tight. It really brings out your... eyes."

"Stop." She tried to hide a laugh.

"So, Axel," Caroline said, "Rena told me you run an auto garage."

"It's a paint and auto body shop," Rena corrected before he could. "His place fixes dents and does touch-ups. But they also do custom paint jobs. You should see some of the work they've done. It's amazing. Lou works for him when he's not at Del's."

"Oh, so you're the big brawler always stealing my niece's people," Caroline teased. "I've heard about you."

He snorted. "From that she-wolf with sticky fingers. Lou was mine before he was ever hers."

Caroline laughed. "*She-wolf.* Oh, that's Del all right."

"Don't call her that though," Rena warned him. "She'll think you like her."

"Meh. Her shop is okay." He gave a small grin to show them he was teasing. "I miss Liam. So much common sense in that man."

"Plus he's less scary than Del," Caroline said.

Axel laughed. "*Ja.*"

Dave cut in. "So, Axel, what prompted you to go into auto body work?"

"My family has long been into mechanical work and cars. The business started in Germany with auto repair. My brother sells cars. And my father runs an auto parts chain."

"Is that what brought you to the States?"

Rena watched him, and he realized he'd never shared the story with her. "I was born north of Stuttgart, in Germany. My mother's people are from Bavaria, my father's near Berlin. But we settled in Stuttgart for my father to work. When I was fifteen, we came to America so my father could open his stores here. Then—"

"Wait," Dave interrupted. "Do you guys own JH Autoteile? They just did a special on that in *Car and Driver Magazine* last month, and I remember the owner's name was something Heller." He explained, "I'm a car enthusiast."

"Jannik Heller is my father. He owns the chain. It's done well in the Northwest."

"Well?" Dave blinked. "It's the highest-rated parts chain on the West Coast, and there are rumors they're planning on opening stores out east."

Axel shrugged, aware Rena didn't look happy with him. "Maybe. My father and I are estranged."

"Oh." Dave looked discomfited. "Sorry I brought it up."

Rena put her hand on Axel's leg under the table. "It's okay. Axel doesn't mind telling you, do you?"

"No." He gave her a big smile. "I have more important things occupying my mind. I've been busy trying to win myself a valentine." He turned to Caroline, who watched them with sharp eyes. "Your daughter is not making my wooing very easy."

"Wooing?" Caroline turned to Dave. "See? That's what you need to be doing."

Dave's smile looked a little strained, to Axel's way of thinking. "Hey, man. You're making me look bad."

"At least you aren't all bruised and banged up. And you dress nice."

Dave sat up a little straighter in his chair. "So, if you don't mind me asking, what happened?" He gestured to Axel's face.

"Rena hit me."

Her mother and Dave gaped.

She did hit him then, on the shoulder, and told the truth. "He got into a fight at Ray's."

Her mother shook her head. "I am *so* glad you stopped working there. Such a rough place."

"Ray's?" Dave asked.

"A bar that caters to bikers and criminals," Caroline answered. "No offense, Axel."

He chuckled. "None taken. I don't have a motorcycle, though I have been called a criminal once or twice."

Rena covered her eyes and sighed.

"Now if we could just get your cousin to stop hanging around there. At least the baby is keeping Del away." Her mother harrumphed. "Maybe we need to get J.T. a baby."

"I think he's hoping that'll happen soon enough, Mom."

Caroline looked delighted. "I can't wait for grandbabies." She eyed Axel up and down then her daughter.

"Nope," Rena said as her mother opened her mouth. "No babies for me yet, Mom. How about you, Dave? Do you have kids or grandkids?"

A pregnant pause filled the silence. Axel sensed tension, but he didn't know what had caused it.

"As a matter of fact, my daughter just informed me she's pregnant."

"Congratulations," Axel said when no one spoke. Then he realized Dave didn't look happy. "Yes?"

"Yes." Dave sighed. "My daughter isn't having an easy time with my divorce from her mother."

"None of us are," Caroline snapped before glancing down. "Sorry."

"Caroline…"

"Excuse me." Caroline left the table.

Dave apologized. "I'd better go after her."

Axel sat with Rena. Determined not to let good food go to waste, he kept eating. He loved a good pot roast.

Caroline started yelling, loudly enough that they heard a few words before a door slammed.

All was not well between the pair, obviously.

Rena started to stand, but he grabbed her arm. "*Nein.* Let them handle this. They wouldn't want you to interfere."

She sat in a huff. "I know. Habit."

"Eat. This is very good."

She took a few bites, but her concentration clearly lingered on the hallway.

After some time, Dave returned with a coat. "I'd better give her some space. Rena, it was nice to see you again. Nice to meet you too, Axel."

Axel nodded.

Dave left, but Caroline didn't return.

"Now I'm going to talk to her," Rena warned him.

"*Ja,* go. I'll clean up."

Her frown eased. "Thanks." She leaned over to kiss him.

"Let me know if I can help, okay?"

She cupped his cheek. "You help just by being you."

He thought that was a pretty nice thing to say.

Then he realized there was way too much roast left over, and he'd be insulting his hosts if he didn't show how much he'd enjoyed Dave's cooking. So after he cleared the table of all the dirty dishes, he put them in the dishwasher and returned to his seat and empty plate. Then he took another helping and enjoyed his food.

Rena found her mother sitting on her bed, crying.

"Oh, Mom. What's wrong?"

Her mother accepted her hug. "You were right. About all of it."

"Mom?" She hadn't felt right. Dave had been open about everything, and he'd been charming tonight. She'd thought about what Axel had said when they'd talked about this. That maybe she felt threatened by her mother finally finding happiness and because her mom had had so many bad boyfriends, Rena didn't want to see her hurt again so imagined the worst of Dave.

"He and his wife have been talking a lot because his daughter's pregnant." Her mother blew her nose. "I'm genuinely happy for him, but I don't like it. He's committed *to me*, or so he said."

"Has he been unfaithful or something?"

"No. I just don't want him talking to her. He tells me she has a new boyfriend, the mom, not the daughter. That they have been over for a long time before I was ever in the picture. I want to believe him. But he gets texts he won't let me see. And he's busy all the time when we're supposed to be together. I don't know if he's cheating on me or this new contract at work really is taking up his time. And he gets so defensive if I ask about the divorce. I can't wait for it to be over, but he acts like he's getting ready to go to a funeral."

"Well, Mom, for him, it kind of is like a funeral. His marriage died. He loved her once, I'm sure. But when he gets divorced, that future he once had will be lost." She didn't want to hurt her mom more, but she had to ask, "Are you sure this is what you want? He hasn't been separated from her that long."

"They've been living apart for a year, just hooking up now and then before he met me."

Rena blinked. "Ah, okay."

"So, if she's got a boyfriend, the daughter's married and ready to have a baby, then where does that leave him and me? I thought he wanted to be with me, but he keeps putting me off. He hasn't introduced me to this daughter yet because it's 'hard for her.'" Caroline swore. "It's fuck-all hard on me too! Damn it!" She broke down crying again.

Rena let her mom ramble, letting all the hurt out. She tried to soothe with hugs and kind words, but Caroline Jackson had balled herself into a meltdown of misery.

This is what I'll be like when Axel and I are over, Rena couldn't help thinking.

As if she'd conjured him to appear, Axel stood in the doorway. "No, no. No more tears." He walked in, sat on the bed, then picked up her mother to sit in his lap. He hugged her, crooning in German, as if he hadn't just met the woman an hour and a half ago.

Her mother didn't seem to mind, sobbing her heart out on his chest.

Rena just stared, wide-eyed.

Talk to her he mouthed, patting her mom on the back, and said to her mom, "No tears, Caroline. You will be happy, *ja.*"

Her mom cried harder. "No."

"You mean *nein.*" He winked at Rena and nodded toward her mother.

"Mom, Axel's right. You'll be happy if you let yourself be happy. I was wrong about Dave. He seems like a nice guy. But he probably needs time." She'd read about these situations a lot in magazines. Rena was a student of the human heart. "I think you need to let Dave grieve his marriage. But maybe don't rush into anything. You said he's financially set, and you know you are. So take it slow. Keep dating, but don't move in together."

"But I l-love him."

"I know, Mom." It hurt to see her mother so unhappy. "And if he loves you—"

"He s-says he d-does."

"Then give him space and time to come back to you."

"Caroline," Axel cut in, "from a man's point of view, you are beautiful and smart. You can have any man you want."

She lifted her head, wiped her eyes, and blinked at Axel. "You think?"

"*Ja.* If Rena hadn't told me, I would not know you are old enough to be her mother. You look so young and pretty. Dave is lucky to have *you.* Believe in yourself. If he's too much a dumbass to go be with another woman, he doesn't deserve you."

"Exactly," Rena agreed. The big guy was *so* getting lucky later.

"Really?" her mom asked, looking at Rena, not at Axel.

"Really, Mom. I just get protective of you with men because we both know you've made some bad choices. But you don't know how pretty and smart you are, like Axel said. You have guys checking you out all the time."

"I do?" Her mom brightened a little.

"I would check you out," Axel added, "but Rena would kill me."

Her mother laughed through her tears. "Oh, stop."

"Mom, the only reason you don't have men lined up to ask you out is because you put out an unavailable vibe. Look, you're an amazing nurse. You're calm under pressure, and you don't have money problems. Heck, you just got promoted."

"I did." Her mom blew her nose again, but this time she was listening.

"Dave found you and is lucky to have you." Repetitive, but maybe if she kept saying it her mom would believe it. "Let him be sad his marriage ended. And if he acts all distant, take some time for yourself. You're not married to the guy. Go out and date. See who else is just waiting to find you available."

"Honey, I hate to break it to you, but there's a shortage of good black men in this town." She glanced up at Axel. "Although if you know any more like this one, I'd make an exception."

"Yes," Axel agreed. "Don't deprive a nice white boy because he's too pale. He could be German, so take pity on him and let him fall in love with you. It will make him a better man."

Caroline chuckled. "Is that what my daughter did with you?"

"Of course."

Rena frowned. Had she made him fall in love with her? Really? *In love?*

"You two are good for my ego." Caroline patted Axel on the shoulder and stood. Then she crossed to the bathroom and closed herself inside.

Rena dragged Axel to the living room. "What nonsense are you telling my mother?"

He hugged her, and she didn't know what to think.

"Axel?"

They stood together, hugging, for a while before he said, "I miss my mother every day. Seeing your mom made me think of her crying, being sad. It's not good for your mother to have so many tears."

She felt for him because she heard his pain.

"My mother too was beautiful, but with a man who didn't love her. My father… He was not good for her. And she spent a long time unhappy and hurt because of it." He pulled away to look down at her. "I'm sorry if I overstepped. I only wanted her to feel better."

Stop being so freakin' perfect! "Oh, I'm not mad."

"*Gut.*"

"But I do wish you would have told me about your dad being all rich. Are you loaded too?" She didn't like the thought.

"No. My father and brother have money. I do not." He paused. "Well, I am comfortable. My business makes a profit. But I don't have the money they do."

"Good. That's okay then." If he was rich on top of looking the way he did and being so loving, she'd definitely feel an imbalance of power in the relationship. Though she'd read plenty of billionaire romances, when it came down to it, she really just wanted a regular guy.

"You're a nice man, Axel."

He sighed. "No, I'm a mean bastard who has a soft spot for you. Tell no one."

She grinned. "My lips are sealed."

"Then take this and think of me." He handed her a small present.

She unwrapped a cinnamon ball. Finally. A Valentine's present she understood and liked. "Sweet."

"No, it's extra spicy. Like you. But the red is for Valentine's Day."

She popped it in her mouth and about died. He hadn't been kidding about the extra heat. As she made a mad dash to the kitchen for water, she heard her mother ask Axel where she'd gone.

"I scare her, Caroline. Her love for me is so strong, it burns her to think of it. So she hides from me in the kitchen, pretending she needs to do the dishes I already put in the dishwasher." He sighed, the giant fibber. "I may have a big heart, but I mean well. I regret that my words to you alarmed her."

"That girl has no sense. Who in their right mind would run from a perfect man like you?"

"*Ja.* That's what I think too."

"I like you, Axel. How about some cheesecake for dessert?"

"Yes, please. And might I add how lovely you look, even after you have cried? That is a gift in itself."

"Yep. If my daughter thinks she can do better, she's surely out of her goddamn mind."

Rena didn't have to see him smile to know he was grinning ear to ear.

♥ ♥ ♥

An hour later in the truck, he gripped the wheel and moaned, pleading with her to end her torture.

Rena had him on the verge of coming then pulled her mouth away. "You big baby. Telling her I ran because I was scared. What's wrong with you?"

Actually, it had been pretty damn funny, him looking so smug, her mother clearly on his side, making Rena out to be the bad guy. Her mom had doted on him, feeding him huge slices of cheesecake and acting as if he could do no wrong.

And wonder of wonders, Caroline Jackson had no longer seemed to dwell on the mess of her love life when they'd left.

"I am sorry. You are right." He gripped her shoulder. "I am so very sorry, *Häschen.* And my dick is so very big right now. You should hop on and make it go down."

"I would, but—"

He held out a condom to her and smiled. "In my pocket."

"Prepared now, are we?" she muttered, trying not to smile back. She shimmied out of her pants and panties while he fitted the condom over himself.

And then she was sliding down, taking him deep while they fucked in his truck parked in his driveway. The windows steamed because of the cold outside, and as she felt his fingers drag over her clit and neared her own end, she didn't care about neighbors, foggy windows, or that the truck continued to shake. Because Axel moaned her name and swore, coming seconds before she did.

He muttered in German while she drew out his pleasure, squeezing him tight.

Rena fixed her hair, pulling the sweaty strands back. "That's what you get for being so nice and sneaky tonight."

He grabbed her by the neck and devoured her mouth. "I am a raiding Viking, and you are my prisoner."

She shivered. "Oh, we need to go inside so we can play that scene again."

He grinned. "I thought so. You like when I'm in charge."

She squeezed him inside her, heard his breath hitch, and corrected him. "When *who's* in charge?"

"Fuck. I love when you hold me like this." He ground against her, digging deeper. "But when I'm spanking you or when I'm shoving deep inside you, don't you like that too?"

"Oh, I do." She relaxed against him. "Okay. One scene where you're in charge then one where I'm in charge."

"*Ja,* that I can do."

"Then for God's sake, I need some rest! I have an appointment first thing tomorrow morning. And trust me, if the girls see me walking funny, they'll make fun of me."

"We can't have that, now, can we?" he asked and kissed her again.

They made it inside to the living room at least.

Monday morning, she gave herself extra time in the morning to get ready. It took her a thirty-minute hot bath to soak away the aches from her weekend with her Viking lover. And Tommie still had the nerve, in front of a full salon and in a loud voice, to ask her why she was walking bowlegged after her date with Axel.

CHAPTER SIXTEEN

Late Tuesday afternoon at the salon, Rena was replacing stock while Nicky worked on a client in the back and Stella did paperwork.

"Um, I don't know, Rena. I mean, the troll could be classified as cute. But that statue of Cupid is just creepy. It has bulgy eyes and a little dick. And that video Heller gave you..." Tommie cleared her throat, glanced around at the almost-empty salon, and added in a whisper, "I've seen it. It's straight-up porn."

"What?" Rena looked down at the innocent looking copy of *Be My Valentine, Charlie Crown*. She looked harder. "It says Charlie Crown, not Charlie Brown."

Tommie tried not to laugh, but Rena could see her struggle. "See, Charlie wears a crown. But he wears it over his, um, penis. It's a cock ring. And only his true valentine can get it off."

Rena just stared. The cover of the DVD had cartoony characters. They looked like the Peanuts gang, but upon closer inspection, she could see they weren't quite the same. "That is so wrong. What if I was a kid or something?" Where had Axel gotten this?

"What exactly is he trying to say to you?"

Stella walked up behind them. “Oh, that’s a good one. The chick with the long red nails gets Charlie at the end, not Lucy.”

“Stella?” Rena couldn’t believe her friend had seen that.

“What? It’s a popular gag gift. Most everyone I know saw it last year. It was a hoot.” She chuckled. “Oh, wait. Is this from Heller?”

“Yep,” Tommie answered. “He’s been trying, but our guy is not great with the gifts.”

Stella shrugged. “Maybe he’s telling her he wants her to be his vag-entine.”

Tommie snickered. “To be his sweetheart and play with his *hard* candy.”

“He wants her to enjoy his Pea*nuts*.”

Rena refused to laugh. “You two are ridiculous.”

Nicky and her very tall, very manly client left the back room. Everyone stopped and watched him move, a walking example of fierce meets sexy.

As Nicky was taking his credit card, the guy did a double take at the video in Rena’s hand. He looked at her and the girls then back at the video. “Charlie Crown, huh? Didn’t think you were into that kind of stuff.”

Rena glared. “Oh, shut up, Grim.”

He chuckled as he left, and the room sighed. “He’s like a dark Heller, only meaner. I’m so in lust with that man.” Tommie groaned. “Do you think he likes Asian chicks?”

“I think he’s gay,” Rena said, knowing full well he wasn’t. The guy worked with J.T. at the tattoo shop and liked the ladies.

The girls looked horrified, Tommie especially. “*What?*”

“But I could be mistaken. Who knows?” She gave Tommie a mean smile.

"That is so wrong."

"*Hard* candy, really? At least vag-entine was creative."

"And Pea*nuts*. Don't forget that." Stella stuck her tongue out.

Tommie laughed. "Touché."

They continued to tease until it was time to go. An early day for everyone, for once, with the sun still out at four o'clock. Stella walked out first and came right back inside. She didn't look pleased. "Guys, something you need to see."

They followed her outside to the back and saw someone had spray-painted a lot of nasty names over the block cement wall, *Bitch* and the C-word being the nicer ones used. But not to leave anyone out who worked in the place, the artist had managed to throw in racial slurs on African Americans, Latinos, Asians, and Italians, though Rena wasn't sure who that had been aimed at since their token white girl, Nicky, was Scottish.

"Motherfuckers," Stella spat. She went off in Spanish and dialed her brother before Rena could tell her not to.

Knowing Lou would tell Axel, she grabbed her phone, took a picture of the graffiti, which covered half the brick wall, and dialed her man.

"Rena, *Liebling*. How are you?"

"I have a small problem."

"What's wrong?" He sounded serious, probably having heard the waver in her voice.

As she told him, she grew more angry than afraid. "I bet it's Fletcher's guys. Who else would it be?"

"I'll be right there," he said and hung up.

"Axel's coming over."

"So is Lou," Stella said. "But then, he's working with Heller, so that's kind of a no-brainer."

Tommie and Nicky stared at the wall in shock until Tommie recovered enough to say, "They spelled *pussie-bitch* wrong. It's not *pussy* with *ie*, it's with a *y*."

"And it's not really a word, even though they used a hyphen," Nicky added. "*Pussy* and *bitch* should not be used together. Now *dumb bitch* or *pussy-whipped* would make more sense. But then that could imply we were whipping people with our vaginas, so maybe not."

"Good point." It was either laugh or cry, and Rena chose to see the humor in the situation. She was laughing by the time Axel showed up.

He pulled into the back, looked at the wall, and shook his head. "They spelled *pussy* wrong."

The girls burst into laughter. His eyes crinkled, but he didn't smile. Instead he walked up to the wall and touched the paint. When some of the paint came off, he took heavy equipment out of the back of his truck along with a hose and a bottle of something.

"Can you hook this up for me?" He handed a hose and cord to Rena.

"What is it?"

"Pressure washer. I have graffiti remover too. When I'm done using the pressure washer to clean this, I'm going to find Fletcher and use it on him."

Lou pulled up with Smitty in his car. "We left Mateo and Rylan to finish the Honda," he told Axel as the pair got out. He stared at the wall, and his scowl grew. "I'll fucking kill him."

Smitty shook his head. "Gotta be Fletcher's guys."

"Get in line," Stella told Lou with a mean smile. "Heller's first."

"Hey," Rena barked. "This is my place. Maybe I want to be the one to kick his butt." If it was even him. They'd all just assumed. But who else would it be?

Axel kissed her on the head—the stupid, patronizing man—and got to work.

"Axel, I can handle this."

"You can. I am going to."

She glared at him. He ignored her and started cleaning the wall.

Rena and the girls went back inside. "He's humoring me."

"He can humor me any day of the week," Nicky muttered.

"It's my shop."

Stella raised a brow. "Want me to tell him to stop what he's doing?"

"No," Rena snapped. "But he should at least ask if I wanted his help before taking over." And like that, her bad mood changed. Mr. Perfect wasn't so perfect after all. "Huh."

"Yo, Ms. Jekyll, what the hell?" Tommie leaned closer, looking into her eyes. "You on drugs? You're mad, you're laughing, you look like you want to cry."

"She does not," Nicky said.

"She did earlier."

"I'm good. I'm just mad at Mr. Perfect out there, and it feels good. Sometimes he's so great he makes it tough to be angry at him."

Stella grinned. "He pissed you off. Make him pay for it."

"But not with more Valentine's Day presents." Tommie grimaced. "He's not a good gift giver. Just sayin'."

Stella shrugged. "Meh. I don't mind. I'll take the possessed Cupid if you don't want it. It'll scare my sister. And she's getting on my last nerve lately."

Axel did his best to keep his anger in check as he took care of the graffiti. Such bullshit. He knew, he *knew*, this had to be Fletcher's work.

"That cheek looks pretty bruised, *Jefe,*" Lou said, leaning back against his car as he watched Axel and Smitty work, applying the graffiti eliminator. The paint had only semi-dried, so it would come off easily. The pressure washer would probably work on its own, but he was taking no chances with Rena's shop.

Axel didn't answer, so Smitty spoke for him. "He annihilated two of Fletcher's crew Friday night. Rabies is out. Scott suffered a bruised jaw and concussion, and no one's seen Daryl or Fletcher for a while."

The guys looked at Axel. He frowned. "Not me. But if I find them, I'll kill them and leave no bodies." He was only half-joking.

"Ah, good thing then no one's seen them since Friday night," Smitty said. "Interesting that Fletcher's been absent. I would have thought he'd have been a part of your attempted beatdown."

That had bothered Axel too.

Lou said, "But didn't someone see him out and about not too long ago? He might be hanging out at those white-power rallies in Spokane. It's been in all the news about how the city's doing its best to get rid of those fuckers." He went off in Spanish.

Axel agreed with most of the words he understood and added his two cents in German.

Smitty sighed. "I don't speak Spanish or German, and I still agree with what I'm pretty sure you said."

The cleaning took little time, and Smitty and Lou decided to head back to the shop to check on Rylan. Mateo would be fine, and Rylan had been doing well, but Smitty wanted to check on the guy. They got in Lou's car and rolled down the windows. "Rylan keeps giving me attitude." Smitty scratched his head. "I don't know why, but I get the feeling he doesn't like me."

Lou gave him a mock gasp. "Not like you, but why not? You're so damn pleasant to be around."

"Yeah? So's your mother."

"Oh, nice, Smitty. You gonna insult my mama like that?"

Smitty grinned. "Man, she's hot. If I wasn't gay, I'd take her out and make a real woman out of her."

Lou rolled his eyes then waved at Axel. "Later. Take care of Rena and the girls. And if you didn't see how much you pissed off your girlfriend, you are one blind son of a bitch."

Smitty chuckled. "We really should stay and watch him try to fix it."

"Watch a grown man cry? Nah, I've seen that before."

"Oh right, being you work at Webster's Garage half the time."

Axel snorted. *Nice one, Smitty.*

"Well, yeah. Those guys are weak. And Del's friggin' scary."

They left in Lou's '73 Duster, and Axel took a moment. He put his gear away and debated the wisdom of confronting Rena in her shop or of apologizing and confronting her later.

Because if she thought he was okay with her working without protection or leaving alone at night without a plan in place to help her, she was way past wrong.

Ignoring a case of nerves, he walked inside and found the women passing around the old-school video he'd given her.

"Oh boy. Good luck." Tommie grinned at him. "And Charlie Crown? Man, what are you trying to say, Heller?"

He frowned "What?"

Stella snickered. "I really want to stay."

"Go," Rena ordered them while glaring at him.

Shit.

Nicky patted him on the shoulder. "Thanks for cleaning up, Heller. I hate when people can't spell."

He nodded.

Then it was just Rena and Axel and angry silence.

She blew out a loud breath. "Well?"

"I'm sorry," he tried.

"Can you be more specific?"

Great. A blanket apology wasn't going to work. "For cleaning your wall."

"No, for cleaning my wall without *asking me* if I wanted you to clean it."

She wore her hair pulled back, and the severe style put all the focus on her face, the anger in her light-brown eyes and the passionate flush on her cheeks a testament that she wasn't playing around.

Neither was he. "Rena, I'm sorry you are upset. But it's not safe for you with Fletcher and his people making trouble."

"We don't know that it was Fletcher." She held up a hand. "But I agree, it's likely him and his boys. That still doesn't explain why you're suddenly making decisions for me." Cute Rena had been replaced by Warrior Rena.

"You *want* the graffiti?" He was starting to get mad, feeling defensive and not sure why. He'd helped her out, dropped everything at work to come over and make sure she was okay.

"No." She took a deep breath and blew it out. Slowly. "I want you to acknowledge you pushed where you shouldn't have."

"Fine. I pushed. I'm sorry."

Her eyes narrowed. "You don't sound sorry." Then she shoved the video at him. "And what's the deal giving me porn for Valentine's Day?"

Now she had thoroughly confused him. "*Was?*"

She brought his hand up and placed the video in it. "Go watch the movie and let me know what you think."

"Would you like to watch it over dinner?" He'd been planning to take her to his place for a nice meal after work.

"Not tonight. I've lost my appetite." Again, she glared at him.

"I didn't put those words on your wall." He felt angry, scared for her and at her because she didn't seem to understand the danger.

Then, realizing that his anger was directed at her, he shut down. He could do happiness, laughter, joy. Around Rena, those made sense. Anger had no place around her. That he'd felt it at all worried him. So, internally, he stepped back, walling off his emotions. Keeping her safe.

"I'm sorry," he said quietly. "I'll wait for you to lock up then go." He turned and left, video in hand.

Rena didn't know what had just happened. All she'd wanted was a sincere apology for overstepping. Period. But Axel hadn't been sincere. He'd been annoyed with her, a first in their new relationship. But just to leave with a quiet *I'm sorry*? No discussion?

She locked up the back and saw him sitting in his truck by her car. She didn't bother saying anything, and neither did he.

Their little fight felt odd. No yelling or theatrics, nothing like the drama her mother would have engaged in. It was as if an icy blanket had smothered the flames of their connection, leaving her on the outs. Still, the big overstepper followed her home and watched her enter her locked townhome before leaving.

Huh. What to make of that?

Two days of silence later, she sat with Chi-Chi, her doggie buddy she'd decided to foster until someone could find the little guy a home, and watched mindless television while her brain raced. She and Axel had never fought. This period of quiet between them would be a good indicator of how he handled conflict.

Which wasn't to say he'd been totally absent the past two days. He'd been waiting in her lot while she opened and was there to watch her close. And he'd left two more gifts on her front step.

A small box of liquor-infused chocolates that had almost made her hurl and a pretty little bunny frame with his picture in it. That she kept at the office, aware the Easter-themed frame had nothing to do with the gorgeous—and stubborn—man inside it but understanding his little rabbit reference.

To date, that was her favorite present.

She grabbed a new book from a pile and started reading. But after rereading the same page for the twentieth time, she put the book down and pulled out her laptop.

After catching up on some book blogs and Facebook, she still found no satisfaction. About to close everything and go to bed early, she almost missed a message from Abby, of all people. Abby, the famous romance author, was also Del's sister-in-law.

You know this man?!?!?

Confused, Rena clicked on the link and saw the picture of Axel taken after his haircut.

Then her phone beeped. The same text from Abby. The phone rang.

"Hello?"

"Oh my God. Answer your messages!" Abby sounded shrill.

"Abby?"

"Do you know the bearded Adonis or what?"

"Um, yes." *He's my angry boyfriend, I think.* "Why?"

"He's viral!"

"What?" Axel wasn't diseased, he was…oh. "Wait. Why?"

"Click on this." A new Facebook message popped up with a link. When she clicked on it, she saw that nearly 500,000 people had liked his picture, with comments from *he's so sexy* to *where can I get my own Viking?* to the more extreme *what I'd do with him* descriptions. She cringed at a few of the more overly graphic ones.

"Where did these come from?" she asked Abby.

"I saw it on Instagram. I think one of your stylists posted this picture a few days ago, and it's taken off. I mean, this guy is drool-worthy, and I'm not the only one who thinks so. A friend of mine shared it to her romance reader group. So of course she tagged me to see it, and I recognized your salon. I have to meet this man!"

"Aren't you married?"

"Rena, do not play with me! He's got to be my next cover model! Come on. Can't you see him on the cover of my new MC series?"

"I thought you didn't like motorcycle club romances."

"I don't. He'd be an undercover DEA agent or something riding a motorcycle. But he'd look like that."

Rena could almost see the book taking form in Abby's brain.

"Well, I could talk to him for you, but only if you let me be the first to read it."

"Oh, would you? Please? I swear you'll get to read the very first draft. I'll even dedicate it to you."

Rena choked, wondering how Axel would take all this. "Um, I can talk to the guy, but I'm not sure he'll be up for modeling for romance books."

"Screw everyone else. I want him for *my* books. Just think, I could have exclusive rights to that body! That face! He makes me want to write a historical with Vikings and plundering heroes. Oh, I love that beard and mustache. He has to be mine!"

"Abby?" Rena heard her husband's voice in the background. "What the hell are you talking about? Who are you talking to?"

"Gotta go. Text me!" Abby hung up.

Rena loved Abby Singer. Abby was the very first romance writer Rena had ever met, and the woman was just as sweet and funny as a reader could ask for.

In any case, if Abby wanted Axel to be her studly model, Rena would make it happen.

But first she had to make him apologize, grovel a little, and communicate like a regular person. If he shut down every time they had a disagreement, they were in for a *world* of drama, and that she could do without.

Axel sat watching…something…that was not at all affiliated with Charles Schultz's Peanuts. "What the hell?"

He'd put it off, too depressed to watch it. But with nothing else to do on Thursday night but pet the cat or work out, he'd decided to see what Rena had been talking about.

The video should have been *Be My Valentine, Charlie Brown.* Instead, he sat watching a live version of Charlie *Crown*, not Brown, apparently, who wore the cartoon character's trademark yellow shirt but no pants. He kept waving around his swollen dick and complaining about his crown—a cock ring. And he was looking for love in *all* the wrong places.

Axel scrubbed his face, peeking only when Peppermint Pussy and Bossy Marcie started going at it.

I'm going to hell for sure.

Unfortunately, he'd missed the boat on this gift. Totally unintentional, but that's what he got for buying shit off the street.

He paused the video before a human Snoopenis and Woody-stock got up to no good and found the box that held the rest of the treasures he planned on giving Rena. There had to be some way to use them to get her to talk to him again.

He double-checked the swag he'd been collecting for her. A few more trolls with different-colored hair, some Reese's Valentine's candies, a big lollipop that said *Love Me*… He peered closer. Damn it. It said *Blow Me.* He pulled that aside. He'd had some latex balloons he'd planned to blow up and leave outside her store. A plastic carnation with artificial scent. That would last. A good gift. And for a real treat, he'd gotten the number for a place that had people come and sing in cute costumes, something he might need to whip out now instead of saving it for last. The card read *Call Us for the Yiffing Experience.*

Maybe he could get them to sing "I'm Sorry" to her.

Except he wasn't sorry he cared. He still didn't understand how helping her had been a bad thing. But—

The doorbell rang.

He rose stiffly from his spot on the couch, his aches and pains taking some time to fade. His leg and ribs still bothered him, but his cheek was now just a colorful reminder of a fight, and his shoulder didn't hurt at all.

As he drew close to the front door, he saw Rena through a side window. His heart raced.

"One minute," he yelled and hurried back to her box to hide it.

Then he rushed to the door, calmed himself, and opened it. "Hello."

She looked a little nervous but still just as beautiful as the last time he'd seen her. Her braided-back hair made her look more sophisticated. Sexy but older. He preferred it loose.

"Can I come in?"

"Yes, yes." He flushed and stood back. "*Bitte.*"

"Thanks."

"I'm sorry," he blurted, wanting her to care for him once more. The days without her had been empty and gray. As if without her near, he'd never feel warm again.

She gave him a guarded look, and even that made everything better. "O-kay." She sighed. "Do you mean it?"

"Yes, I don't want you mad at me. I'm sorry." He'd say it a million times if she'd forgive him.

"Good. So you won't make decisions for me again, right?" She looked him in the eye.

He didn't want to lie, but… "I will try not to."

"I guess that works." She sounded grumpy. Then she handed him something. A pet carrier, and it had something in it.

He held it up to see what she had in there. "The Chihuahua? You still have him? I thought you had left him at the vet to foster."

She shrugged. "I was going to, but they had a huge intake of dogs from a pet hoarder and needed my help. Plus he's so small. I worry he'll just sit there with his blind eye and ripped ear and get passed over. And his attitude isn't helping." She glared down at the dog, but he could see her fighting a smile. Especially when the dog looked at her and barked on cue.

"Hey, little guy. I missed you." Axel crooned to him, and the dog calmed at once, so he set down the cage.

"That is *so* unfair. I've been the one feeding you, Chi-Chi."

"Nice name." He wouldn't smile.

"Yeah? What do you call your pregnant cat?" Who happened to waddle up to them, sniffing at the cage.

"I do not have a cat."

Chi-Chi yapped once then put his nose at the bars. The cat sniffed him back, and they touched noses.

Axel knelt to let the dog out, prepared to scoop him up if he tried to hurt Queen. But the dog sniffed her for some time, and the cat let him. Then he started investigating Axel's home, his nose to the floor, the cat trailing.

"Well?" Rena asked.

"Well what?"

"What's her name?"

"Queen," he muttered, beaten.

"Ha. You are such a softie!"

He frowned at her and went back into the living room. For a little payback, he turned on the video. "And for this, I am sorry as well."

She stared at it, dumbfounded. "Oh my God. That's… What is wrong with Snoopy that Woodstock—wait, that's not… That is NOT the cartoon I remember!" She leaned closer. "Um, he, ah, he's very excited right now."

Axel grinned. "He does seem glad to be around all his naked friends."

"Poor Charlie Crown." She shook her head and turned away. "That is just so wrong."

He chuckled. "Never again. I swear. Your next gift will be—"

"*No.* No. You don't need to keep buying me stuff." She sounded adamant.

"Now, *Häschen,* how will I prove myself if I cannot shower you with gifts?"

She gave him a pained smiled and said weakly, "Oh, sure. Okay." She cleared her throat. "Actually, there is something I need from you."

"Tell me." He leaned against the back of the couch and crossed his arms over his chest.

"Well, remember when those girls took your picture at the diner?"

"That was odd."

"I think it's your haircut."

"Huh?"

"Tommie ended up taking a picture of you in the salon right after I did your hair. She shared it on Instagram the other day. And it went viral."

He thought about that. "Okay. This should be good for business, *ja*?"

She nodded. "You know, I did wonder why the phones started ringing off the hook. And why so many of the new clients seem to be guys wanting a Ragnar 'do, whatever that is."

"What?"

"Never mind. The thing is, my friend, the one who writes romance books, well, she wants you to be the cover model for her next book."

"Me?" He started laughing.

"Yes, you." She didn't laugh with him, so he forced himself to stop. "What's so funny about romance books?"

"Nothing. But that you want my face on a cover? That's crazy."

She studied him. "Not really. You're hotter than any of the guys on my book covers."

"Really?" He was interested in the once-over she was giving him, especially when she stopped at his fly and stared.

"Um, yep." She swallowed. "So if you really want me to forgive you, you should say yes to Abby's book."

"And you'll forgive me, *Häschen*? No more silent treatment?"

"I think it was the other way around. And speaking of which—"

"*Nein. Nein.* We are forgiving each other."

"Wait. I'm not the one who's sorry." She looked confused and irritated.

"I am. So much. So sorry I have waited so long to give you pleasure."

"I—what?" Stopped in mid-rant, she just stared as he unbuttoned his jeans and watched him unzip.

"Turn around and I will show you how sorry I am."

CHAPTER

SEVENTEEN

He'd been dreaming about this forever. Bending his woman over and taking her. Fucking her until she screamed his name.

Constantly prepared for any chance to be with Rena, he always kept a condom in his wallet. He pulled it out and shoved his clothes down to take himself out. Having her watch him put it on made him even harder.

"Y-you're really big."

"And ready for you. Can I get you ready for me?"

She groaned and dragged him the last few inches closer to kiss him. The press of her mouth stole his breath, but it was her hand over his cock that shocked him even more. He hadn't felt her move. One minute he was waving in the wind, the next he felt her hand through the latex.

He continued to kiss her as she stepped out of her shoes and lifted her skirt. A filmy, loose-flowing fabric that slid up her thighs easily.

"Axel," she moaned when he kissed his way up her neck.

"I will fill you up while you cry my name," he promised and turned her around. He pulled her back, which thrust her hips out, and lifted her skirt to rest over her back. Then he slid her panties down, following the path of her smooth skin, palming an ass he couldn't get enough of. So he kissed each cheek and smiled. "I'm kissing your ass, Rena. So much do I care for you."

She laughed. "I'll remember that." Then she groaned when he slid his hands between her thighs, widening her stance, and rose behind her.

"You're so wet," he breathed, trembling with the need to fuck her. But the sight of her, waiting, all his for the taking, forced him to savor this time.

He pushed himself inside her so slowly, moaning as her heat enveloped him. From behind, he felt even bigger, stretching her as he thrust.

"Oh yes, *yes,*" she hissed as he reached around and fingered her.

She jerked, and he slid deeper.

"Fuck." He pulled back and slowly pushed back inside.

"More," she insisted.

But he wouldn't be rushed. He tortured them both, giving her the whole of him but at such a slow pace she started flexing her hips to rush him.

And then he pressed harder over her taut flesh, and she cried out.

More warmth surrounded him, a flood of pleasure knowing she'd come, and he started fucking her harder. With wilder strokes, until he couldn't hold back any longer.

He surged one final time and stiffened, jetting into her and feeling finally at home.

When he finished, he lay over her, kissing her skin wherever he could reach without pulling out.

"Axel." She sighed. "You're so good at this."

"So are you," he said, and she murmured something he couldn't make out.

As he started to soften, he withdrew. "I'll be right back." He tossed the condom in the bathroom trash and hurried to straighten his clothes. Then he came back with a warm washcloth and wiped her between her legs.

"Axel, I can do that." She turned around, looking embarrassed.

"It's my pleasure to do this. I want to take care of you. The way you take care of me," he said when she looked as if she'd argue.

"You think I take care of you?"

He finished cleaning her and watched as she stepped back into her panties and pulled down her skirt.

"You make me a better man. Around you I'm calmer. I feel good. Your smile makes everything bright."

She just watched him. "That's so romantic."

"No, I don't know romance. I just know the truth. And you are the most wonderful woman I have ever known." He paused. "Well, not counting my *mutter*."

She smiled. "I knew what you meant. You're so sweet."

"Not sweet. Honest."

"Well, Honest Axel, something we need to get straight."

"Yes?"

"No more hurrying away from an argument. We should talk it out."

He nodded to make her happy. But he knew he'd leave her the next time they argued and wouldn't feel bad about it. Better he take some time to cool down than say—or *do*—something he'd regret.

The next evening, Axel took Rena out to a movie. He'd argued against her choice but eventually gave in to a romantic comedy he'd secretly been wanting to see.

She offered a compromise. "We'll see the new superhero flick next week, okay?"

"Fine." He couldn't wait for the movie to start and had just muted his phone when he saw a message from J.T. that said *URGENT* in big bold letters.

"You need to turn your phone off," she whispered as the lights went down for the previews.

But when he read what J.T. had to say, he knew their evening wouldn't be filled with laughter and smiles. Not at all.

They arrived at Rena's salon to see a fire truck and several bodybuilder types standing around the back, watching as firefighters put out the fire.

"Oh no." Rena bolted from the truck before he'd turned off the vehicle.

"Wait," he cautioned too late and hurried to join her.

One of the bodybuilders caught her before she could rush toward the truck. "Hold on, Miss."

Axel reached them and drew Rena into his arms, feeling for her as they watched her shop burn.

The back half of her shop, where the graffiti had been, was black, but the firefighters continued to hose down the inside. "How much damage? Does anyone know?" he asked, though it was probably too early to tell.

"We were driving by and stopped to try to help. We're firefighters off duty," one of the men said, turning around. He had sandy-colored hair and a large build. He saw Rena, now sobbing in Axel's arms, and expressed sympathy. "At least it looks like they got here in time to stop any major damage."

Axel had no idea what that meant. "What happened?" He turned to Rena. "No one was working tonight, were they?"

She gasped. "No, they shouldn't have been."

J.T. pulled up and soon joined them. "This sucks."

Axel nodded.

The off-duty firemen in front of them lasered in on Rena. All of them looked athletic, fit, and strong. The two white guys wore shirts with an animal rescue logo on them. The one with a darker tan and the African American with huge biceps wore Seattle FD shirts.

"Are you the owner?" the sandy-haired one who'd spoken earlier asked.

Axel answered for her since Rena had a tough time not crying. "She is. And she had a problem a few days ago with some graffiti. This might have escalated."

"Well, shit—er, shoot," the black firefighter said. "That's awful. Did you report the graffiti?"

"She took pictures," Axel said, aware of J.T.'s scowl. "But reporting it would have done little. We only think we knew who did it."

"Racist assholes," J.T. muttered.

Axel wanted to change the subject because Rena's tears were tearing him up; he hated that she'd been hurt again. And he hadn't been able to stop it. "Are you all firefighters, or are you two"—he spoke to the guys in the vet rescue shirts—"animal people?"

The darkly tanned man smiled. The tallest of the bunch, he spoke with a Southern accent. "We're all FD, part of the new station as a matter of fact. I'm Tex."

"Brad," the sandy-haired man said and held out a hand. "That's Reggie, and that's Mack." He pointed to the black man and the other white guy. "We actually do both. Firefighting and helping rehome strays."

"Oh." Rena wiped her eyes while Axel kept close for support, his hands on her shoulders. "I've been fostering a stray Chihuahua I found outside the shop a week ago. And Axel's got a pregnant cat. Unless he's planning on keeping the cat and her kittens, they'll need good homes."

Axel nodded. "Axel Heller. This is Rena Jackson and her cousin, J.T."

Tex and Mack gave her more interest than Axel appreciated.

Brad frowned at them and stepped forward, holding out a hand. "It's a pleasure to meet you. Sure am sorry about your shop."

"Come on, guys." Reggie sounded disgusted. "Rena's got enough to worry about."

"What?" Tex sounded sincerely confused. "I'm thinking about those kittens. Wonder if we could get a station cat."

"We can help with the dog too if you want," Mack said. He looked at Axel's face. "Or not."

"Blink, Heller," J.T. murmured. "Can one of you guys find out what happened here? I was driving home when a friend saw flames and called 911, then called me to let me know."

"J.T. texted us at the movies," Axel said. "I swear, when I find Fletcher, we are going to have a serious talk. And then I'm going to beat him to—"

"Ah, Heller, might not want to share with guys from the fire department. Who know the police."

"Fletcher, huh? We can pass that name around, see what comes up." Reggie smiled. "We're always down with cleaning up the city."

"One racist prick at a time," Mack muttered, saw Rena's gaze on him, and coughed. "I mean one racist jerk at a time."

She finally relaxed and squeezed Axel's hand on her shoulder while wiping her eyes. "It's only a place. No one was hurt, right?"

"I'll be right back." Brad left.

One of the guys asked Rena a question about her salon, but Mack kept glancing at Axel.

"Problem?" Axel finally asked.

"You look so familiar." Mack frowned.

Then Rena laughed, almost hysterically, but at least she wasn't crying, and said to Mack, "This is the Viral Viking."

J.T. blinked. "Seriously? That's you, Heller?" He started laughing as well.

"It's not funny."

Mack nodded. "Oh, right. The guy all the women are getting so excited over. Dude, you're a minor celebrity."

Tex looked him over. "Huh. Maybe we could get him to come to one of our adoption weekends."

The others stared at Axel and made him uncomfortable.

"Ah, I—"

"I would think having hunky firemen at the adoptions would be enough to generate interest," Rena said in a flirty voice.

He blinked down at her then at the firemen, realizing she'd probably find them attractive, that was if she liked muscular idiots who ran toward fire and not away.

"Well, I don't know that I'd say hunky," Tex responded, his grin a little too wide.

"More like sexy or incredible. We like those adjectives," Mack rallied.

Reggie rolled his eyes. Axel liked *him.*

Then J.T. asked about the site for Seattle's new fire station because he couldn't remember from the news.

Axel grew bored with the fire department guys until he overheard mention of a sweet little Chevelle parked by the side of the road. He turned. Even in the dark it looked pristine, shining under the lamplight overhead.

"What do you think, Heller?" J.T. asked.

He saw Rena engaged with Reggie and found it safe to step away for a minute. He took a few strides to the car and noticed some spots that could use a touch-up.

Mack, Tex, and J.T. joined him.

"Not bad. Needs new paint."

"I know." Mack sighed. "I've been trying to find someone."

J.T. said, "You want the best paintwork in town, you should come to Heller. His custom work is insane."

"If this were mine, I'd restore the mirror finish." Axel nodded. "A classic tuxedo-black paint with white SuperSport stripes. That fading white is no good."

Mack looked interested. "This was my dad's car. You think you could make it shine again?"

"Maybe." He saw Reggie smiling at Rena a little too long and left the car to return to her side.

Brad returned, not looking happy. "It's an obvious case of arson, I'm afraid. The cops have been called."

"What was it?" Reggie asked.

"This isn't official, but it looks like someone threw a rock through a front window and tossed a lit bottle of gasoline after it. They found two other bottles near the front as well, one that hadn't caught fire, so that's the assumption of the incendiary—what started the fire. The truck got here in time, so the damage looks worse than it really is. I imagine if the fire had spread to the chemicals in your salon, it would have been a real blaze and still burning."

Rena clutched Axel's hand.

"When can she start the cleanup?" Axel asked for her.

"That I don't know," Brad said. "Cops will be asking questions, and if I were you, I'd let them know about the graffiti."

Rena sighed. "I still have a picture of it on my phone."

"Man, I'm sorry." Reggie patted her on the shoulder. "But trust me, it could be a lot worse."

She nodded. Axel waited with her while another firefighter, this one suited up, came to talk to her. She answered what she could, but in the end she had a burned-up shop and no idea when she could get back to work.

Axel drove Rena back to her home and prodded her to pack whatever she needed to feel comfortable staying with him for the weekend. That she didn't argue at all spoke to her volume of pain. Once she had a bag, he drove them to his house, where he drew her a bath.

She sat in bubbles, tears tracking down her cheeks. "Will you come in with me?"

He joined her and held her tight, comforting as he whispered sweet words of compassion. And promised himself he'd take Fletcher apart piece by piece, and he'd make sure to leave the body where everyone could see.

Rena snuggled next to Axel in his big bed. The cat and dog slept together on the memory-foam doggie bed he'd bought for the cat. It was too cute, and something she hadn't processed earlier, too caught up in her own drama.

She studied her sleeping giant, watching his chest rise and fall as a sliver of moonlight bathed him through the blinds.

He had tattoos of thorns and the Grim Reaper, as well as a snake devouring its own tail which wrapped around his biceps, and what looked like monsters hiding in flames. Spooky and a little off-putting. Yet they covered a man who showed her in so many ways that she could count on him.

She didn't know what to do about the shop. But that would come. In the morning, she'd text the girls to let them know work would not be happening Monday morning. And she'd need to find alternate accommodations for her clients. She had a pretty good feeling she could find herself and the rest of them temporary accommodations. She knew a lot of other stylists in town, was friendly with most of them.

Then too, the girls might know where they could set up temporarily. With any luck, she wouldn't lose too many clients or her stylists because of something over which she'd had no control.

A sniff worked its way out, then another.

"Shh," Axel murmured, his voice thick with sleep, and turned to her. "I will protect you, *Liebling.*"

She turned so he could spoon her, tucking her into his much-larger frame. She felt toasty warm and cared for. And no longer so sad.

Recalling her evening felt surreal. From a movie to a fire. The girls would be shocked and annoyed they'd missed out on hunky firemen. The men had all been handsome and strong, with that protective aura firefighters had. Reggie had been particularly good-looking, and Brad too. But it had been Axel who'd been there, who'd given her that strong shoulder to cry on. He'd shown her in so many ways how much he valued her.

I think I love him.

The bath had been for her comfort, and she'd shed her share of tears. He hadn't once tried to sex her up or demand she do anything but "Cry it out, *Häschen,* you deserve it."

She fell asleep with his arm holding her close.

And she awoke to the smell of something fabulous.

A kiss pulled her out of a dreamless sleep. "Time to get up." A slap on the butt made her frown, but his deep chuckle earned a smile out of her. "I let you sleep in. Time for strawberry French toast and coffee."

Her favorites. She blinked her eyes open and saw that fine ass leaving the room. When she sat up, she realized her favorite silk scarf covered her head. She'd been so out of it last night before coming to bed. She remembered him helping her dress and asking about what she wanted to do with her hair.

She hurried to the bathroom and found he'd done a halfway decent job of wrapping her curls.

Then she noticed what she was wearing. The same bunny pajamas he'd seen the first time he'd come to her house. As well as the same scarf.

She fixed her head wrap and joined him in the kitchen, trying not to feel self-conscious that he'd seen her with her face off—sans makeup and her hair not done. So when she came into the kitchen, she paused, feeling shy.

He had two plates in his hands on his way to the dining area and placed them next to each other, with fancy glasses and crystal candle-holders, complete with long red tapers he'd lit.

"You're here. *Gut.*" He looked up, saw her, and got the goofiest smile. One full of what she'd swear would look like love on any other man. On Axel, she wondered.

"Thanks for last night" came out softer than she'd intended. She coughed. "I was in no condition to help myself."

He drew her into a hug, and she sighed, sniffing him and loving his scent. Was it his cologne? His soap? Maybe his laundry detergent? Whatever it was, it gave her comfort.

He leaned down to kiss her, and his lips lingered. "You feel better?"

"Yes, thanks."

He took her by the hand and led her to a seat at the table. After pulling out a chair for her, he waited for her to sit.

She felt nervous and feminine and cared for. And weird for being nervous around a man she knew intimately.

"Eat, *Häschen.* You need your energy." He frowned. "But I'm glad you slept. You needed it."

"What time is it?" she asked as she sipped her coffee. Axel, she noticed, wore a pair of jeans and a heather-gray T-shirt, showing off a hint of those amazing tattoos on his right arm. His hair looked styled, his eyes smiling. *Soooo handsome. And all mine.*

Isn't he?

"It's after one."

"Oh my gosh. I have so much to do." She started to stand, but he stopped her.

"Don't be mad at me, okay? I called Del and explained to her what J.T. already had. She called your employees, though I imagine Lou already told Stella. The ladies will come here later to talk to you about your options. And I've already discussed with some friends about things you can do once you have talked to your landlord about insurance and everything."

She just stared at him.

He fidgeted. "I am not trying to take over. I just—"

She left her chair and flew into his arms. "Thank you."

"Oh, Rena. Don't you know I would do anything to make all this go away? You deserve to be happy, *Liebling. Ich liebe dich.*" The German words again.

She pulled back and took his face in her hands. "But I am happy when I'm with you."

His eyes seemed full of emotion, and their stare seemed to connect them on a deeper level.

"Rena." He sighed. "I have to tell you. I—"

Someone rang the doorbell.

They glanced at the door.

"Are the girls supposed to be here?"

He shook his head. "Not until three."

She'd have time to freshen up before then, to put on her armor, so to speak.

"You eat, please. I'll get the door." He leaned way down to pet the dog, once again followed by the cat, she noticed with a smile.

A moment later, he opened the door.

No one spoke.

She looked over but couldn't see past Axel's big body blocking the doorframe.

"What the fuck are *you* doing here?" came out in a low growl.

She ate her French toast, knowing she'd need sustenance to survive this next bit of drama.

Because for whatever reason, she and Axel seemed to be magnets for it.

CHAPTER EIGHTEEN

Axel stared in shock at the older brother he hadn't seen in five years. Maksim Heller looked like a slightly shorter version of their father—and exactly like Axel save for a few superficial differences. He wore his hair back in a sophisticated short cut, was clean-shaven, and wore a suit that likely cost what Axel paid himself each month as a salary.

"Hello, brother." Maksim greeted him in German, and Axel figured German was the best way to converse, to keep Rena out of family business she had no part of.

Unfortunately, Rena entered the living room and stopped dead.

Maksim stared with curiosity but said nothing.

"Who's this?" she asked, comparing them, her eyes wide.

"Rena, this is my brother, Maksim. Maksim, this is Rena, my girlfriend. *Häschen*, would you mind giving us some space to talk?"

"*Häschen*?" Maksim smiled. "Appropriate." He nodded to her and said in English, "I do like your pajamas."

She bit her lip. "Thanks. Nice to meet you. I'll, uh, go grab a shower."

She darted away, and he forcibly tugged his brother inside to close the door behind him. Queen had been looking a little too hard at the open door.

His brother spotted the cat and dog and grinned. "What is going on in this country? Dogs getting cats pregnant? Rabbits looking so fetching in yellow?"

"Why the hell are you here?"

"Father said he told you we'd be coming. I decided to come earlier. I have business in the city."

"And?"

Maksim sighed. "Might I have a cup of coffee? I think I smell some brewing."

"Fuck. Fine." Axel stomped to the kitchen, not caring whether Maksim followed. His brother had always been a huge pain in the ass. So polished and prissy. Always dutiful, the perfect son and heir to take over the family empire. He'd stayed behind in Germany when their mother had chosen to stay in the States with Axel. And when their father had wanted the company to branch out into other interests, it had been Maksim who'd made their first million with a car dealership that now had branches in northern Germany, France, and the United States.

Axel poured a cup of coffee into a mug and shoved it at his brother.

Maksim lifted a brow. "No milk or sugar?"

With a growl, Axel fetched him both. "Now talk fast so you can get out."

It still hurt that he'd never had a close family, something Axel had always wanted. A brother with whom he could play, share stories, seek advice. To have each other's backs, the way his friends and their siblings and cousins rallied around each other, family through thick and thin. But Maksim had always belonged to Jannik. Never to Ilse or Axel.

Truly his father's son, Maksim had treated their mother horribly. Not with the beatings as Jannik used to, but with an arctic silence.

"Your inheritance is waiting," Maksim stated. "What do you plan to do about it?"

"That's not your business." Frankly, he had no idea.

"Father expects you to invest it back in the company."

"Fuck that."

Maksim smirked.

"What?"

"I had a feeling you'd say that."

"Doesn't that bother you? That your precious father might be upset?"

Maksim paused. "Things are not the same with Father anymore. He is...how should I say this..."

"Batshit crazy? An abusive asshole who should be buried alive? A narcissistic creep who used our mother, turned you against her, and then lied about all of it?"

"Strong feelings."

"Fuck you too."

"I don't mean to make light of it. I—" He looked down into his cup, swirling the milky liquid. "I didn't know."

"You didn't *want* to know," Axel corrected him.

"Yes, you're right."

Axel frowned. He hadn't expected agreement. "So why do you believe now? What changed your mind?"

"A letter came a few weeks ago. Mother had left it with Aunt Hester. But Aunt Hester didn't want to tell me because she knew it would cause me pain."

So what? Axel had lived with pain for a very long time. Why shouldn't his perfect brother?

"Mother wrote about the abuse. All of it."

And that still stung, to know why she'd suffered for so long. For her children, two unworthy sons. One who had never stopped the abuse, the other who hadn't cared enough to believe it had occurred. The remembrance hurt so much. "Why believe her after death? You thought her a liar when she was still alive and told you the same thing."

Maksim frowned. "This isn't easy, Axel. Please."

"You know what? I lived with it all. With him beating the discipline into me while he held you up as the perfect son. And when I found out he was hitting Mom too, I tried to stop him. But not you. You called her a whore and a liar to her face. Do you have any idea how much that hurt her?"

Maksim's eyes, a shade lighter than Axel's, grew cold. "I only knew what he told me. That she had cheated on him, that you knew and covered it up. That you hated him and me and wanted to leave with her."

"So he beat me because I hated him? I hated him *because* he beat us." Axel scoffed. "And he hurt her why? Jannik Heller, the man who buried his dick in half the women in Bavaria, cared about fidelity? That man? She was loyal to him, and she shouldn't have been. I only wish she would have had an affair for some happiness in her marriage."

Maksim sighed. "I was young, and he was my father. I was supposed to believe him. And you weren't the only one he disciplined. The reason I was so perfect was because he'd beaten it into me. That's the way children should be raised, with a firm hand." He paused. "That's what I used to think. But you were a lost cause, always so violent with those episodes, so Father gave up on you. I had no idea he was hitting you too."

Axel frowned. "You saw my bruises."

"And when I asked Mother about them, she told me you got them from being an active little boy."

"She wouldn't say that."

"She would in front of Father. I think she did her best to protect us both. I'm only sorry I wasn't a better son." He paused. "But, Axel, you did have anger issues. Just like Father. I watched you lose your grip too many times to believe you hadn't earned at least a spanking or two."

"With a fucking belt?" Axel just stared at his brother.

"You don't remember how bad you would get. You hit Mother."

"I know what I did," he snapped. "But I didn't hit her on purpose. I was trying to hit you, you bastard."

"And you missed and hit her. So hard she had to be hospitalized for a fractured cheekbone. And you wouldn't calm down. They sedated you."

All Axel remembered was hurting his mother, the way his father had too many times. He'd lost control. "And I have never forgotten that. Ever. We left Germany and stayed in the U.S. She made sure I got a dual citizenship but never got one for herself." He paused. "Because she knew she was going home. I never understood why she wouldn't stay here. But at least she had her sister and nephews to help. Not you or Father."

"Yes, she had that." Maksim put the coffee down, his gaze sober. "Father intends to force you to turn over your shares in the company to him. And Mother's as well."

"The fucking shares. Of course. But how will he force me? I don't give a shit about his money. I don't want it."

"But you have it. And unless you do something with the shares at the next shareholders meeting, yours and Mother's can revert to him. And he can vote me out."

"Ah, so that's what this is all about. Keeping a place in the company so you don't lose it all."

"Axel, I'm a wealthy man in my own right. The original dealership is mine. But the company isn't a hundred percent his. Give me yours and Mother's shares, and I'll invoke my right to assign subsequent parties to handle them, namely Aunt Hester and Erik. Let them deal with him from now on."

"You expect me to believe that? That you'll just turn everything over to them?"

"No, I don't. But you don't have the authority. You can only vote the power to me, him, or the minority vote, and they'll never give everything to anyone but Father." He sighed. "I want you to think about this. I will see you next week when Father comes. But if you would, keep this between us. I don't want him to have time to prepare when I take everything he ever cared about."

Maksim walked to the door and switched to English. "And your girlfriend? Be warned. He's going to hate her."

"Fuck him."

"Is that why you're with her?"

Axel answered in German, "I'm with her because I love her. Not that I owe you any explanations."

"Of course not. But I'm happy for you, Little Brother." Maksim let himself out.

Confused and not knowing what to believe, Axel stared at the back of the door, lost in memories. The feel of his fist hitting his poor mother overwhelming.

"You don't know what I want," he yelled at Maksim as they stood on their aunt's farm on a crisp fall day. The sun shone overhead, and the pigs and chickens made noise as his cousins saw to the feeding. Jannik had spent

the weekend in the city, leaving them with their mother, who'd taken them to be with her family farther south. "You and Father always planning my life, trying to order me around. I just want to be with Mother and work on the farm."

"Well, you can't. We have responsibilities." Even at fifteen, Maksim was well aware of the Heller name and all that came with it. "Father says you grow soft around our weak mother. That you—"

"Father says this. Father says that. Maksim, can't you for once stop being his puppet?" Axel got up in his brother's face, nearly as tall as the older teenager, and pushed him. "He hurts Mom. Why do you always defend him?"

"He does not." Maksim shoved him back. "He works hard for us, putting food on the table, doing all he can to support his family. She's a liar."

Axel gave an angry laugh. "We have enough support, you idiot. And that's thanks to Grandmother and Grandfather and you know it! Dad is just a proud asshole who only inherited his money. What has he done to earn it?"

Maksim slugged him.

And it hurt. So he hit back.

The fight turned vicious, as it normally did when Axel grew angry. Even though Maksim tried to pull away, Axel wouldn't let him.

Their mother found them rolling around outside. "Maksim, no. You know Axel can't handle his aggression. Son, stop. Both of you. Please."

Enraged, Axel fought without thought or care. Tired of always being the one everyone dumped on. The stupid brother. The ill-disciplined brother. The disappointment.

He rolled and bit, kicked and punched. And when someone pushed between them, he didn't distinguish his mother's body from his brother's. He struck out.

The crack reverberated down his arm and bruised his hand.

But to the beautiful, thin, almost frail Ilse Heller, he did so much worse. She sailed back to the ground, in a daze, and lay there.

"Mom? Oh no. Mom?" He scrambled to see her, but his brother, and soon his aunt and cousins, pushed him back.

"Axel, what have you done?" Aunt Hester asked.

"I didn't mean to." He started crying, ashamed because he'd hurt her, ashamed because the anger had yet to abate. He wanted to strike out again, to keep on hitting.

"You're a monster, and you always have been," Maksim said, his voice cold.

But though Maksim had called her a liar, he hadn't yet fully turned on Ilse. That would come a few years later, when their father's lies wormed through affection and loyalty and shattered the family for good.

"Axel?"

Lost in bad memories, he was surprised by Rena's voice, and he jumped.

"Sorry. Did your brother go?"

He turned to see her looking at him oddly. "*Ja.*"

"I heard shouting. I guess you two still aren't getting along, huh?"

"No. And I don't think we ever will." He felt raw, his brother a reminder of all the reasons dating Rena was a bad idea. Remembrances of a violent past making him loath to talk or even think about seeing Maksim or Jannik again.

"Do you want to talk about it?"

"No," he said firmly, needing space, unable to process the happiness he'd so briefly touched with Rena. Because that fight with his brother had been one of many that he'd had at school and with classmates. He'd been a violent, moody teenager, and his sweet mother had deserved so much better.

It had taken a long time to get past his outbursts, to be able to control his violent tendencies. Yet not so long, he thought, recalling what he'd done to Rabies. The way he'd laid out Scott with one punch.

What if Rena had come between them? What if she'd put a hand on his shoulder and he'd turned and punched her instead?

"Sweetie, are you okay?" she asked softly.

He wanted to be. Very much. She needed him now. But he couldn't.

"I need to be alone for a bit," he managed without screaming his frustration, his voice cool. How had the day gone from so good to so bad in so short a time? "I'm sorry, but you should go."

"No, that's okay." Her smile looked too bright, and it didn't reach her eyes. "I'll get my things and go home." She had no car because he'd driven her last night.

"I'll drive you."

"No. I'll grab an Uber."

"No, I will…" At the sight of her mulish expression, he swallowed. "Okay. But text me when you get home, okay?" He paused. "Please."

She gave a stiff nod.

He wanted to follow her, to apologize and explain why he was scared and hope they'd work it out. But instead he did what came naturally. He distanced himself and watched in silence as she pushed past him and walked out the door.

"Be my Valentine, my ass," Rena snarled as she waited on an Uber to come pick her up. There had been one in the area, and it scooped her up and dropped her at home in no time.

She let herself inside and realized she'd forgotten the dang dog. Oh well. Chi-Chi would have to put up with that aggravating man's moods.

Honestly, it was like he was on his period. Happy one minute, kind and gentle, then angry and distant the next.

This pattern didn't bode well for a future between them. Rena liked to talk things out. Holding shit inside just made it worse. But Axel didn't seem to see that. Quiet, contained, and God forbid he get upset with someone. Then he'd either pound the crap out of them or ignore them.

Though she had to admit she'd prefer being ignored to being hit.

But the thought didn't fit because Axel had never once, in all the time she'd known him, been aggressive with her in any way. Well, not counting sex, and that happened only if she asked for it. If they started to argue about something serious, and not just what TV series to binge or which flavor of ice cream was best, he clammed up. *Yeah, well, silence is not always golden, Ragnar.*

She grumbled to herself as she returned her landlord's calls, pleased to hear sincere concern and a desire to get the building back up to code as soon as possible. Then she sent a group text to Stella, Tommie, and Nicky to meet at her place and spent her remaining hour cleaning up so she didn't look like a complete slob for company.

The girls, at least, gave her sympathy. Between the four of them, they managed to scrounge temporary places to work. It took a few hours, lots of phone calls, and an order of Chinese food to get everything right.

"So Tommie and I will be out in Green Lake," Rena recapped. She and Marla had gone to cosmetology school together and been friends ever since. "Stella, you're filling in at Winnie's."

"Yep." Stella munched on a second helping of cashew chicken. "Works for me."

"And Nicky, you said you're going to work out of your house?"

Nicky sighed. "It's not ideal, but I did that before I joined you. And I'd rather be there for my kids when they come home from school. We're having homework issues lately."

"Okay then." Rena sighed. "That took a lot of work. But we've updated the clients, so it looks like we're all set…for however long it takes to get the place fixed."

Thinking about the hell they'd gone through and how hard she'd worked to fund her store and find the right location made everything seem unbearable.

"Whoa. Now you cry?" Tommie pulled her into a hug.

"What's up, *chica*?" Stella asked, joining the hug. "We'll be good. You'll see."

Nicky nodded. "It's hitting you, isn't it? I thought you seemed pretty calm. Hell, I'm feeling stressed too."

Embarrassed she'd lost it when she'd been doing so well, Rena reached for the box of tissues and grabbed one. She blew her nose and everyone backed off.

"Whoa."

"Ew." Tommie made the sign of the cross. "What demon just screamed through your nose holes?"

"You mean her nostrils?" Nicky rolled her eyes. "But, yeah, that big old blow ain't very ladylike."

Rena snorted, then her eyes leaked some more. "It's not just the salon."

"Let me guess." Stella said some words in Spanish. "Heller's being a dick."

"Kind of. He's confusing the crap out of me." Rena wondered how much to share, then decided to share it all. When had she ever not? "Axel's been so supportive. He's been kind and sweet. And even though his gifts are weird, he means well." Which made her sad because she hadn't gotten anything today. She didn't care about the actual present; she loved the thought behind the gesture. "I mean, last night he was nothing but supportive. He ran me a bath and held me when I cried. And he told me how pretty and great I am. Then this morning he looked *through* me and told me to get out. He needed space." She sighed. "I just don't understand the man."

Stella shrugged. "Does he take medication?"

"Stella." Nicky shook her head.

"What? It's a thing. I've got a few friends who need medication to balance their moods."

"Well, I guess that's true, he could have a condition." Rena frowned. "But I don't think that's it. He was fine until his brother showed up."

The room grew silent.

"*Oooo.*" Tommie leaned forward. "What's his brother like?"

Rena had to smile. "Like Heller but without the facial hair, wearing a killer suit, with a killer haircut and looking like a million bucks. They look like twins, except Maksim, his brother, is maybe an inch or two shorter."

Tommie fanned herself. "I'm in love."

"His brother arrived, so I left them privacy with an excuse about grabbing a shower. But I made it a fast one because I didn't want to miss too much. They were arguing in German, so I couldn't really understand anything. But Axel sounded so mad. Then I think his brother saw me because he switched to English and said that their dad would hate me."

"Oh boy." Tommie winced.

Stella's eyes narrowed. "What did Heller say?"

"That's what's weird. First he said, 'Fuck him.' Then when Maksim asked if that was why Axel was with me, because his dad wouldn't like me, Axel switched back to German."

"Frankly, I can't see Heller doing anything he doesn't want to do," Stella said.

Nicky and Tommie seemed to agree.

"I know, but… This is the second time we've argued, and he just pushes me away. Is this what being in a relationship with him will be like? When it's good, it's great, but when it's bad, we don't exist?"

Nicky shrugged. "That's a good question. Personally, when my guy and I argue, we yell a lot until we're through. Then we have makeup sex."

"I've been with the cold-shoulder types," Tommie said. "It sucks. I'm not into passive-aggressive."

"Me neither." Stella and Tommie high-fived. "Which is why my guy is such a catch."

"That and he's gorgeous," Tommie said dryly.

"Well, that doesn't hurt." Stella grinned.

"Ahem. We were talking about *my* problems?" Rena cut in.

Stella coughed. "Sorry. Go on."

"So Axel's nonsense on top of the fire at the salon makes me feel like I'm spinning my wheels and not going anywhere." Rena sighed. "That's it. All of the rest of what I had to say. And I'm sorry for dumping on you guys."

"We're friends. That's what we're here for." Tommie and the others nodded.

Someone banged on the door.

Her heart raced. Axel. She stumbled to her feet and nearly tripped in her haste to reach it. But when she pulled it open, she found Del, Colin, her mom, Uncle Liam, and Sophie standing there.

"Here, Aunt Rena." Colin handed her a little red bag with hearts all over it. "This was on your doormat."

She took it and let them all in. And did her best not to burst into tears all over again when Colin gave her a big hug and said, "Mom said you needed this. But don't worry. I brought you some gum too. And I'm going to find out who burned your hair place and beat them up for you."

Del chuckled. "He heard a lot from Mike and the gang last night. We had dinner together and were talking about what we could do for you. We came up with a plan."

Her mother kissed her cheek. "I see we aren't the only ones planning. You all have Chinese?"

"Yep. The gang and I have been moving around appointments."

Stella waved. "Hi, Liam, Del. Hey Colin! And everyone else."

Caroline waved back. "I'm Rena's mom, Caroline." She made introductions while Rena tried to disentangle herself from Colin, who was still clinging. "I brought pie and cookies. Now let's see what you've all come up with."

Colin put a piece of gum in her hand and shot a glance at his mom, who was talking with Tommie and Nicky. "Don't tell. It's the sugar kind."

"I won't. Thanks, sweetie."

That he let her kiss him told her just how much Colin worried. He held her hand and wouldn't leave her side.

Sophie smiled at him and looked around at everyone. "I love your family, Liam."

He smiled back then yanked Colin away so he could hug his niece.

"Hey," Colin scowled.

"Go get pie."

That scowl disappeared in a heartbeat, and Sophie followed the boy into the kitchen.

"Now, Rena, you tell me exactly what happened. Starting from the graffiti," Liam ordered. "But first, what's in the bag?"

She glanced down. "You didn't bring it?"

"Nope. It was sitting in front of your door when we arrived."

She opened it and saw another grotesque little troll, this one with bright-yellow hair. This troll held a tiny printed card that read *Be Mine.* Written underneath it was the word *bitte.*

She sighed. "It all started with an angry, ragey,"—*lovable*—"confusing German and a fight at Ray's."

CHAPTER NINETEEN

By Wednesday morning, Axel couldn't handle much more bullshit. He had only fifteen days and counting until Valentine's Day, and he was no closer to fixing things with Rena than he was to finding Fletcher. The bastard had gone to ground.

On top of being on the outs with Rena, he'd had two cancellations that he'd slotted important time for, so he'd been tap-dancing to move around the schedule while dealing with drama at the shop and the ever-present threat of his family ready to drop in on him at any time.

He'd made it clear to his brother over the phone that their father was *not* welcome at his house. About Maksim, he'd done a lot of thinking.

He and his brother had never been enemies, not until Maksim had turned on their mother. With only two years separating them, they could have been close. Their father had seen to it that neither would have the chance, grooming Maksim to take over the business while shuttling Axel to one family member or another, keeping the boy well away from him because of his "mood issues," what their mother had called his episodes.

Looking back on it, he had to acknowledge he'd had a problem.

He'd been angry and prone to violent outbursts when young, though never to his mother. As he'd gotten older, his moods had worsened. He recalled taking medication and being sent to work on the farm, talking a lot to his aunt—a licensed therapist. Working on Aunt Hester's farm had done much to soothe him, and he'd gotten to spend extra time with his mother.

They'd grown so close, and then he'd struck her, something he'd sworn never to do. It had changed something inside him, hurt him in a way no beating ever could. Though she'd forgiven him immediately, he'd never been able to forgive himself, conscious he was a lot more like his father than he wanted to admit.

For years after that, he'd focused that anger, worked on controlling it. He did his best to make his mother proud, protecting those who couldn't protect themselves. He kept in shape and got bigger and stronger. He fought to challenge himself, drawing on the numbness, taking anger out of the equation so that brawling became a form of exercise, a therapeutic outlet. One he was good at.

As time passed, his rages turned more sporadic, until he was simply a man who dealt with anger by either pounding his fists or suppressing the emotion until it went away. Mostly he never allowed himself to feel too much. Love for his mother. Loyalty to a few friends and family—Aunt Hester and a few cousins. For all intents and purposes he and his brother ignored each other.

So his mother's passing had hit him hard. With it came responsibilities. And a lot of money he didn't want or deserve.

Hell, he didn't want to deal with any of it, but he knew the time had come.

He groaned and sat in the dark in his office, needing more time to deal with his fluctuating moods. Rena had filled that void so well, keeping him happy and balanced. He now felt empty all the time. He'd fucked up by sending her away. Now that he could think about it rationally, he knew he wouldn't hurt her.

He hoped he wouldn't.

Hitting his mother had been an accident. But dealing with his family brought up his ugly past.

"I'm talking to you," Rylan shouted.

And then there was all the bullshit in the shop. Mateo normally kept himself busy sanding and dealing with the smaller one-man jobs. Unfortunately, that left Rylan and Smitty to work together. And lately, Rylan had become a constant headache. How Smitty hadn't yet shoved the guy's head up his ass was anyone's guess. Even Lou had commented on it, and Lou got along with everyone in the shop.

"Okay, Rylan. It's just you and me now. Let's have it out." Smitty sighed.

Apparently they hadn't realized Axel was here, though his truck sat in the parking lot. But he hadn't turned on the office lights, the room lit by a light-sensitive nightlight he liked to leave in the office. He had the shades drawn, so it looked as if the office sat empty.

He glanced down at his new office mates, Chi-Chi and Queen, who lay together on Queen's cat bed. Rena had left the dog behind on Saturday, and the poor canine whined whenever he tried to pull the pair apart. Since Queen seemed to like Chi-Chi well enough, Axel left them together.

Rena hadn't called to complain.

He rubbed his heart. She hadn't called at all. Not to yell at him, to respond to his texts checking in, or to say she'd been receiving his presents.

Fifteen days seemed like too short a time to win her back.

If he'd ever had her in the first place.

Maybe she'd seen the real him, and she'd been gently trying to get away for days. Maybe she realized that great sex couldn't hold them together and that she needed a *hunky firefighter* to make it all better.

He frowned, wondering if any of those bastards had reached out to help her.

"You have a real problem with me, don't you?" Rylan snapped.

"I do. You're too emotional," Smitty growled. "I'm tired of playing nursemaid. You have skills, kid, but—"

"Who the fuck are you calling kid? You're maybe two years older than me."

"Then why do I feel like your daddy? Because you act like a teenager. Quit with the moods and get to fucking work. It's a job, not recess, dickwad."

Ouch. Smitty could be the king of put-downs, and he insulted in a calm, low voice that could be all the more annoying because he didn't seem to care whether you got mad or not.

"Fuck you."

"Oh, that hurts." Smitty snorted. "Look, you're not half bad at the job. You know what you're doing, mostly. So what the hell is the problem? Mateo comes, does the job, goes home. Same with me. Same with Heller."

"Please." Rylan gave an angry laugh.

Axel tensed.

"The boss is one snarl away from going rabid. The guy is either quiet or pissed off with no in-between."

Smitty said sharply, "And he's your boss, you dumb shit. How many guys do you know who'd offer an ex-con a job with the way you've been acting?"

"No, that's not it. You don't hate me because I was in jail. Tell the truth."

Smitty's loud sigh echoed in the otherwise quiet bay. "I don't hate you at all, Rylan."

"You fucking do." Rylan swore. "Fuck, I *know* you do. You saw me. Outside that bar with that guy."

What? Axel stood and crossed the room to peer through the slats in the blinds.

Rylan and Smitty were so focused on each other they didn't spare a glance back at the office.

Smitty scrubbed his hair. "Look, Rylan, I don't care who you fuck or where. I mean, not here. It's the shop. But what does that—"

"I knew it! So I was getting some action. I'm not a fag. I was just hard up, that's all." Rylan sounded panicked. "I'm not gay."

Smitty's fists clenched. "Okay, that's it." He stalked Rylan, but instead of pounding the guy, he shoved him up against the wall with little effort.

Axel watched, impressed. Smitty in a mad was nothing to play with. The guy had muscle and knew how to use it. And he'd done his share of time behind bars long ago. Rylan didn't corner the market on mistakes.

"Let's get this straight," Smitty enunciated very clearly. "You think I'm anti-gay and that I hate, and I quote, 'fags.'"

Rylan blinked a lot. "Y-yeah." A big guy himself, he seemed awfully weak in the face of Smitty's anger.

Smitty just held him there, Rylan up on his tiptoes. "You're a prick, you know that? *Fag* is not a nice word. You say it again in this shop or anywhere around me, I'll fucking knock your head off."

"But—"

"Second, *I'm gay,* you asshole. You want to get a blowjob against the wall of a scummy bar? That's up to you. But I could give you a ton of other, cleaner places to go to get some action." Then he leaned forward and planted a kiss on Rylan's mouth that left Axel speechless.

That he hadn't been expecting at all.

"And third, you're cute. A dumbass, but you'd rock a leather harness. You figure out what you want to use that dick for instead of stepping all over it, you let me know." He moved back, and Rylan sagged against the wall. "Bitch, quit acting like the world revolves around you and your sexual proclivities and get to work. We're all about professional, and the clock starts now."

Smitty turned on the radio and went about his day as if he hadn't just kissed his coworker against the wall.

Axel turned and went back to his seat, laughing to himself. That had been one huge can of worms he hadn't had to deal with, at least. *Well, now, do I leave the office and pretend nothing happened, or do I say something?*

Awkward.

"Hello. We are looking for Axel Heller?" That voice he recognized. Maksim.

"My son," came another voice.

Shit.

Axel threw open the office door and stalked toward the unwelcome intruders.

Smitty's eyes grew wide, and Rylan turned beet-red when they saw him. Mateo entered behind his family with Kelly in tow.

"Hey, guys. Look who's back!"

Kelly grinned, the scruffy paint expert a welcome arrival, and asked, "What did I miss?"

"Not much," Smitty said after clearing his throat. His cheeks looked slightly pink, but he met Axel's gaze with an amused one of his own. "I'm gay and proud of it. Heller's dad and I'd guess brother just arrived. Oh, and we now have a pregnant cat and a half-blind Chihuahua as mascots."

"Whoa. Big news." Kelly blinked. "I was kinda hoping you could just fill me in on the detail work for today, but okay."

Mateo took a good look at Jannik and Maksim and whistled. "Is everyone from Germany seven feet tall?"

Jannik Heller looked at Smitty and Rylan with disgust, apparently having overheard their private conversation. Maksim made no comment and didn't express much of anything.

Axel crossed to the conference room and opened the door with more force than needed. The door slapped against the wall. "In here," he growled.

Once his family had followed him, he reminded the guys about the new work orders on his desk then shut himself in with his enemies. Well, enemy and one he wasn't so sure about.

"Son, I am here to talk business."

Axel ignored him on purpose. "Maksim, would you like a coffee?"

"Please."

"Fine. Wait here."

He left and returned half an hour later. He brought the guys two dozen donuts and had two coffees to share with his brother as well as a breakfast sandwich for himself. He interrupted his brother and father arguing in German. They stopped when he entered.

"Where the hell did you go?" his father snarled. "My time is valuable."

"Then get the fuck out." He passed a coffee to his brother, who nodded his thanks.

Jannik blinked. "What did you say to me?"

Axel hadn't seen his father in years. Though they argued on the phone every few months, his contact with his relatives in Germany had been with his mother.

"You heard me. But you know, let's talk." He unwrapped his sandwich and took a bite, famished. His brother, he noted, sipped his coffee, remaining watchful. "Before we get to business and mother's and my shares, let's talk about how you lied for years about what you did to her."

"I did nothing." His father sniffed and tugged at his cufflinks. "She was not a good wife. She cheated on me."

"You're a fucking liar," Axel snapped back. Maksim, he noticed, kept quiet. "I haven't been the best son, I admit. But Mom ignored all your cheating and lies. She was a good woman, and you hurt her so much."

"That's not true." From Jannik's tone, it didn't seem as if he cared if they believed him. "Your mother did as she was told. But she clearly failed with you." His sneer didn't win him any favors with Axel. What was his father playing at? If he wanted cooperation, he was going about it the wrong way. "Ilse's shares should have come to me upon her death. But I'm fixing that. Axel, your time in the company is done. I'm buying you out, and as majority holder and committee chair, I can. It will take time and a lot of lawyers, but it's doable. But if you *sign* Ilse's shares to me, I promise to give you twice what they are worth and stock in JH Autoteile."

Axel snorted. "I don't need your money, old man."

"I am your father. You will talk to me with respect."

"Or what?" He prayed Jannik would try to hit him. Now as large as his father, Axel didn't need to cower. And he could certainly take the bastard in a fight. The need to pay his father back for all the times he'd hit their mother and she'd suffered in silence. For all the times he'd made her feel like nothing. The fights behind closed doors that would leave his mother feeling "sick" for days while she recovered from a beating.

He could have his revenge now. Hurt his father with the same size fists that had once landed on his own smaller body.

Forgiveness soothes many burdens, little bear, he could hear his mother say so clearly. *The pain comes from hate and anger. But letting it go will heal you better than any kisses from your mother.* She'd kissed his cuts then.

Young Axel hadn't understood. *But Mom, your kisses are better than anything.*

She'd smiled. *Well, maybe not better than kisses from your mother. But forgiveness heals where rage does not. Be better than him, Son. Don't be the same.*

"Or what?" His father barked a laugh. "Or I'll cut you from everything. The company, my will. You won't see one penny. Ever."

An inheritance his mother had been worried that he might not receive. So she'd put up with Jannik's bullshit, all to protect her sons' legacy.

Axel met Maksim's gaze, reading nothing.

And he didn't care. Not about any of it. He didn't want to fight them. He didn't want the money, and he hoped his mother would understand. She'd needed him to be well, never to want the way she had growing up poor. She'd wanted Axel to have a good life. But he'd made that for himself on his own.

He laughed, long and loud. Outside the office, he heard nothing but silence. "Fuck you and your will. I want nothing from you. And I don't own the shares anyway. Maksim does." He'd made the decision easily, uncaring of anything but getting under his father's skin. He'd given consent Monday and had gone to a partnered legal firm in the city yesterday and signed papers.

Millions of dollars, no longer his.

Instead of looking angry, his father smiled at Maksim. "Good work. I knew I could count on you." He turned to Axel with a smug grin. "Don't you see what you've done? You've lost after all. That money is *mine,* and I won't give you a cent. You failed her again. Ilse wanted that money for you, but you blew it. And why? Because you're a sorry little bastard I should have smothered at birth. Maksim makes me proud." His father gave a disgusted sigh. "*You* are a waste, a disgrace, a… What are you doing?"

Axel had grabbed the back of his father's jacket and trousers and was dragging him toward the door. He pushed through it, ignoring Jannik's threats. "Smitty, the door."

Smitty hurried ahead of him to open the front door. Axel tossed his father's ass right on out. In an unemotional voice, he said, "Get lost. You come back in here, I'll beat you to death. And no one will care. I have no money. No shares. Nothing you want. Don't ever talk to me again."

Then he turned and walked back to the conference room, aware of the stunned silence around them. He sat back down and stared at his brother, who'd helped himself to Axel's sandwich. "Hope you're happy with yourself."

Maksim ate, watching Axel with curiosity. "You don't mind that you have lost thirty million dollars?"

He shrugged. "It was never mine anyway. Our mother lived a nightmare to earn that money. I don't want it."

Maksim frowned. "She'd want you to have it."

"So what? Give it to him if you want. You lied to me to get it. Congratulations." He felt numb. "I really don't care."

"That's too bad." Maksim finished the egg sandwich and grabbed his coffee. "Because I do care, and I do want it. I'm giving it to Aunt Hester and Erik." He paused, maybe waiting for Axel to change his mind.

Axel sensed something different about his brother. "You're really not working with Jannik, are you?"

Maksim finally smiled. And it was an expression filled with ill intent. "Oh, I'm working with Jannik. When I'm done with that prick, he won't have his claws in the family company anymore. Sadly, he'll still be wealthy, but legally I can only do so much."

Knowing how pissed off their father would be, Axel nodded. "Okay then."

Maksim walked with him toward the exit. "You don't want any of the money? You could… You could come back home, be a part of the business. We could find something for you to do. Cars are in our blood."

Surprised Maksim would even offer such a thing, Axel paused by the door and studied his brother. "My home is here," he said slowly. "But maybe you could come and stay for a while. Take a vacation sometime and enjoy Seattle."

"Maybe I could." Maksim blinked in surprise. Then he smiled. "I'll make sure to record Jannik's expression when he learns of all he lost."

"Now that is a real gift."

Maksim chuckled. "Best of luck to you, Brother." He held out a hand.

Axel shook it. "And you."

"I will take you up on that offer of a vacation."

"See that you do." He stared after his brother and watched the car pull away.

When he turned, he saw everyone looking at him.

"What?" he barked.

"Nothing, Boss," Kelly was quick to reply.

Axel sighed. "Ah, Kelly. I missed you."

Kelly grinned.

"Suck up," Mateo muttered.

Rylan looked nervous and darted a look back at Smitty. "Heller, um—"

"*Nein.* No more drama." Axel groaned. "And no more kissing in the garage. It's a shop, not a singles bar."

Smitty laughed. "Rylan, if you could see your face."

"Shut up, old man." But Rylan had to bite back a grin.

Then Kelly turned on some God-awful country music, and the shop got back to normal, arguing over radio stations, the sound of a spray gun and sander filling the garage.

Axel sat back in his office and put his hands behind his head, aware he'd crossed a huge hurdle today. He'd shoved his father out of his life, hopefully for good. And he'd partially mended a bridge with his brother. Now if he could just figure out how to handle the heartache left by the beautiful woman who no longer seemed to want him in her life.

I have fifteen days to win her over. He prayed it wasn't too late.

Noise by the cat bed made him take a second look, and he froze. Queen was circling her bed and panting. Then she lay down, still panting, and started cleaning herself while the dog stood like a sentry off the bed, his focus on the cat.

The kittens were coming.

"Shit." He hurried out of the office and grabbed some clean towels and rags.

"What's up?" Smitty asked.

"I think Queen's about to have her kittens."

"Seriously?" Smitty dropped paint samples to the table and followed Axel back into the office.

The others soon followed.

Axel placed towels under the cat and crooned to her in German, petting her hesitantly until she purred and rolled to her back.

"Don't touch her too much," Smitty cautioned, looking at his cell phone. "It says here some cats don't want you to touch them."

Axel started to pull his hand back when the cat wrapped her paws—and dug in with her claws—around his wrist.

"I think she likes it," Mateo said, his voice reverent.

Axel glanced up at his crew. A bunch of knuckleheads he'd cobbled together over the past seven years had come together to form a weird kind of work family. Rough and tumble yet they stared at Queen in wonder.

Yeah. He could do worse.

CHAPTER TWENTY

Five days after her not-quite-a-breakup with Axel, Rena heard the knock on her door and answered with a tired "Yeah?" She hadn't looked through the peephole, thinking it was J.T. coming back to check on her since he'd just dropped her off. In addition to having to work at someone else's faraway salon, her car had up and died.

Del and her guys were working on it, and J.T. had volunteered to give her a ride home that evening since she'd just cut his hair. But it wasn't J.T. on her doorstep.

She suddenly felt wide awake. "Axel?"

He gave her a thorough once-over, his expression shuttered. "Hello, Rena. May I come in?"

She almost said "As long as you haven't brought any more wacky gifts" but didn't. It had become almost comical how bad the presents were. A plastic flower that smelled like dirty socks and lavender, a red-heart lollipop with a scorpion inside it that read *Stung through the heart*, yet another troll doll—this one with puke-green hair—and a candy bracelet that had turned her mouth purple. That one she'd handed off to an excited Colin.

She hadn't received a gift today and frankly didn't want one. Except she did, because she was as big a doofus as the man standing in her doorway, apparently. "Come in." She stepped back to let him in and winced when he handed her a small red gift bag covered in hearts.

"Two more weeks until Valentine's Day." He just stood in her living room looming over her, his hands in his jeans pockets, his black sweater looking too damn good on him.

"Yep."

They didn't talk. He glanced at the bag then at her.

Swallowing a sigh, she opened it. "A Reese's heart." It was white chocolate and peanut butter, a combination she found utterly disgusting, but she still warmed at the thought behind the gift. "Thank you, Axel."

They stared at each other.

"I waited for you to call," he said at the same time she said, "I didn't call because—"

They stopped and stared at each other again. And waited. When they both started to talk at the same time again, Rena took charge. "Okay, me first. Axel, I like you. You're great, but we can't have a relationship if you—"

"I saw my father," he blurted.

Thank God. She'd been gearing up to give him the old heave-ho speech for days but still couldn't make herself do it. She'd fallen in love with the big idiot and his terrible Valentine's presents. She felt so weak for wanting to pretend his shutting her out didn't hurt. She should just take him as he was. All her friends wanted the hottie. He was sweet and kind, and, sure, he beat people up sometimes, but they had it coming to them. Rena should accept what Axel was willing to give.

Bull. Shit.

She wanted Mr. Right, the kind of man she read about in her books. And, yes, she knew they were fiction. She'd been told so many times by so many exes that they'd never live up to her exacting standards. As if loyalty and good communication should be an unachievable goal.

Well, Axel seemed to be loyal. But that pulling-away crap had to go. Living without that two-way trust would eat at her until she hated him for making her doubt herself for loving him. If he couldn't talk to her, what did they really have outside the bedroom?

So she waited while he gathered his thoughts. Tired, she moved to the couch and sat down.

He paced, watching her warily. "I've been wanting to talk to you since you left me on Saturday."

"Uh-huh."

He looked to be trying to gauge her responses, but she was too tired to care about being nice. He continued, "But I didn't know what to say." He looked confused and sad, and she squashed the nice side of her wanting to offer comfort. "When I told you I needed space, I meant it."

That hurt. She cleared her throat. "Well, I'm here. You live there, so..."

"I don't want to hurt you."

She swore his heart shone in those deep-blue eyes then wondered just how much wishful thinking could kill a girl's hopes and dreams.

"No," he clarified. "I mean, I worry I might someday hit you."

"You do?" She hadn't expected that, though she'd not once, in all the time she'd known him, sensed any violence toward her.

He sighed. "My father used to hit my mother. Like he hit me, and, I just learned, like he hit my brother. But I deserved it. I didn't listen well. I had violent outbursts when I was young. Episodes, my mother would call them." He looked away, as if ashamed.

Rena didn't know what to say, so she just listened.

"My mother wanted to be a good wife, so she stood by his side, no matter how he abused her, with fists or words. She grew up in poverty, and she didn't want that for us. She truly loved my father when they married, but when she learned what he was really like, by then it was too late. She had two boys she would do anything for. My father had a lot of money, and if my mother played the good wife, he promised to take care of us always." He met her eyes, his full of grief. "Cancer runs in her family, and her sister already had enough mouths to feed. My aunt's husband left her, and I think my mother worried my father would do the same if she didn't follow his rules."

"I'm so sorry."

He nodded, his pain stark. "My brother believed my father's lies about *Mutter*, and one day I fought with him about it. One of many arguments, sadly. My mother tried to interfere. And I hurt her." He closed his eyes. "I didn't mean to, but I struck her so hard I gave her a concussion and a broken cheekbone. I was only thirteen years old, much smaller than I am now, and I did such damage, Rena."

He opened his eyes, his expression bleak. "I have never fought like that again. Never so lost in anger. I like to fight, *ja*, but I'm in control. I'm ice. Nothing touches me." He paused. "But with Rabies and Scott, I lost it. What if you'd been there, and I'd accidentally hurt you?"

She couldn't watch him looking so sad and not do something about it. "Oh, Axel." She stood and moved to hug him. He let her, hugging her back tightly, before he stepped back.

"When I rage, and the feeling is there, I worry I'll strike out."

"But Axel, relationships are *about* feeling. Acting out. You laugh, and you cry. You shout, and you whisper."

"I don't."

"Have you ever loved a woman? And not your mom or other family."

He just looked at her.

She swallowed a boatload of nerves, wanting so badly to believe he loved her. Now a little afraid he did. "Ah, do you think maybe you're afraid of feeling so much? So you keep drawing back instead of trusting yourself to know you won't hurt me? What happened to your mom was an accident."

"I hit her," he whispered.

"Yes, but you never did again. And you didn't hit her on purpose in the first place. Or did you?"

"*No,* never. But I'm worried. With you, I don't feel control." He cupped her cheek. "I burn and rage. I want to kill anyone who hurts you. And when you get mad at me, I don't like it."

"I don't like it either, but that's life."

"But—"

"Honey, you can't tuck away the bad stuff. You have to let it all out. Within reason, I mean. And there are people you can talk to who can help you deal with emotions."

He paused. "My aunt is a therapist."

"See?"

"But I don't talk to her about that. I want to put it in the past."

"But it's not in the past," she said gently because he looked so miserable. "The other day, why did you want space?"

"I felt all the hurt that comes with my father. Maksim brought it back. I didn't want you around all that ugliness."

"But I want your ugliness."

He frowned.

"Let me ask you something." She grabbed his big hands in hers, hands that could be so strong and do so much damage then touch her with such care. "Did you miss me?"

He groaned. "So much. It was like the sun went out and all was dark and cold. I don't want to be without you."

That was *so* much better than a troll doll. And he said he had no romance inside him. "I missed you too. But Axel, I can't live with a man who shuts me out. I told you I don't do lies. Well, only giving part of yourself is living a lie. It's not sharing with your partner the whole truth. When I'm scared or afraid, I want to know I can come to you and tell you how I feel."

"You can."

"I need to know you can share with me too."

"It's a man's job to take care of his woman."

She gave him a look.

He flushed. "It is."

She just kept staring at him.

"Okay, maybe I could rely on you too. But I just, sometimes I feel…" He took a deep breath and exhaled loudly. He seemed nervous. "I think I'm not…"

"Axel?" He seemed *so* close to opening up.

Instead he kissed her. Her libido almost managed to override her disappointment. But she pushed him back. "Sex is not the answer." Which would sound so much more like she meant it if she could catch her breath and ignore his huge erection pushing against her belly.

"I know." He leaned down to press his forehead to hers. "I miss you so much."

"Just open up with me, Axel. It's not hard. I won't judge you."

He pulled back and cupped her cheeks, his gaze wistful. "But you might not be able to help yourself if you see the real me. My ugliness, it's deep down." He sighed. "I'm sorry."

He left before she could stop him.

Huh. Now what to do?

Go after that moron.

"Axel, wait." She chased after him and nearly got run over when he started to back out and turn.

He slammed on the brakes just as she stepped back, leaving an inch from making contact. She heard him cursing through the driver's-side window, grateful she didn't recognize half the words spoken in German.

"Are you crazy?" He rolled down the window, looking furious. "I could have hurt you."

"But you didn't." She jumped up on the sideboard, grabbed his sweater by the collar, and yanked him close for a kiss. The warmth of his mouth and skill of his lips had her melting when she pulled away. "Okay, bozo. Look. You can be scared of a lot of things. I know I am. Spiders, a bad perm, *troll dolls.*"

He blinked. "You don't like the trolls?"

"But if you want something, you'll fight for it. So the question you have to ask yourself is this—would I rather hide my ugliness from Rena and lose her to some hunky fireman?" She wasn't too proud to remind him he had competition. "Or do I want to figure out a way to deal with my issues so Rena and I can be forever valentines? Only you can figure it out. But, Axel, I'm not going to sit around and wait for you to decide for years on top of years. Get it together and get it right, or you're going to lose the best thing in your life, *Liebling.* And that's me."

She jumped down from the sideboard of his truck and strutted back up the walkway to her townhouse. "You have two more weeks, Axel. Don't blow it."

Axel thought on what Rena had said all night long and into the weekend. Each day, he gave her a new gift. And not one of them was the last blue-haired troll. Friday he left her a pet rock with a heart on it…and made an appointment with a therapist. Not for Rena's sake but for his own because he had to stop fucking things up.

On Saturday he left her a whoopee cushion. It was pink, and he thought it would make her laugh. And on Sunday he texted her a video of Queen and her kittens with Chi-Chi standing guard.

He would have given her an actual kitten, but he didn't know if she'd like a living creature to take care of. As it was, he'd taken Queen, her litter, and Chi-Chi home while the cat looked after her babies. To his amusement, Mateo, Kelly, and Smitty had already chosen kittens to take home once they'd been weaned.

Which left three more, the mama, and Chi-Chi to deal with.

Sunday afternoon, he drove to a local pet supply store in Green Lake to the Pets Fur Life adoption day. He hoped these were the same guys he'd seen outside Rena's salon.

He walked to the store, surprised to see it so crowded and especially with women. An advantage to being tall meant he could see over almost everyone's heads, and he saw Brad, Reggie, and Mack talking to different people and handling animals.

He also bumped into his friend Sam's girlfriend on the way in.

"Oh, hi, Heller." Ivy smiled, a pretty blond who looked way too sweet and classy to belong with Sam. "Are you here to adopt a pet? I think they've run out."

"*Nein.* Are *you* getting a pet?"

"No. Sam helps out sometimes with animals, and recently his group has been fostering for Pets Fur Life."

He looked around and saw Sam talking to two older ladies toward the back.

"I need to talk to Sam then."

"I'll take you." She threaded her way through the throng, but he lost her midway in.

And then it happened.

"It's the Viral Viking!" someone squealed.

Half the room hushed and turned to him.

Shit.

Before he knew it, women were asking to take pictures with him and crowding him with cell phones. Then a few guys stepped forward to flex. He did his best to look tough, and it must have done the trick because they all seemed pleased.

One man sauntered up, looking like a model himself, and shook his head. Didn't stop him from taking a selfie in front of Axel though. After he'd taken it, he frowned. "Way too much with the facial hair. Not my type, sadly. But if you want to make money modeling, I can totally introduce you to people." He paused and winked, giving Axel another once-over. "For a price."

"Elliot, cut it out." A tall woman wearing a leather jacket dragged the man away. "Wasn't flirting with the fire department enough?"

Confused and not sure where to turn, Axel desperately sought salvation.

"Sorry, folks. We're closing in ten minutes," called one of the store employees. "So if you're not already in line, could you please make your way to the exit? I promise we'll share on our store calendar when we have our next adoption. And maybe the Viral Viking will come too!"

Amid cheers and more picture taking, the crowd slowly dispersed.

"Yo, Axel. Over here." Brad waved him over.

The firemen all wore Pets Fur Life shirts.

Mack tossed a shirt at him. "2X work for you?"

"*Ja.* But—"

"You promised to come to an adoption," Mack reminded him. "This one doesn't count."

Reggie raised a brow.

Brad waited.

Rena would like it if he helped out.

"Okay, just let me know when."

Brad smiled. "Rena said you'd agree."

Axel scowled. "When did she say this exactly?"

"She was in earlier. Bought some dog and cat treats and gave us a ten-dollar donation. She's sweet."

"And not for you," Axel growled.

Brad raised his hands. "Apparently her landlady already contacted her. She has the police report and the insurance adjuster should be out there soon. The police report definitely said arson, but none of it is Rena's fault."

Sam joined them with Ivy under his arm. "I need to talk to you about that," he said to Axel. "After."

"Okay." Axel turned back to Brad. "I came to talk to you about some pets that need homes, actually. Three kittens and…" He paused. Queen and Chi-Chi seemed too attached to separate them. But kittens normally found good homes pretty easily. "Three kittens." He could always rehome the dog and cat later. "They're too young right now to separate from the mother, but when they are, can I bring them to you?"

"Sure, man. We'll find them a place to live."

Axel nodded. "Thanks." He added wryly, "Good job flirting your way to big donations. Very social-minded of you."

Mack gave him a thumbs-up.

Reggie seemed to recognize his sarcasm. "Don't knock it, Viral

Viking." He sneered then laughed. "We got a lot of money to help with the animals."

"Yeah, Heller." Sam frowned. "Quit picking on the guys. They have fragile egos. You know, handling all that hose to compensate for small dicks and all."

"Sam!" Ivy turned scarlet.

"Oh, you heard that?" He glared over her head at Mack.

"Ignore him, Mack," Ivy said. "I think you all do *great* work."

Mack winked at her.

Brad rolled his eyes. "Reggie, muzzle Mack before Sam turns his face inside out."

"Roger that." He put Mack in a headlock and dragged him away, which the stragglers in the shop found hilarious.

"Be right back, honey," Sam said to Ivy as he and Axel moved to a quiet spot in the back.

"What do you know?"

"Rumor has it Fletcher's gonna make a scene at Ray's with a bunch of his white brothers next week."

"When? And how do you know this?"

"We think anywhere from Thursday night through Saturday night during Ray's busiest times. It's some kind of power play to get rid of the 'colorful' crowd at Ray's. And Daryl told me."

"He just volunteered the information?"

"Let's say I promised him he'd be safe from you if he cooperated and laid low until we took Fletcher down."

"Okay."

"I let Ray know a few hours ago. He's beefing up security, whatever the hell that means, until this shit's over. Thought you'd like to know."

"Oh, yes. I'm planning to be there every night this week."

Sam sighed. "Thought so. I'll be there too."

"Why?"

Sam glared. "Face it, Heller. You have friends. Deal." Sam clapped him on the shoulder, told him not to be a dumbass, then left with Ivy.

"Huh." Axel wondered what to do with himself. He took a list out of his back pocket and scratched *Find Fletcher* off it. Which left him with a therapy session and just eleven more days to figure out how to win his lady.

He eyeballed the firefighters again.

Hmm.

"Yo, Axel. Before you leave, I wanted to talk to you about my car," Mack said.

"Perhaps I can fit it in. But I need something from you as well."

Late Monday afternoon, Rena was well into her third appointment, a simple haircut for a seven-year-old, when one of the stylists came over to her and whispered, "You need to come see this. There's someone here for you." She choked with laughter.

God, help me now. "Be right there," she murmured.

She had one more snip, and the child was finished. "And you look lovely, milady."

The little girl giggled and stared at herself in the mirror. After a moment, her mother took her by the hand and started out the back exit. "Thanks, Rena. I'll text you to book our next appointments."

"Sounds good." She smiled, wondering what Axel had brought this time, and froze when she reached the lobby.

Three people dressed in fuzzy animal costumes, one a duck, one a dog, and one a rabbit, stood waiting.

The duck nodded, then the rabbit must have pushed a button on a phone because music came out of a small Bluetooth speaker on the counter. "From the Yiffies," sang the dog.

The three animals started singing some weird song with the lyrics "I love you furry long time" and made suggestive movements that animals likely wouldn't be making. Then she heard, "Axel wants you, baby, one more time. Come on out tonight and party like it's 1999." An amalgamation of song lyrics smashed into one cheesy tune with a continual thread of sexual invitation to fuck a duck, do it doggy style, and go at it like bunnies.

Rena blinked. "What?" The music stopped. The small adult crowd—thank goodness the child had already left—clapped and hooted. Then the duck handed her a card. "Yiffie party Wednesday night. Your invite is on the back. Later, chickie."

They left, and Rena still didn't know what had just happened.

On the other side of the room, Tommie was laughing so hard she was crying. "That's his best one yet!"

"What is going on?" Rena asked, dragging her away.

"The Yiffing crowd are part of the furries—but these guys don't just wear animal costumes. They like to dress up in furry costumes and have sex." Tommie started laughing again. "Oh my God. That was awesome. I have it all on video. You look so confused." She started snorting and had to bend over to breathe.

Rena stomped back to her temporary station, not sure whether Axel actually meant such an invitation or if he'd had no idea he'd invited her to dress up like a rabbit and have sex.

But she planned to ask him soon enough.

Her day ended, and she grabbed a ride with Tommie to Axel's shop. He rarely closed before five, and she'd texted him earlier to hang around so she could stop by to say hello.

Tommie parked, insisting on coming in with her. "Please. I have so little in my life. Let me show him the video."

Rena bit back a grin. "Oh fine. But stop singing 'I love you furry long time.' It's creepy."

Tommie laughed and laughed.

They entered the shop to see the guys cleaning up.

Smitty waved. "He's with Mateo in the paint bay."

Before she could ask which one that would be, Axel exited one of the rooms and unzipped a yellow suit down to his hips, pushing his arms out to expose one glorious chest covered in a white T-shirt.

"It's like peeling a banana and finding a Yiffie inside," Tommie murmured.

"Stop it," Rena insisted, and Tommie snickered some more.

"You have truly outdone yourself, Heller." Tommie grinned. "Seriously."

The guys looked interested.

"Would you like to see my present today?" Rena asked, trying to be kind.

Axel lit up. "*Ja, bitte.*"

Tommie whipped out her phone and waited to be surrounded before hitting play.

Everyone watched in stunned silence.

When it was over, they all looked at him.

"What was that?" He looked adorably confused.

Rena socked him in the stomach, which only bruised her hand. "You sent sex animals to my workplace. I was serenaded by Yiffies inviting me to a party on Wednesday. Was that something you set up or what?"

"Party?" He frowned. "And why were they thrusting so much and talking about fucking?"

Smitty had to turn away. Mateo gaped at the phone and asked to see it again. Kelly joined him and watched along with Tommie.

Rylan didn't even try to hide his gales of laughter.

It took Rena two more tries to explain what the costumed dancers really meant, and when he finally understood, Axel started laughing. Great booming laughs that left him breathless.

Rena's lips twitched, and she coughed to cover her mirth. "I hope you're proud of yourself."

"No wonder they were so expensive and had me sign an adults-only form to rent them. I thought it was just expensive for the holiday. Oh, *Häschen*. That is… *Häschen*. Little rabbit." He started laughing again.

Rena was done. "Tommie, let's go."

"I'll text it to you," she whispered overly loudly to the guys.

Mateo gave her a thumbs-up.

"Ten more days, Axel Heller. And if I see one more troll doll or one more horny duck, you're toast."

Then she got in the car with Tommie and laughed until she cried.

CHAPTER TWENTY-ONE

By Wednesday night, Axel's nerves were strung tight. The therapy session he'd had the previous day had been hard to handle. The therapist had been quiet, understanding, and extremely easy to open up to. He hadn't planned on saying much, and he'd ended up saying a lot, learning how much he hadn't realized he'd held in.

He had an appointment to see her next week as well. But the best thing he'd learned was that what he felt made sense. He wasn't crazy, and keeping himself apart from the very thing that seemed to be helping—namely, Rena—didn't make sense.

It was like he had a pass to start living again.

Though he figured Fletcher wouldn't show until the end of the week, he wasn't taking any chances. Neither was Ray, apparently. Axel saw Sam, Lou, Foley, Smitty, and Rylan sitting together, and he recognized a bunch of regulars who spent their time between Ray's and a jail cell, but a lot of the crowd in the bar looked…unfamiliar. Not people he knew, and they all had a vibe that told him he didn't want to know them. Then he saw Mantego sitting in the back and understood.

Lou had painted Mantego's car, a cherry Shelby Mustang, and turned the already-classic car into a work of art. And Mantego, as most of those acquainted with Seattle's underbelly knew, ran a major crime network in the city. Big J said something to the guy that had him laughing.

So, Mantego must have been Big J's connection, and a big connection it was.

Fletcher had no idea who he'd pissed off.

Axel sat with his guys.

"Rylan, you probably shouldn't be here," he said, just in case the law showed up.

"The more the merrier, Boss." Rylan shrugged. "I like Ray's, and I don't like Fletcher's guys."

"See, he's cute and smarter than he looks," Smitty said under his breath, though Axel heard him.

Rylan blushed under his scowl.

Axel had no urge to know why the hell the two had been so chummy lately.

"Why are you three here?" he asked Lou, Sam, and Foley. "You all have women now, and you don't come in that much anyway."

Foley frowned. "We come in enough. This is our place. And we love Rena. What else is there to say?"

Lou said a few words in Spanish. "There's no place here for Fletcher's kind. Ray's belongs to all of us." He shot Axel a knowing look. "It's not just you and your girlfriend who have a problem with this asshole."

"Ah, *gut*." Axel tossed back his beer. "Just don't damage your hands. I need you."

"So glad to know you care," Lou muttered, but Axel caught his grin.

He spotted Liam talking with a few big guys with bad reputations.

Men who liked to tear apart cars and sell their parts for money for some heavy-hitters who hated cops. "Liam is here?"

"Yeah. We were told to stay away from him." Foley grinned. "Liam's still badass. I respect the hell out of him."

Axel looked around. The bar belonged to all of them labeled by many as outcasts, degenerates, and troublemakers. Axel didn't see anything wrong with that. He just liked to have a good time. To go to a place where a guy could fight or drink or just forget about things without worrying about a dress code and twenty-dollar cocktails.

Ray's was all about inclusiveness. So having some dickhead players trying to limit anything rubbed everyone the wrong way.

"I need some air," he said and left out the front.

He wasn't surprised by the crowded parking lot and looked up at the stars. He missed Rena, and he knew he needed to go to her, to come clean about all of it.

Lou joined him. "I'd keep far away from the big tree and those Escalades over there."

Axel looked over and spotted a familiar car circled by a bunch of others under a huge oak. "Is he insane? He brought the Shelby?"

"You going to tell him to take it home?" Lou raised a brow.

"No. I'm not stupid." He paused, Mantego's presence hinting at something he'd wondered about but hadn't believed. "Is Fletcher part of Righteous?" The Righteous were a white-power gang in the city, often at odds with the WSW—the West Side Wolves. Lately, both gangs had been all over the news, the law cracking down on gang-related activity in the city. Even among the coffee drinkers and millionaire techies of Seattle, gangs fought and struggled to hold onto territory.

Lou snorted. "He's not Righteous, but he wants to be. I had a conversation with Mannie earlier." Only Lou called Mantego Mannie.

"From what he thinks, this is probably Fletcher's last chance to prove himself to his white brothers. When he gets his ass handed to him, it's not going to be pretty. The only worry is if they're bringing guns. Then we need to get gone."

"*Ja.*" Axel wanted to break Fletcher's neck, but he was no fool. A fist rarely won when up against a bullet.

He wondered what Rena would think about tonight. Or about what he'd done for her preceding tonight. He still couldn't believe he'd hired a group of Yiffies to serenade her. Not one of his better presents, though the guys at work considered it a gift to *them*. They continued to razz him about it.

But none of it bothered him because he'd been doing a lot of soul searching lately, and he'd come up with some answers he hoped she'd like. But with only six more days until Valentine's Day, he felt put on the spot. He could only hope he hadn't totally ruined things by keeping his distance and working on his own problems.

He texted her every day, and they talked on the phone about anything and everything. He loved talking to her, hearing her voice. But the time had come to see her, face-to-face, and really talk. And this time he'd promised himself he'd share. Whatever she wanted to know, he'd tell her. No matter how much it hurt. He couldn't lose her. Not again.

A large cavalcade of trucks and cars pulled alongside the road by the bar. Cops usually ignored this area, as mostly rundown homes and businesses populated the side streets. Nothing of notice except for Ray's.

So when Fletcher and Scott stepped out leading a bunch of redneck-looking assholes, Axel was ready. Someone must have alerted the bar because people started pouring out.

Fletcher sneered as he and his crowd stopped in the small area between the lot and the bar. There didn't seem to be more than fifteen or twenty guys, and none of them seemed to be carrying.

Facing so many people, Fletcher looked uncertain. And then he spied Axel and concentrated his hate in one direction.

"Look at all the diversity in the crowd. It's like a rainbow out here." He sneered at Axel.

His guys laughed.

Axel just stared, saying nothing, his intent to destroy Fletcher and his friends clear in the look he shot the bastard.

Fletcher looked nervous and tried to cover it up with bravado. He obviously hadn't expected a lot of people on a Wednesday night. "How's your girlfriend? So sad that her place burned down. But you know, it's hard for their kind to run a business without someone to tell them what to do. Now if I were the one giving her orders, she'd be on her hands and knees thanking me." He snickered.

Even knowing the man wanted to start a fight, that he needed to hold onto his control, Axel had a difficult time not playing Fletcher's game. Because when he imagined how Rena could be hurt, he wanted to kill the man. Break his fucking neck.

He continued to stand there, his hands on his hips, and wait.

Fletcher started to sweat. "What's wrong, you big pussy? Too scared to talk? How about we fight instead?"

"Take a swing," Axel finally growled. "I won't stop the first one."

Behind him, Sam muttered, "Nah, man. I'd totally block it and hit back."

Oddly, no one made a move. Not Fletcher and not any of his guys, who seemed to realize they were vastly outnumbered.

Axel sighed. "Today. I have things to do." Behind him, people laughed.

It was sadly anticlimactic. Before Axel could take a step forward, someone from behind tapped him on the shoulder.

He turned to see Mantego flanked by half a dozen ballers, tats on their necks, brass knuckles on a few fists. He recognized gang tats. The guys around Mantego looked like straight-up convicts. Mantego wore slacks and a black T-shirt, no jacket, and could have passed for one of the millionaires in the city.

He had a slight Spanish accent and spoke in a cultured voice, his words precise. "Excuse me, Heller. I think this is my fight."

Axel stepped aside. "You sure? I'm happy to take the lead."

Mantego smiled. "I'm sure. There's been some miscommunication at this establishment, and I need to make a few things clear. Perhaps you should join the others back in the bar." He paused. "Oh, and I have a Corvette needing some love. Can you fit me in?"

Axel sighed. "You mean can Lou fit you in? *Ja,* sure, Mantego. Bring her around. But I need just one thing." He pointed to Fletcher, who looked ready to piss himself. "Maybe when you're done, you could let me know so I can have a talk with that one. He's been bothering my girlfriend."

Mantego blinked. "You have a girlfriend?" That Mantego kept tabs on people was a known fact, but Axel hadn't realized he'd been on the guy's radar. He should have though. Anyone who did business with him probably factored into account.

He growled, "It's not a big deal, you know." Axel had no idea who'd taken over his mouth. This guy could carve him up like a turkey and truly bury the body. "Rena Jackson. She's mine."

"Ray's Rena?" His eyes narrowed on Fletcher. "Oh, yes. I heard about graffiti and the fire. Hadn't put two and two together though. *Sure,* I can do that. I'm happy to. And call me Mannie." He stepped forward with his friends, and the others who'd converged in the parking lot joined them, stopping Fletcher's buddies from running away.

Axel knew when to cut bait. He joined the others back inside.

Ray shouted, "Who wants drinks half off?"

A ton of cheers erupted, and people flocked to the bar.

Liam had been waiting and pulled Axel to the side. "What the fuck are you doing talking to *him*?" He nodded to Mantego and the gang outside.

"We do his cars. He promised to drop Fletcher off once he's done with him."

Liam sighed. "Well, as long as he's cleaning up outside, why not, right?" Then he smiled. "You know, I have some duct tape in my car. I think there's a way we can work with that."

Rena sighed. Wednesday night and she had nothing to do but count how many days it had been since she'd seen Axel. Only two, actually, but it felt like forever. Even worse, he hadn't given her a valentine yesterday, though Monday he'd given her that white chocolate Reese's heart. How sad that she'd actually choked it down, but only because it had been from him.

She missed being with him. Talking and texting were all well and good, but she missed seeing Axel's smile, hearing his laugh. And, God, she missed having sex. How was he lasting so long? It had been a week and a half since they'd been intimate.

Her phone rang.

"Hello?"

"Hi, Rena." Axel's low voice. She sighed. "I need you to come to my shop. Can you get here as soon as you can?"

"Why? Are you hurt?" Had he gotten into another fight at Ray's?

"I'm fine. I have some things to say to you. To apologize as well. And I would like to do it here. Now."

"Um, okay." Weird, but since she had her car back and nothing else to do *and* she missed Axel like crazy, she met him at his shop.

The lights were on, and her uncle's car looked to be in the parking lot. Odd. She got out and went through the front. There, in the middle of the shop, tied up in duct tape and sitting on his ass, was Fletcher. On either side of him stood her uncle and Axel.

Fletcher saw her and tried to talk through his gag. Someone had clearly worked him over. He had black eyes, a bloodied and broken nose, and bruises on visible skin.

"You kidnapped Fletcher?" she squeaked, imagining her lover and her uncle going to jail for a very long time.

Uncle Liam grinned. "No. He's with us voluntarily, aren't you, son?" Her uncle rubbed his hands together, and Fletcher nodded so hard she feared he'd snap his own neck.

Axel kicked him, not hard, but enough to get his attention. "You have something to say to her, *ja*?" He removed the dirty rag from Fletcher's mouth.

"I'm sorry," Fletcher said, for once sounding sincere. "So very, very sorry. I shouldn't have burned your salon or painted those ugly words." Okay, that part didn't sound so true. He scowled, saw Axel and Liam watching him, and swallowed hard. "I won't bother you again. Ever. I swear on my life."

Liam chuckled. "You got that right."

Axel nodded, looking satisfied.

"Why? Why did you do that to me?" She had to know. "I was never anything but nice to you."

"I..." He looked at Axel.

"Go ahead. Tell her the truth. Because you will never, *ever*, see her again. What he does to you is nothing compared to what I'll do."

She felt the menace in the air but had no idea what Axel was talking about. "He" who?

Fletcher swore and turned back to her. "You teased me. Acted like you could give me a taste of that sweet pussy then dumped me for this fuckhead. And I shouldn't want you," he muttered. "I don't. Not at all, really. I don't know why I wanted a piece."

A piece, as if she were a slab of meat. She loathed his answer, but she noticed Axel watching her, his hands fisted at his sides, no doubt ready to pummel Fletcher some more.

"Axel?"

"You have the right to decide what we do with him. I slit his throat and dump the body. I can beat the shit out of him first then slit his throat and dump the body. Or I can—"

"You know what? How about if I just kick him in the balls and we call it even?"

Fletcher didn't look so good as her uncle and Axel lifted him to his feet and held him steady. The man kept cringing and crossing his legs.

She wanted to laugh. "Not so much fun now, is it? You could have hurt someone at my shop. Just like I could hurt you now. I won't because I won't sink to your level."

His relieved smile just made her sad. That and the fact he had blood stains in a lot of places and his breathing didn't sound right. She looked at her uncle and Axel and didn't see any damage on them though. Which still didn't mean they hadn't caused Fletcher's injuries.

"Yes, I'm better than you. I'm a nice person. I never led you on. I knew you were prejudiced, but I thought if I treated you kindly, you might see there's more to me than the color of my skin."

Axel smiled at her.

"Ain't she something?" Uncle Liam asked, beaming.

"So much something. Yes." Axel sighed. Then he slugged Fletcher, hard, in the gut.

Fletcher wheezed and sagged to the floor.

Rena wanted to feel bad for him, but she couldn't.

"Now that had to hurt," Liam said.

Axel stood over him, staring down at Fletcher as if he shouldn't exist. "*Gut.* So, *Häschen*, do we kill him or turn him over to the police?"

"Well, crap. I was hoping to make him disappear." Uncle Liam winked. And she hoped to hell they were both kidding. "I'll take him down to the police station. You two enjoy your evening." He speared Axel with a look. "Make it right."

Axel sighed. "I know."

Uncle Liam left with Fletcher through the front, and Axel took her by the hand out the back. He locked up and led her to his truck.

"But my car…"

"It'll be safe here. We'll come get it later. Rena, I have to talk to you."

The dreaded words she'd longed to hear, but now that she had them, she didn't know what to think.

In the truck, Axel reached for her hand and held it on his knee the whole way to his home. Once there, he let her in and took her to the front room, where Chi-Chi sat with Queen and six tiny baby kittens.

"Oh my gosh. They're adorable." She wanted to pet them but didn't want to disturb Queen's feeding, so she settled for a few quick strokes and instead petted Chi-Chi, who rolled onto his back, begging for a belly rub, his tail wagging like crazy.

"He's like a whole new dog."

Axel looked pained. "He's in love with Queen. I don't think they can be separated."

She tried not to smile.

"Stop it."

"So…you have a cat *and* a dog. Good for you."

"Laugh it up," he muttered. "Come, *Häschen.* I have things to say." He led her back to his bedroom, and she wanted to jump for joy. A bed, so close…

She sat on the edge of it and looked up at him.

"You were right about everything," he confessed. "I was scared. I *am* scared. I don't want to be like my father."

She'd been waiting so long for him to talk to her. She was so happy she could have cried. But she didn't, wanting him to get it out. "You aren't like your father."

"I could be," he said with a frown that eased as he looked at her. "I talked to that therapist you told me about. And I'm going to keep seeing her."

"Oh, Axel. I'm so happy for you."

He sighed. "I've missed your curls. Your smile. Those bright eyes." He paused and got down on one knee in front of her.

What the hell?

He took her hand and kissed the back of it. "I love you, Rena Jackson."

She stared, wanting so much to have heard those words that she feared she'd imagined them. "What?"

"*Ich liebe dich.* I love you."

Oh my God, he's been saying that for weeks! "Y-you do?"

"I have loved you since I first saw you, back in April last year. You served me chocolate-chip cookies and beer. And it was so strange, and the beer tasted like piss. But seeing you, I felt truly warm for the first time in a long time."

Her eyes teared up. "You are so romantic."

"*Nein.* But if you think so, I can be okay with that." He stayed on one knee, speaking to her with such an earnest expression. "I will never want to hurt you. But I am not so good at communicating. I think sometimes I'm a very ugly person inside." He glanced down before meeting her eyes again. "I don't want to be. I'm afraid I'll never be good enough. That my mother is truly the only person who could ever love me." His eyes shone. "I still miss her so much, Rena. She was so kind and loving. She made me a good person. But I will try to be that man for you. I would give you anything you wanted, you know."

"Oh honey. I love you too." She wiped her eyes. "I've wanted you for so long. And not romance-book-hero you. I wanted a real man to love. You're beautiful inside and out. You're generous and protective. And you have the best body. I love touching and kissing you."

"I'm not perfect," he warned.

"Oh, I know that too." She laughed, so filled with joy. "You give the worst Valentine's Day presents ever."

He looked hurt, and she laughed even harder. "Axel, you gave me troll dolls, a red hot that almost burned my mouth off, a porn DVD, a lollipop with a bug in it, and an invitation to Yiffie sex."

He flushed. "What about the chocolates?"

"Okay, the first bunch was delicious. But the alcohol-infused ones were plain gross. And fake flowers are not a good idea."

"Oh." He frowned.

She tilted his chin up to look into his eyes. "But that's why I love you. Because you try and you're thoughtful. You have a huge heart, and it's all mine."

"But I haven't gotten you your big Valentine's Day present yet." He smiled.

"The only thing of yours I'm dying to have is in your pants, buddy, because you already gave me your heart."

His eyes lit up. "Oh, *gut.* I've been dying to have you again." He rose and pushed her back on the bed, stripping her of her clothing until she wore nothing but him.

He leaned over her, kissing and stroking, and his mouth followed. From her breasts to her belly and farther down to her sex. His lips scorched her, leaving her teetering on an orgasm. He laved her with his tongue and lips, drawing her clit into his mouth so he could suck her into oblivion.

She was still coming when he, still dressed, his pants pushed down to shove the condom on, entered her in one thick, forceful push, which brought on an even more powerful climax.

As he rode her through to his own bliss, she knew she'd finally found her Mr. Right. And he'd been in front of her all along.

They made love all night and each night until the weekend, where they spent their time at Axel's, taking breaks only to eat, laugh, and love, simply enjoying each other.

"Will you come with me to my uncle's wedding?" she asked. "The ceremony is actually on Valentine's Day."

"I would be honored," he said Sunday evening as he drove her home. "The wedding party is on the weekend, *ja*?"

"Yes. But you already knew that because my uncle invited you."

He grinned. "Yes, he did. But I had been hoping to come with you." He gave her a big kiss. "Have a good day at work tomorrow, *Häschen*. Then we go to your place, okay?"

"Deal."

Rena spent her Monday lost in a world of sheer joy, compounded when her mother called to break the good news that Dave had filed for divorce and that they were again talking, taking their relationship day by day.

When Rena shared the news with Axel later, he nodded. "I knew your mother would find happiness. She's too strong not to make her own way." He kissed her. "Like her daughter."

The next week passed in a blur of perfection. Axel stopped giving her presents, thank goodness, instead swamped with work. They spent every spare moment together, usually at his place so they could watch over the cat and dog he *still* said he didn't have along with Queen's adorable kittens.

By the time Valentine's Day rolled around, Rena knew she'd never have a better day. The only thing marring her happiness was the slow process of getting her salon back on its feet. But she didn't worry. Mike had said he'd get to it just as soon as his current project wrapped up, and the insurance company had agreed that she was due coverage, since the police report and Fletcher's arrest attested to his guilt.

But what really drove Rena to bursts of happy laughter for no reason was her uncle's pending wedding. He would finally be getting married to the woman he loved later that evening. Today was a day that felt even more special because she wanted to truly commit to Axel. And she planned to do it with a ring.

It went against all the romantic tropes she lived and breathed, but it felt right.

She only had one appointment scheduled, with a girl Tommie couldn't fit in. She hadn't planned to work, but Tommie had been such a trouper through it all. So that morning, she did her hair, put on makeup, and dressed in jeans and a cute top and ankle boots, prepared to go home and change into a gorgeous red wraparound dress and heels later. Fortunately, the weather looked dry and clear. The sun shone, like an omen signifying good times ahead.

She chatted with the girls in the salon as she waited for her client to show up.

"Man, it's crowded today."

Tommie nodded. "Totally." She stood working on a friend's cut. "Are you doing hair tonight for the wedding?"

"I would have, but Sophie and my uncle wanted me to relax. So no. Just mine and I'm done."

She'd spruce it up a little before the wedding took place, but she'd opted for her natural look. And not just because Axel loved it so much.

A fire truck pulled next to the salon, lights flashing.

Everyone stopped and stared.

"Uh-oh. I wonder what's going on," she said, even as she recognized several of the men now walking toward the salon.

Brad wore dark-blue pants and a dark-blue Seattle Fire Department shirt. With him were Reggie, Mack, and Tex. Honestly, they looked like they'd just walked off a man-of-the-month calendar. That or they were headed in to strip for money.

"Hubba hubba," Marla said with a sigh.

Chatter grew loud as the four hotties drew closer and entered the shop.

Rena smiled with welcome. "Hey guys. What are you doing here?"

Then she saw Del's car pull in the front, and Del waddled out, taking pictures.

Confused, Rena didn't know what to think.

CHAPTER TWENTY-TWO

"Ma'am, if you could please come with us," Brad said.

Someone raised their hand. "No, take me!"

"Take me," Tommie shouted.

Then the rest of them chimed in.

"Why?" Rena managed to get a word in. "What's going on?"

Reggie winked. "Everyone's okay. Just enjoy the ride."

"*Oh,* I'm telling him you said that," Tex said with a laugh.

"Shut up, Tex."

Tommie was taking pictures behind her, as were a whole host of smiling customers and stylists. Apparently, everyone was in on the joke but her.

Reggie, Brad, and the others escorted her outside and helped her into the fire truck. It was smaller than the ladder ones she'd seen but still big enough to fit the four of them and her.

"We're not doing anything special," Mack said. "We're actually off duty and doing a favor for B Shift. Just taking Big Red out for a spin since she just got back from maintenance. You just happen to be doing a ride-along if anyone asks."

"What?"

"Just roll with it," Tex said, his accent sexy, but not as sexy as her boyfriend's. "Boy, Rena, you sure look good."

"Enough to eat," Brad said with a wink and pulled out.

"Axel put you up to this."

Reggie raised a brow. "You think?" Then he looked her over and whistled. "Do you have a sister?"

The guys teased her but would say nothing of where they were headed.

Mack held up a red half mask meant to cover her eyes. "You have to put this on, I'm afraid."

Mystified and thrilled Axel had gone to so much trouble, she put it on.

A few minutes later, the fire truck stopped.

"I'm gonna hand you down to Tex, so don't panic," Reggie said and helped her down.

Tex carried her in his big strong arms to another man, one whose sexy scent she recognized.

"Thanks," Axel said, cradling her to him.

She was *so* in love.

"Oh, you'll pay." Tex chuckled. "Good luck. See you at the adoption in two weeks."

Whistles and cheers sounded, and Rena recognized Tommie, Stella, J.T., and Del among the catcallers.

She plucked at her blindfold and got scolded.

"Not yet, *Häschen.*"

He set her on her feet. "I have something to say." He seemed to be addressing a crowd.

Darn it. She wanted to see.

"I fell in love with Rena at first sight many months ago. I have never seen a more beautiful woman. She is lovely inside and out, and a man would have to be crazy not to see that."

People clapped. Her eyes burned, and she feared her makeup would run when she teared up.

He pressed a tissue into her hands and kissed her cheek.

"So I was stunned to find a few rotten people trying to hurt my precious Rena. They made a mess of her shop, a place she has worked tirelessly to see come to being. It wasn't enough they wrote terrible things on the walls. They tried to burn it down."

"Are we at my salon?" She had tingles.

"Shush," he told her then said to the crowd, "But no one can keep Rena down. Not even me and my big mouth."

People laughed and clapped again.

"So it is only fitting that my Valentine's Day gift to my lovely Rena is to tell her I love her and to give her back her dreams." He took the mask from her eyes, and she looked up into his smiling face. "For you, *Häschen.* Because I love you."

Axel prayed she'd like it. He hadn't done all the work himself. Far from it. But for the past two weeks, he'd had friends and her family working together with the landlord to get the place back up and running, making sure she stayed well away to surprise her.

Axel had footed the bill, willing to wait for the insurance to reimburse him later. In hindsight, he could now appreciate how taking the money from Maksim would have helped. As it was, he'd used up a huge chunk of his savings to make things right for Rena. But she was so worth it.

Getting around-the-clock work done at such short notice hadn't been cheap, even with family and friends pitching in for free. Parts still cost, as did paint and furnishings.

"Rena, what do you think?" They'd painted the exterior of the building a flat gray with a sparkling new pink sign that read *Rena's* in capital letters. It had a stylish flair, looked all hip-designer to him, but would she like it?

"It's amazing." She kept wiping her eyes. "Oh, Axel. This is the best gift ever!" She hugged him.

"Better than Yiffies," Tommie yelled, and a bunch of them cracked up laughing.

Del's kid asked his father, "Dad, what's a Yiffie?"

Rena grabbed Axel by the hand and tugged him with her into the building. "This is…"

"Do you like it? If you don't, you can change it to anything you want."

"It's incredible. Even nicer than what I had." They'd fixed up the interior to reflect what had been there before, but everything was new. This place is so cool!"

She darted from room to room, *ooh*ing and *aah*ing. Then she noticed the table with the large cupcake tower, bowl of punch, and grand reopening sign overhead.

"It's a celebration?"

He nodded. "I'm sorry they stole your joy. It's my job to bring it back for you."

She burst into tears and hugged him hard. "Oh, Axel. I love you so much."

He sighed, having finally gotten it right. He smiled. "So do you think we can watch *Charlie Crown* later and figure out what the dog and the bird do in the doghouse?"

She laughed. "Only if we blindfold the trolls first. I mean, come on, Axel. They're creepy."

He pointed to one sitting on the front desk.

She leaned close to it, pushed the troll aside, and picked up the framed photograph.

"Is this… Is this you?"

He nodded, thinking the fake book cover did kind of look like a book she might read. "It's a mock-up image. Abby said her publisher definitely wants to use me. And when I told Abby about what I wanted for you—all this—she knew just what book to propose to her editor. A Viking romance." He grinned. "And you and I get to be on the cover."

Rena looked as if she was going to explode.

"Are you okay?"

Rena kissed him then raced out screaming about her Viral Viking being on a book cover.

Axel joined her outside, seeing her with friends and family, all of them here to support the woman he loved.

She turned and held out her hands. "Come on, Axel. Come meet the old Mr. Sexy."

Mike McCauley groaned. "It's a curse I'm happy to hand over to you."

His family laughed. Little Colin hugged his aunt. Then he turned to Axel and gaped.

"Oh my gosh, Aunt Rena. Your boyfriend is even bigger than J.T.!"

J.T. gave him a sour smile. "He's not that big."

"He's my own hero," Rena told her nephew. "He can even pick you up with one arm."

"Do it. Do it!"

Axel sighed and put on a display to please Rena. Colin gazed at him with adoration…and a conniving grin.

He leaned closer to the boy. "So this puts you in the winning, *ja*?" He'd met the boy two weeks ago when one of the kid's uncles had dropped by to check out the shop. And they'd had an interesting conversation about the betting board.

"Yep. Thanks, Axel," Colin whispered. "But don't tell, okay?"

"*Nein.* It's a secret."

The boy rejoined his parents, and Mike shot Axel a suspicious look before Del tugged him with her toward the salon.

"Hero worship, that's what that is," Rena teased him as they joined the others for cupcakes and punch.

He wasn't used to being anyone's hero, and he didn't know if he felt comfortable with her thinking of him in that way.

As if she read his mind, she said, "Get used to it. Your family just got a whole lot larger."

He smiled. "All I need is you." He glanced over at the front desk. "I told you trolls bring good luck."

Liam and Sophie's ceremony brought tears to Rena's eyes. The entire day had been magical. From all her friends and family gathered to celebrate her new salon to a love match for her uncle she'd been *dying* to witness.

The happy couple walked away from the simple service arm in arm and disappeared into a stretch limo.

Rena walked with Axel out to his truck, and they drove back to his house, unable to take their eyes off each other, though Axel did do his best to get them home safely.

Home. To *his* home, though he'd given her a few subtle hints about moving in.

She had a feeling her townhouse was soon going to be ready for a new occupant.

Once inside, she stopped him. "Today has been absolutely perfect. So this is your chance. What else do you have to tell me? Anything I should know?"

"Ah, you see…" He swallowed.

Her heart raced. She usually had a tough time looking away from him in jeans and a T-shirt, but in a suit and tie, he stole her breath away. At this point, he could tell her he was an undercover DEA agent or an assassin working for aliens and she'd be okay with it.

"Just tell me. It's the perfect time." She fiddled with the back of her dress and saw his eyes widen. He licked his lips.

"I could have bought your salon, but I didn't."

She froze. "What?" How did he have that kind of money? Had she thought she'd be okay with anything?

"I told my brother I didn't want any of my mother's inheritance. The store I fixed using my savings."

"Axel. You shouldn't have." She hadn't considered how much it had cost to fix the salon. Stupidly, she'd just been so happy to have it back.

"Rena, I love you. I want you to have everything. Including a rent-free place to work. But I just couldn't touch that money. My mother took so much abuse to earn it, it feels wrong."

"I get that. I do." She couldn't get over the fact he'd actually even considered buying her salon. "So you're not rich?"

"Not really." He sighed. "Maybe I should have taken the money for you. I could have had access to a lot."

But she understood why he hadn't, and she loved him even more for it. "Enough to buy a castle?" she teased, not expecting an answer.

"A small one."

Her eyes widened. "A yacht?"

"Maybe."

"A sleigh?"

He frowned. "Why a sleigh?"

"For romantic sleigh rides in the winter."

"It hardly snows here. It's all slush."

"So?"

He sighed. "Yes."

She blinked. "I just… Seriously? You had that kind of money and you turned it all away?"

"Yes."

"For your mother."

"I did. I know that doesn't make me sound very smart, that I'd so something that foolish. But I couldn't."

She paused, wanting to get this right. "Axel Heller, I have a very important question to ask you."

"Go ahead." What did she want? A way for him to get that money back, probably. In hindsight, he couldn't blame her. He'd let feelings get in the way when the practical answer to his brother should have been to take the money or to at least talk it over with Rena first before saying no.

She gave him the most beautiful smile. "I got you a ring. I was going to propose earlier."

He stood there, unable to form a response better than "Really?"

She was everything he'd always wanted. Maybe she had a point about Valentine's Day being the best day of the year.

"But now you might think I only want to marry you out of pity for throwing away a fortune," she teased. "And I'm kidding because I totally understand why you did it, and it makes me love you even more. Your mom must have been a special lady to have you for a son."

He'd never heard words that touched him more. He blinked so as not to cry, not wanting to spoil the moment. "*Ja,* I'll marry you." He paused, seeing Chi-Chi staring at him in the doorway before the dog trotted away. "But there are conditions."

"Oh?" Her eyes shone with joy.

"I come with a cat I'm keeping and her half-blind sidekick, a house that needs remodeling, and a lot of smartasses calling themselves my friends. I'm in therapy and might be for a while. Oh, and my brother may be visiting soon." He wiped a tear from her eye, feeling so much. "But the important thing you need to know is that once I have you, I'm never letting you go. You're *it* for me, and you have been since I first saw you."

Rena cupped his face and smiled through her tears, then wiped *his* cheeks dry. "I've been looking for you my whole life. You're my own hero and Mr. Right all rolled up in one."

"*Ich liebe dich, Häschen.*"

"Back at ya, Viral Viking. You're all mine." She kissed him until they were both breathless. Then she shoved him back, and he fell on the bed. "There's just one more thing I've been dying to say to you for days."

He waited, wondering what else she could say to make this day better. She looked adorably smug as she waited, so he knew it had to be good.

"Tell me," he insisted. "I must know."

She grinned in triumph. "Happy Valentine's Day! Now let's get naked and party like it's 1999, Charlie Crown."

And they did.

ACKNOWLEDGMENTS

Huge thanks to Elisa Schwake for giving me the real scoop about stylists and for always giving the best cuts! And to the folks at Sourcebooks for being so terrific to work with. I truly appreciate all your hard work. Cat, you rock. And to my agent, Nicole, you are a joy to work with. To all the readers who wanted Heller and Rena to have their happily ever after, I couldn't have written this book without you. And especially to Donna, Joanne, and Lisa, thank you so much for your valuable feedback.

ABOUT THE AUTHOR

Caffeine addict, boy referee, and romance aficionado, *New York Times* and *USA Today* bestseller Marie Harte is a confessed bibliophile and devotee of action movies. Whether biking around town, hiking, or hanging at the local tea shop, she's constantly plotting to give everyone a happily ever after. Visit marieharte.com and fall in love.

ALSO BY MARIE HARTE

The McCauley Brothers

The Troublemaker Next Door

How to Handle a Heartbreaker

Ruining Mr. Perfect

What to Do with a Bad Boy

Body Shop Bad Boys

Test Drive

Roadside Assistance

Zero to Sixty

Collision Course

The Donnigans

A Sure Thing

Just the Thing

The Only Thing

Veteran Movers

The Whole Package

Smooth Moves

Handle with Care

All I Want for Halloween